*Signature Select™*
SHOWCASE

# JAYNE ANN
# KRENTZ

*Lady's Choice*

# HARLEQUIN®

TORONTO • NEW YORK • LONDON
AMSTERDAM • PARIS • SYDNEY • HAMBURG
STOCKHOLM • ATHENS • TOKYO • MILAN • MADRID
PRAGUE • WARSAW • BUDAPEST • AUCKLAND

ISBN 0-373-83694-5

LADY'S CHOICE

# One

"I love you, Travis. Hold me, hold me."

"*Juliana.*"

Travis Sawyer heard his own muffled shout as he shuddered heavily over the flame-haired woman in his arms. The last of his white-hot passion spent itself in a blinding, driving storm of pure release. He lost himself in his lover's arms, surrendering to her fire even as he exulted in his victory. She clung to him with all her sleek strength, drawing him into her until he felt as though he'd stepped into another universe.

It had never been this good with anyone else. Travis Sawyer was thirty-eight years old. He'd never been a womanizer but he considered he'd lived long enough to make the judgment. This was special. Nothing had ever been this good before in his life.

It was everything he had instinctively sensed it would

be with this woman. Hot, wild, powerful. He had never felt so alive, so strong. Satisfaction swept through him in the wake of the slowly dissipating passion.

She was his now. Reluctantly he disengaged himself and rolled to one side, his hand trailing heavily over the gentle curve of Juliana's breast. She smiled up at him from the pillow, the expression as dazzling as always, even here in the darkness of her bedroom.

The thick, untamed mass of her hair was an elegant, pagan crown framing her vivid features. Travis stared down at her, captivated by huge, long-lashed eyes, a noble nose, an arrogant, yet surprisingly delicate chin and a luscious mouth. Her long leg slid between his in a languidly sensual movement. Then she closed her eyes and snuggled into his warmth.

He had done it, Travis thought triumphantly as his arm tightened around her. He had claimed his red-haired, topaz-eyed queen.

And then, in the next moment, reality settled back into place around him. What the hell was he doing here, holding her like this? He'd never intended to take his revenge this far; never intended to wind up in bed with Juliana Grant.

He stared deeply into the shadows of the bedroom, searching for answers that weren't there. He felt dazed now that the fiery passion had receded.

Vengeance led a man down strange paths. Juliana Grant had been an unexpected detour in the long road he'd been walking for the past five years. But he could not, would not allow the detour, no matter how exotic, to deflect him from his chosen course. He had come too far. There was no turning back now, even if he wanted to do so.

Travis Sawyer was very good at what he did, and

when he had set out to orchestrate his revenge he had left no loopholes. There was no escape for anyone, not even for himself.

The clear, bright California sunshine danced across the bay and slammed cheerfully through the condominium's bedroom windows. Juliana opened her eyes slowly and watched the early-spring light as it bounced around the dramatic white-on-white room. It sparkled on the thick white carpet, bounded off the white walls, struck the chrome and white leather chair and tap-danced over the gleaming white lacquer dressing table. It sizzled when it struck the only color accent in the bedroom, an egg-yolk-yellow abstract painting that hung on the wall over the chrome and white bed.

Mesmerized, Juliana followed the trail of sunlight as it ricocheted between the mirror and the painting and splashed across the foaming white sheets of the rumpled bed. There, in a final burst of dazzling brilliance, the morning sun revealed the alien male being who had invaded her room last night.

A man in her bed. That, in and of itself, was a rare enough event to excite wonder and curiosity, but in this case it was an even more notable occurrence. Juliana hugged herself with her secret knowledge.

Because she knew beyond a shadow of a doubt that this particular man—this hard, lean, sexy man named Travis Sawyer—was *the* man. The right man. The one she'd been waiting for all her life.

She savored the delicious secret and held herself very still so as not to awaken the exotic creature lying next to her. She wanted a moment to luxuriate in the thrilling certainty that she had finally encountered her true mate.

He was not exactly as she had fondly imagined over the years when she had indulged in a little harmless fantasizing. He wasn't quite as tall as he should have been, for one thing. She, herself, was just a sliver under six feet and she had always envisioned her true mate as being somewhere in the neighborhood of six feet, four inches or so. Tall enough so that she could wear high heels comfortably around him. Travis was barely an inch over six feet. In two-inch heels she was eyeball to eyeball with him. In two-and-a-half-inch heels she was taller than he was.

But whatever he lacked in height, he more than compensated for in build, Juliana assured herself cheerfully. Travis was sleekly muscular and as solid as a chunk of granite. Last night she had been in no doubt of his strength. The masculine power in him had been totally controlled and all the more exciting for that sense of control. This was a man who exercised a sure command over himself, a man who had learned the techniques of self-mastery. She admired that kind of control in a man. It gave a woman a sense of security—an old-fashioned, primitive assurance that his greater physical strength need never be feared but could be relied upon for protection.

Travis did not quite match Juliana's inner image of her perfect man in a few other minor respects, either. His eyes were the wrong color. Juliana preferred sensual, warm brown or hazel eyes in those of the male persuasion. Travis had cool, crystal gray eyes that did not betray his emotions except in the most intense situations. Last night had been intense, however, she recalled with delight. She'd seen the passion blazing in his eyes and it had sent shivers of excitement through her.

This morning she was quite prepared to drop her old

standards regarding eye color in view of the fact that Travis's eyes were not only capable of reflecting his passion, but also an intelligence that complemented her own and a rare sense of humor that delighted her when it showed itself.

His hair was a bit off, too, unfortunately. It was a far darker shade than she'd fantasized. Juliana had always liked men with tawny-colored or blond hair, but she had to admit that Travis's severely trimmed, night-black hair seemed to suit him. The hint of silver at the temples was not at all unattractive.

There were a few other minor discrepancies between the real Travis Sawyer and Juliana's fantasy version of her true mate. If she were inclined to be picky, for example, she could have carped about the undeniable fact that his rough, grim looks would probably forever keep him from gracing the cover of *Gentlemen's Quarterly* magazine. Ah, well, it was *GQ*'s loss, she told herself. He looked perfect here in her bed.

Then, too, there was Travis's apparent total lack of interest in style and clothes. She had known him for almost one whole month now and she had never seen him in anything but a pair of dark trousers, an austere white shirt, a conservatively striped tie and wing-tip shoes. His jackets were all muted shades of gray. But Juliana figured she could fix the problem. After all, she had more than enough style for both of them, she told herself. She glanced at her closet and smiled as she pictured the rack of expensive, high-fashion clothes and the boxes of shoes inside. Shopping was high on her list of hobbies.

All in all, Juliana was more than willing to make allowances for the few areas in which Travis Sawyer fell short of her idealized image of Mr. Right. She was used to working for what she wanted, and she was quite prepared to put in whatever time and effort was required to polish her very special diamond in the rough. Last night she had received ample assurance that the effort would be worth it. She still tingled from head to toe with the hot memories.

Having finished her perusal, Juliana stretched slowly, deliberately stroking one toe down the length of Travis's muscular calf. When there was no response, she sighed and accepted the fact that the man probably needed his sleep after last night.

Juliana grinned with amused regret, pushed back the sheet and got to her feet. She was mildly startled to discover she ached pleasantly all over. Travis had been a demanding as well as a bold and generous lover. He'd taken everything he could get but he had given back passion with equal intensity. If she closed her eyes she could still feel his strong, sensitive hands on her this morning. She felt as if she'd been imprinted with his touch.

Standing in the middle of her bright white room Juliana allowed herself one last, fond gaze at the man in her bed and then she headed for the bathroom with a long, exuberant stride.

She would welcome her true mate with a proper display of feminine domesticity, she decided. Might as well give the man a little foretaste of the wonders that were in store for him.

Half an hour later, showered, her mass of red curls caught up in a dramatically cascading ponytail and dressed in a pair of fashionably cut, high-waisted slacks and wide-sleeved painter's shirt, Juliana made her way back into the bedroom. She was carrying a black enameled tea tray. Perched on the elegant tray was an art deco teapot and two cunningly designed, bright red cups.

"Good morning." She smiled brilliantly when she saw that Travis was awake. He sprawled on his back, watching her through half-closed eyes.

"Good morning." His voice was husky with sleep and very sexy.

"Beautiful day, isn't it? But, then, it always seems to be beautiful here in Jewel Harbor. That's one of the things I had trouble getting used to when I first moved here four years ago. It's the perfect California seaside town, and perfection always makes a person a little suspicious, doesn't it?" Juliana busied herself with the tray. "Even the fog, when it shows up, is different here than it is anywhere else. Soft and romantic and eerie. You don't take milk or sugar in your tea, do you?"

"Uh, no. No, I don't." Travis sat up slowly against the pillows.

"Didn't think so. You're not the type."

"There's a type?" He watched her, as if deeply intrigued by the whole process of pouring tea.

"Oh, definitely. But I knew you wouldn't be one of those." She handed him a red cup. "Just as I knew the day you walked into my shop that you drank just plain coffee, not espresso or latte or cappuccino."

Seemingly bemused, he glanced down at the strong, dark tea and then up to meet her expectant gaze. "No offense, but it is a little surprising to discover that the queen of the local coffee empire serves tea in bed."

Juliana laughed and helped herself to the second cup. "I'll let you in on a little secret," she said as she sat down in the white leather and chrome chair. "I really don't like coffee, especially all those fancy French and Italian variations I serve at the shop. The stuff upsets my stomach."

Travis's mouth curved faintly. "I know most of your secrets but you've hidden this one well. I would never have guessed you're a closet tea drinker. What would the patrons of Charisma Espresso say if they knew?"

"I don't intend for them to ever find out. Until, that is, I get ready to open up a chain of tea shops."

Travis frowned, shaking his head in an automatic, negative gesture. "Forget the idea of tea shops. Your goal is to expand Charisma, remember? There are a lot more coffee drinkers than tea drinkers around here."

"Never mind about my tea shop idea. I don't really want to talk about it this morning, anyway." Juliana eyed him with great interest. "Did you think you knew all my secrets just because you've been looking into my business affairs for the past couple of weeks?"

"Most of them." Travis shrugged, his bare, bronzed shoulders moving with masculine grace against the white satin pillow. "I'm a business consultant, remember? I'm good at what I do. And I've learned that once you know someone's financial secrets, you usually know all the rest of his or her secrets, too."

"Sounds ominous." Juliana shuddered elegantly and took a sip of her Darjeeling. "I'm glad that in our case there are still a few surprises left. More fun that way, don't you think?"

"Not all surprises are pleasant ones."

The warning was soft. And, predictably enough, it went unheeded. Juliana figured Travis was still a bit sleepy.

"Oh, in our case I'm sure the surprises will all be at least interesting, if not downright pleasant," she said with assurance. "I'm looking forward to each and every one." A rush of happiness sizzled through her as she studied him. He looked so good lying there in her bed. She loved that mat of dark hair on his broad chest. To think she had ever wasted time fantasizing about fair-haired men. She shook her head in disbelief at the recollection of her own foolishness.

"Something wrong?" Travis asked.

"Not in the least."

"I thought you might be having a few regrets—" he paused carefully, his eyes meeting hers "—about last night."

Juliana's stared at him in astonishment. "Of course not. If I'd worried about having regrets, I wouldn't have gone to bed with you in the first place. I knew exactly what I was doing."

"Did you?"

"Absolutely. I'm sure you did, too."

"Yes," he said, looking contemplative. "I knew what I was doing. You look pleased with yourself this morning, Juliana."

"I am." She smiled widely, vastly pleased indeed, with him, life and the world.

"I'm glad you weren't disappointed."

"Disappointed?" She was shocked. "How could I possibly have been disappointed? It was glorious. Perfect. Everything I imagined. You are a fabulous lover, Travis Sawyer. Magnificent."

An unexpected telltale red stained his high cheekbones. For a few seconds Juliana could have sworn Travis looked embarrassed by the expansive praise. She was instantly touched by his lack of ego in that particular department.

"No," Travis said, concentrating on his tea, "I don't

think it was anything special I did. We just sort of clicked, I guess. It happens that way sometimes. Two people meet, find each other attractive and, well, things work out in bed."

Juliana's brows rose and she pursed her lips thoughtfully. "Has it happened that way a lot for you in the past?"

Travis blinked and his crystal eyes gleamed behind his lashes. "No," he admitted quietly. "It hasn't happened that way a lot for me."

Juliana relaxed immediately, satisfied to know for certain that the emotions in this situation were not one-sided. "Good. I knew last night was special."

"I take it that it hasn't happened that way a lot for you, either?" The question was reluctant, as if Travis did not want to know the answer but was unable to stop himself from asking the intimate question.

"Never in my whole life," she assured him with perfect honesty.

He grinned slightly. "Maybe you just haven't had enough experience to judge."

"I'm thirty-two years old and along the way I've had to kiss a few frogs to find my prince."

"But you haven't slept with too many of those frogs, have you?"

"Of course not. Frogs can be very slimy, you know. A woman has to be cautious."

"Ummm. These days it works both ways."

"I'm aware of that. And I know you're not the kind of man who jumps into bed with any willing body that comes along." Juliana wrinkled her nose with distaste. "I could never fall for a man who didn't have enough sense to be extremely discriminating when it came to his sex life. More tea?"

"All right." He held out the red cup, watching with amusement as she leaped out of the chair to pour from the stunning little art deco pot. "I could get accustomed to this kind of service."

She laughed. "You've caught me in a good mood. Either that or the novelty of the situation has inspired me." She handed him back the cup, enjoying the brush of his fingers against hers. "Well?" she asked, barely able to conceal her impatience. "Would you like to talk about it now or later?"

"Talk about what?"

"Our future, of course." She was aware of Travis going very still against the pillows, but she ignored the implications. "When did you plan to ask me? I wouldn't want to spoil the surprise, but it would be helpful to know what date you had in mind so that I could start making plans. So much to do, you know. I want everything to be just perfect."

Travis stared at her, his tea forgotten. "Plans? What the devil are you talking about?"

"Are you always this dense in the morning?" She smiled at him indulgently. "I'm talking about our marriage plans, of course."

"Our *what*?" The red tea cup slipped from Travis's hand, spilling its contents on the white sheets. It rolled off the edge of the bed and landed on the white carpet with a soft thud.

"Oh, dear. I'd better get something on that right away. Tea stains, you know." Juliana jumped to her feet again and scurried into the white-tiled bathroom to fling open a cupboard.

"Juliana, wait. Come back here. What the hell did you mean a minute ago? Who said anything about marriage?"

She turned around, sponge and carpet cleaner in her hands and marveled at the sight of Travis standing fully nude in the doorway. For a few seconds she forgot about the risk of tea stains in the other room. "Who cares if you're a little on the short side?" she asked softly. "You're just perfect."

"Short?" He scowled at her. "I'm not short. You're too tall, that's the problem."

"It's not a problem. We can work it out. I'll wear flats or short heels most of the time," she vowed. Her eyes traveled wistfully down the length of him. "And certain parts of you are not very short at all."

"Juliana, for Pete's sake." Travis snatched a white towel off the nearest rack and wrapped it around his lean hips.

"You're blushing. I didn't know men could do that."

"Juliana, put down that sponge and start talking sense. What did you mean about getting married?"

She remembered the carpet with a start. "Hang on a second, I have to get that tea out right away. That's the trouble with a white carpet. You can't let anything sit on it very long or the stain sets." She brushed past him and hurried over to where the brown stain was slowly sinking into the beautiful white fibers. "This thing is supposed to be stain resistant, but unfortunately that doesn't mean it will take just any sort of abuse. I probably shouldn't have put in white but it looked so terrific in here I couldn't resist."

Travis stalked slowly across the room to stand towering over her while she knelt and began to scrub industriously. "Damn it, Juliana, I'm trying to talk to you."

"Oh, right. About our marriage. Well, I've been thinking about it and I've decided there's no real reason to wait, is there? I mean, we're hardly kids."

"No, we are not kids," Travis shot back. "We are adults. Which means we don't have to start talking marriage just because we went to bed together on one occasion."

"You know me well enough by now to realize I like to get going on things right away," she reminded him airily. "Once my mind is made up, there's no stopping me. Just ask anyone."

"Juliana, stop scrubbing that damned carpet and pay attention."

"But while it's true there's no real reason to wait, maybe we shouldn't move too quickly on this." Juliana chuckled. "I mean, you're always telling me that I should take my time and plan major moves carefully, right?"

"Damn right."

"And I do want to plan this wedding carefully. I think I'd like to have a big, splashy one with all the trimmings including an engagement party first. After all, I only intend to go through this once, you know? I'd like to do it right. I'd want the whole family present, naturally. My cousin Elly and her husband live just a few miles down the coast and my parents will be able to come down from San Francisco quite easily. Uncle Tony lives in San Diego so that's no problem, either. Then there are all my friends here in Jewel Harbor. There are also several good Charisma customers I'd like to invite."

"Juliana…"

"We could use that lovely little chapel that overlooks the harbor."

"Does it occur to you, Juliana," Travis interrupted in a grim voice, "that you're rushing this a bit?"

She paused in her scrubbing and looked up curiously. "Rushing?"

"Yes, rushing." He seemed gratified to have her full

attention at last. "I recall everything that happened last night as well as every detail of everything we've discussed for the past three and a half weeks and I know for a fact that nothing, I repeat *nothing*, was ever said about marriage."

"Oh, dear. I've gone and ruined your big proposal scene, haven't I? You were probably planning a romantic evening with wine and caviar topped off by a stroll along the harbor front and a formal proposal of marriage." Juliana bit her lip contritely as she got to her feet. "I'm sorry, Travis. But there's really nothing to worry about. We can still do all that tonight or tomorrow night. That restaurant where we ate last night, The Treasure House, makes a great location for marriage proposals. We can go back there this evening."

"How would you know it makes such a great location for proposals? Oh, hell, what am I saying? Forget it." Travis's gray eyes glittered with anger and exasperation. "Damn it, Juliana, I have no intention of asking you to marry me."

There was a heartbeat of silence while Juliana absorbed that information. For a moment she was convinced she must have misunderstood. "I beg your pardon?"

"You heard me," he said, rubbing the back of his neck in a gesture of irritation and frustration.

"But I thought…I assumed…" Juliana ran out of words, a stunningly unusual event. Vaguely she waved her hand, the one with the sponge in it, in a helpless little gesture. "I mean, last night we…"

Travis's mouth twisted wryly. "You think that just because we'd been dating for the past couple of weeks and we went to bed together that it automatically followed that I intended to marry you? Come on,

Juliana, you're not that naive. In fact, you can be pretty damn savvy when you choose. You're one heck of a sharp businesswoman. You now how to take care of yourself and as you pointed out, you're thirty-two years old and you've kissed a few frogs. So don't give me that wounded doe look."

The accusation stung. Juliana instantly narrowed her eyes as a slow anger began to simmer through her veins. "I will have you know, Travis Sawyer, that my intentions were honorable all along. I knew the minute I met you that I was going to marry you."

"Is that right? Well, maybe you should have warned me. We could have avoided this whole silly, embarrassing scene. Because I have no plans to marry anyone at the moment."

"I see." She drew herself up proudly. "You were just using me, is that it?"

"No, I was not using you and you damn well know it. We are two adults who happened to be very attracted to each other physically. We have professional interests in common, we're both single and we're working together because you hired me as a consultant. It was perfectly natural that we start an affair. But right now, that's as far as things have gotten. We're involved in an affair, nothing more."

"You're not prepared to make a commitment yet, is that it?" she challenged.

"Do you always hit your dates over the head like this the morning after?"

"As we've already discussed, there haven't been that many morning afters and no, I don't generally hit them over the head like this. But, then, I haven't wanted to marry very many of my dates."

"How many have bothered to ask you to marry them?" Travis asked sarcastically.

"Lots of men have asked me to marry them. I get asked all the time, as a matter of fact. Usually at The Treasure House. That's how I know it's a perfect setting."

"If you've had all those opportunities, why haven't you taken one of the poor jerks up on his proposal?"

Juliana was furious. "Because none of them have been the right man. I've turned them all down. Except for one that didn't work out, anyway."

"So I'm one of the lucky two you've considered suitable, huh? What happened to the other sucker?"

Juliana felt hot tears gathering. She blinked furiously to get rid of them. "There's no need to be so rude. He wasn't a sucker. He was a wonderful, charming person. A caring person. He was also a real hunk. Beautiful hazel eyes and tawny blond hair. He was a handsome, golden god. And he was a lot taller than you."

"I don't care what he looked like. I just want to know how the guy escaped."

"Why? So you can escape the same way? All right, I'll tell you how he escaped my clutches. He turned tail and ran, that's what he did. Straight into the arms of someone else. Someone who happened to be very close to me. Someone petite and blond and sweet natured. Someone who never argued with him. Someone who never presumed to question his judgment. Someone who didn't overwhelm him the way I did. There. Satisfied?"

"Hell, Juliana, I didn't mean to rake up old memories." Travis rubbed the back of his neck again. "I was just trying to make a point."

"Consider it made. Go ahead, take the same way out my fiancé took three years ago. Run away if you're that skittish. But I have to tell you, Travis, I expected more from you. I didn't think you were the kind of man who was intimidated by a woman like me. I thought you had some guts."

"I am not going to run anywhere," Travis bit out. "But I am also not about to let you pressure me into marriage. Do I make myself perfectly clear?"

Juliana dashed her hands across her eyes, nodding sadly. "Perfectly. It's obvious there's been a terrible mis-understanding here. I guess I misread all the signals." She sniffed back the incipient tears. "I apologize."

Travis's hard face softened. He stepped closer and lifted a hand to stroke the side of her cheek. "Hey, there's no need to upset yourself over this. I've known you long enough to realize you're the impulsive type."

"My cousin Elly says I'm very spontaneous."

Travis smiled, and the rough edge of his thumb traced the line of her jaw. "That, too."

"This is so embarrassing."

"Forget it," Travis said magnanimously. "Last night was very good. I can see where you might have read more into it than…uh…"

"More than you intended?"

"Let's just say more than either of us intended."

"Speak for yourself." She turned away, ducking out of the range of his hand. "It's getting late. You'd better get dressed. I'm sure you've got a lot to do today."

"Nothing that can't wait until Monday." Travis watched her closely. "What do you say we spend the rest of Sunday at the beach?"

"No, thanks." She bent down to take one last swipe at the carpet. Then she picked up the empty red cup. "I've got a million chores to do today," she added grimly. "You know how it is. I think I'll start with washing my hair and move on to the laundry. These sheets definitely need to be cleaned."

Travis didn't move. "Are you going to sulk?"

"I never sulk," she assured him grandly.

"Then why the excuses? Last night we both made plans to spend today together."

"Everything's changed now. I'm sure you can comprehend that." She moved into the white-tiled bathroom and replaced the carpet-cleaning materials in the cupboard. "I wish you would hurry up and get dressed, Travis. It's disconcerting having you standing around in my bedroom wearing nothing but a towel."

"I could take the towel off."

She glared at him through the open doorway. "You're not suggesting we go back to bed together, are you?"

"Why not? We both agreed last night was very good."

"I don't believe this." She braced one hand against the door frame. "Travis, you surely do not expect me to jump right back into bed with you now that I know your intentions are not honorable?"

"Will you stop talking like a nineteenth-century heroine who thinks she's been compromised?"

"You don't seem to understand," Juliana said with seething patience. "I am throwing you out. Now. Get dressed and get out of my condo. Everyone makes a mistake now and then, but I do not cast pearls before swine twice. And I have no intention of wasting any more of my valuable time with a man who is as muddle-brained and stubborn as you are."

"Is that a polite way of calling me stupid?"

"You got it. I'm the right woman for you, Travis Sawyer. I was made for you. And you were made for me. If you're too dumb to see that, then there's no point taking this relationship one step further. Get out of here."

His eyes were narrow slits as he snagged his trousers from off the dresser. "Does this mean you're going to try to terminate your contract with Sawyer Management Systems?"

Juliana was startled. If she actually fired him she might never see him again. The thought was too terrible to contemplate. "No, it does not. SMS is the best business consulting firm in this part of California and the future of Charisma Espresso is too important to jeopardize by getting rid of you. Unfortunately."

"Is that right?" Travis yanked on his pants and reached for his white shirt. "Nice to know I'm still appreciated in some respects. But aren't you afraid of mixing business with pleasure? That's how we got into this situation in the first place."

Juliana lifted her chin. "No, I am not the least worried about it. I am quite capable of separating my business from your pleasure."

"Yeah? Well, we'll see just how good you are at it, won't we?" He finished buttoning his shirt and grabbed his wing-tips.

"Are you threatening me, Travis?"

"Wouldn't think of it." He tied his shoe strings with short, savage movements of his fingers and stuffed his tie into a shirt pocket. "But we both know you're the emotional one in this equation. And you want me. Hell, this morning you woke up convinced you were in love with me."

"I never said that."

"Yes, you did," Travis countered coldly. "Last night

when you were lying under me, hanging on to me as if I was the only man left on earth. I heard every word."

Juliana felt herself grow very warm with humiliation. Her chin lifted defiantly. "All right, so I said it. I won't deny it. I wouldn't have wanted to marry you if I wasn't in love with you. But you brought me back to reality this morning. Love is probably no worse than the flu. I'll recover just like I did three years ago when my engagement ended. Now go on and get out of here before I lose my temper. You are becoming very annoying."

Travis stalked toward the door. "You'll be sorry you're kicking me out like this."

"Hah. Not a chance. Life is too short for foolish regrets. Like I said, I'll recover. But I warn you, Travis, someday you're going to look back on this whole thing and call yourself a fool."

"Is that right?" He was in her turquoise and apricot living room now, his hand on the doorknob.

Juliana hurried down the hall behind him. He was practically out the door she thought with horror; practically gone. "Yes, that's right. I'm the perfect woman for you, and one of these days you're going to realize it."

He swung around to confront her, the door open behind him. "I already realize we're good in bed together. What more do you want from me?"

She skidded to a halt a couple of feet away from him, breathless. "I want you to realize you love me. And then I want you to ask me to marry you."

"You don't ask much, do you?"

"I never do anything by half measures. You should know me well enough by now to realize that. But—" she paused, gathering her courage "—maybe I should make allowances for the fact that you're a man and therefore not as in touch with your own needs and emotions as you should be."

"Gosh, thanks for all the deep psychological analysis and understanding, lady."

"I'll tell you what, Travis. I'll give you one month. One month and that's all. If you haven't come to your senses by then, I won't give you any more chances."

His brows rose in an intimidating fashion. "One month to do what?"

"One month to figure out you're in love with me and ask me to marry you."

"One month, hmm? I'm surprised at you, Juliana. You should know me well enough by now to realize that I don't react well to ultimatums."

"Don't think of it as an ultimatum," she urged. "Think of it as a breathing space in which you can sort out your options."

He shook his head, amazed. "You never give up, do you?"

"People who give up don't often get what they want."

Travis went through the door. "I don't need a breathing space. I already know what I want. I've known all along."

"Just exactly what did you want from me?" she demanded, moving to stand in the doorway. "A night in bed?"

"No, Juliana. Getting you into bed wasn't the important thing. Believe it or not, it wasn't even part of my original plan. Just icing on the cake, I guess you could say."

He walked away into the bright, sunny morning. Juliana stood on the brick steps of her Spanish-style white stucco and red-tiled condominium. She watched with dismay as the man she loved climbed into his tan, three-year-old, nondescript Buick.

How could she have been such a nitwit as to lose her heart to a man who drove such a wretchedly dull car and wore such old-fashioned ties, she wondered.

# *Two*

The whole thing had gotten far too complicated, unbelievably complicated, disastrously complicated.

Revenge should have been a simple, straightforward matter filled with strong, clear, uncomplicated emotions. There were just two sides to this thing, Travis reminded himself—his side and the other side. And anybody with the last name of Grant was on the other side.

He sat behind the wheel of his car and stared broodingly out over the Pacific. From the top of this bluff the view was postcard perfect. The town of Jewel Harbor sparkled down below, an artistically charming mixture of Spanish Colonial-style homes and the latest in California Coast modern architecture. There was an air of trendy prosperity to the whole place that was a bit unreal at times. It would make a good setting for the headquarters of Sawyer Management Systems.

The streets were lined with swaying palms and every yard was lush and green. A lot of the backyards had sapphire-blue swimming pools and orange trees. The cars parked in the wide drives tended to be of German manufacture with the occasional Italian or classic British model thrown in for variety.

The downtown business section of Jewel Harbor looked as casually upscale as the rest of the town. Strict ordinances kept the shops and office buildings low in height and architecturally reminiscent of the Spanish look. White stucco and red tile predominated, just as they did in Juliana's condominium complex. Travis narrowed his eyes momentarily, searching the vista. From here he could just make out the busy shopping plaza where Juliana had opened Charisma Espresso.

He thought about the fateful day nearly four weeks ago when he had walked into the trendy watermelon-red and gray interior of Charisma. He had told himself at the time it was a simple reconnaissance move. He was like a general with a carefully arranged battle plan and he wanted to be sure he had covered all the angles. He had timed everything else involved very carefully, right down to making sure that his trap would close while he was here in Jewel Harbor setting up the newest office of Sawyer Management Systems.

Juliana Grant was the one member of the Grant family he hadn't met five years ago, the one unknown quantity in his equation. She had not lived in Jewel Harbor back then. He vaguely remembered being told that she was working in San Francisco at the time.

Travis wasn't quite certain what he'd been expecting when he pushed open the glass doors of Charisma Espresso, but he had been immediately struck by two powerful forces. The first was the heady aroma of freshly ground coffee and the second, far stronger force, was the vivid, red-haired, incredibly dressed, six-foot-tall goddess behind the counter. The electric-blue jumpsuit she'd been wearing should have looked tacky or at least overpowering, and on anyone else it probably would have. But on Juliana it looked just right. It was as bold and animated as she was.

Juliana Grant was unlike any of the other Grants, and that was probably why he had allowed the situation to get so complicated. Travis remembered the men of the family as being of average height, the women petite and delicate.

Juliana, by contrast, was almost as tall as Travis. Hell, he thought wryly, when she put on heels she was as tall or taller than he was. Her flaming red hair might have been inherited from her father, but it was difficult to be certain because Travis remembered Roy Grant as being gray. The same with Tony Grant, Roy's brother. She had probably gotten her eyes from her mother, Beth. But there was no one in the family with quite the same combination of coloring and height that Juliana had. In her, the genes had obviously come together in a whole new, exotic mixture.

But it wasn't Juliana's looks that had caught him off balance; it was Juliana, herself. She was different. Not only different from the other members of her family, but different from every other woman Travis had met in his life.

*Too much,* he thought, seeking the right words to describe her. That was it. Juliana was a little too much of everything. Too colorful, too tall, too emotional, too dynamic, too assertive, too smart. The kind of woman who, a thousand years ago, would have carried a spear and ridden into battle beside her chosen mate. The kind who would give everything and demand just as much in return.

She was, to put it bluntly, the kind of woman most men found overwhelming except in very small doses. Travis knew his own sex well enough to realize that the average male would find Juliana riveting for about fifteen minutes. Shortly thereafter, that same man would be frantically searching for an exit, running as fast as he could in the opposite direction.

No question about it. Women like Juliana could be downright intimidating to the average male.

Travis didn't consider himself average and he refused to be intimidated by Juliana, but that didn't mean he was prepared to jump through hoops for her, either. The lady was a handful but he had no real doubt he could handle her. That was not the problem.

The problem was that he wanted her and, given his current situation vis-à-vis the Grant family, he had no business getting any more involved with her. It had gone far enough. How in hell had he let himself get hired by her as a consultant? He must have been temporarily out of his mind. He hadn't taken on a tiny client like Charisma Espresso for over ten years.

Travis exhaled deeply, trying to think his way through the mess. In the beginning it had seemed simple enough. Juliana was a Grant and he had vowed revenge against the entire clan of Grants. He had told himself that seducing Juliana would add a nice fillip to the masterpiece of vengeance he had concocted. And it was obvious Juliana wasn't going to object to being seduced.

But looking back on it now, Travis wasn't quite sure who had seduced whom. It was Juliana who had paved the way for the affair when she had talked him into taking her on as a client. The moment she had discovered what he did for a living, she'd started bombarding him with questions about how to successfully expand Charisma Espresso.

Travis had taken what seemed an obvious opening and proceeded to play it for all it was worth. One more Grant scalp for his belt.

His mouth twisted grimly at the thought. He didn't need Juliana's scalp. She'd had nothing to do with what had happened five years ago. She didn't even know who he was. It was her misfortune, however, to be related to all the other Grants, and three and a half weeks ago when he had first met her, he'd told himself he might as well make use of her.

Last night he'd stopped thinking in terms of using her for revenge and started thinking in terms of satisfying the craving that had been building up inside him.

This morning he had been too bemused by events to think at all until Juliana had breezed into the bedroom with her chic little art deco teapot and started making marriage plans. That had brought Travis back to reality with a thud.

Juliana was taking over, threatening his plans for vengeance. After all the planning and hunting and patience he'd been obliged to exert during the past few years, Travis was not about to lose control of the situation now.

He rubbed the back of his neck and switched on the Buick's ignition. He should have seen it coming, he told himself. Juliana had fallen in love with him sometime during the past three weeks. He'd known that for certain last night when she had given herself freely, without any reservations. That was the way she did things. And if he was honest with himself, he had to admit he had taken everything she had to give.

He had to keep reminding himself that she was a Grant, Travis thought as he headed back toward his apartment. And he would be damned if he would let any Grant give him an ultimatum.

One month to figure out he loved her? One month to come to his senses? Who did she think she was? Before the month was out he was going to have reaped his revenge on all the Grants.

He would be lucky to have a week with her, at the most.

Because when the manure hit the fan, as it surely would very soon, everyone would have to choose sides. Travis didn't need to be told which side Juliana would choose. Her choice was preordained by the fact that she was a Grant. Travis faced this reality with stoic acceptance. He was used to being the outsider, to being the one not chosen.

But all he could think about as he drove back down the winding road into town was that last night had been something else. The memory of it would haunt him as long as he lived and he knew it. He could still feel the imprint of her nails in his back. Juliana Grant was the kind of woman who left her mark on a man.

Suddenly the prospect of stealing even one more week with her was more than he could resist.

"Hey, how was the big date, Juliana?"

"Saw you having dinner down at The Treasure House last night. You two looked so involved I didn't want to interrupt. Thought maybe the man was about to pop the big question."

"How about it, boss, you wearing a ring this morning?"

Juliana glowered fiercely at the expectant faces of her staff as she came to a halt in front of the long gray counter.

"Don't the two of you have anything better to do this morning than stand around asking personal questions?"

"Uh-oh." Sandy Oakes, her gelled hair sleeked back behind her ears to show off the three sets of earring she was wearing, eyed her co-worker. "Looks like all is not well with our supreme leader this morning. Best go grind a little coffee, Matt."

Matt Linton, whose hair was even shorter than Sandy's and who wore only one earring, frowned in sudden concern. "Hey, we were just teasing. Is everything okay, Juliana?"

"Everything is just fine. Absolutely peachy. Fabulous." Juliana hurled her oversized leather tote into her cubbyhole of an office and then reached for one of the watermelon-red aprons that bore the Charisma logo. "I couldn't be happier if I had just found out I had won the lottery. Satisfied? Now get busy. The morning rush will be starting in a few minutes. Sandy, why aren't those biscotti in the display case?"

"The bakery just delivered them five minutes ago," Sandy explained in soothing tones. "I'll have them out in a sec." She slid a speculative glance at her boss as she arranged the biscotti in a glass case near the cash register.

"Matt, try to look useful. The counter needs straightening. And where's the cinnamon shaker?"

"Ouch." Matt shook his hand as if it had just been bitten by a savage dog.

Juliana groaned. "Look, I apologize for being snappish this morning. But the truth is, I am not in a good mood."

"Funnily enough we could tell that right off," Sandy said. "I take it the turkey didn't ask you to marry him as planned?"

"Not only did the turkey not ask me to marry him, he was apparently stunned to find out I expected him to do so," Juliana informed her. "The whole thing was a complete misunderstanding. I made an absolute fool out of myself. If I ever show any signs of wanting to get involved with anyone else of the opposite sex ever again, I want you to promise to remind me of what happened this time. I refuse to repeat my mistakes."

Matt grinned. "You're going to swear off men forever just because Mr. Right turned out to be Mr. Wrong?"

"He isn't Mr. Wrong. He just doesn't know he's Mr. Right." Juliana turned her back to the door and busied herself with grinding an aromatic blend of beautifully roasted Costa Rican beans. She raised her voice to be heard over the roar of the machine. "But I guess if he doesn't have enough sense to know he's Mr. Right, then he really is Mr. Wrong, isn't he? I mean, the real Mr. Right wouldn't be that dumb, would he?"

She was so busy working through that train of logic that she failed to hear the shop door swing inward.

"Uh, Juliana," Matt began nervously, only to be cut off by Juliana's diatribe.

"But I have to tell you, I think my heart is broken. And what does that say about my intelligence, I ask you? How could I let Mr. Wrong break my heart? I'm too smart to do that."

"Juliana, uh, maybe you'd better…"

"What's more," Juliana plowed on forcefully, "if Travis Sawyer is so stupid he doesn't even realize I'm the right woman for him, then he's probably too stupid to be planning the future of Charisma Espresso. This morning I told him I didn't intend to fire him, but now I'm not so sure. I've had time to think about it and I really don't believe I want to put the future of my company in Sawyer's hands…"

"Juliana," Sandy broke in hurriedly. "We've got a customer."

"What?" Juliana finished grinding the last of the beans and the machine stopped.

"I said," Sandy repeated very clearly, "we've got a customer."

"Oh. Well? Why make a big deal out of it. Go ahead and see what he wants."

"What he wants," Travis Sawyer said calmly from the other side of the counter, "is the one month you promised him in which to come to his senses."

*"Travis."* Juliana couldn't believe her ears. Relief and happiness rushed through her. She swung around to confront him, knowing she was smiling like the village idiot, but not caring in the least. Her heart was not broken after all. "You came back."

"I never left. At least, not willingly. You're the one who kicked me out."

"I knew you'd see the light. I knew you just needed a little time to get your head screwed on straight." Juliana tossed the sack full of ground coffee toward Matt and dashed around the counter to hurl herself into Travis's arms.

Travis braced himself as she landed against him with an audible thud. He only staggered back a step. "I'm touched by your faith in my intelligence." Travis looked straight into her glowing eyes. She was wearing two-inch heels today. "Does this mean you're not going to try to find a way out of our business contract, after all?"

Sandy spoke up firmly from the other side of the

counter before Juliana could respond. "I don't think he's groveled enough yet, Juliana."

"Give the man a break, ladies," Matt growled. "He's here, isn't he? How much more can you ask?"

"Thank you," Travis said gravely, nodding at Matt. "I agree completely. How much more can you ask?" He turned his attention back to Juliana who was smiling with delight, her arms around his neck. "Would you mind very much if we conducted the rest of this grand reconciliation scene in private? I like Matt and Sandy, but once in a while I find I like to operate on a one-to-one basis with you."

"Don't mind us," Sandy said quickly. "We're only too happy to help out."

"Right," said Matt. "We're just like family."

"Not quite," Travis said, taking a firm grip on Juliana's arm and leading her toward the door.

Juliana was bubbling over with laughter by the time Travis had led her to the outside seating area. Morning sun poured warmly through the decorative wooden lattice overhead, dappling the white tables and French café-style chairs.

"They mean well, you know," Juliana said easily as she sat down across from Travis.

"I know they do but I feel like I'm in a goldfish bowl every time I go into the shop. Do you tell them everything?"

"No, of course not," Juliana assured him quickly. "But they've been sort of monitoring our relationship right from the start. They were there that first day when you walked in and ordered a cup of coffee, remember? They knew how I felt about you at the beginning. They guessed right away this morning that something terrible had happened."

Travis sighed and leaned back in the small chair. It creaked under his weight. "You're a full-grown woman, Juliana. Not a starry-eyed teenager. You'd think by now you would have learned to be a little less, well, less obvious about your personal feelings."

"I'm a very straightforward person, Travis." Juliana grew more serious as some of her initial euphoria subsided. "People always know where they stand with me and I like to know where I stand with them. Life is easier that way. Keeps the stress level down a little."

"You're an odd combination of ingredients, you know that?"

"You mean, for a woman?" she asked dryly.

"For anyone, male or female. When it comes to business you're as shrewd a small-businessperson as I've ever met. The success you've made out of Charisma speaks for itself."

"But?"

Travis's mouth kicked up at the corner and his eyes glinted. "But when it comes to a lot of other things, you're a little outrageous. No, that's putting it mildly. You're more like a keg of dynamite. I can't always predict when and how you'll go off. And you always do it loudly."

She shrugged. "You don't know me as well as you think. And I obviously don't know you as well as I thought I did or I wouldn't have put my foot in my mouth the way I did this morning. But that's okay. We've got plenty of time to learn all we need to know about each other, don't we?"

Travis studied her for a long moment. "I'm not going to make any promises, Juliana. I want that clear this time right from the start."

"Are you one of those men who can't make a commitment? If so, just say it straight out because I really don't want to waste any time messing around with a male who's uneducable."

"Damn it, I'm one of those men who won't be rushed into anything, including a commitment. And I just want that fact on the table before we try this relationship again. Knowing that, are you still willing to give me my month?"

Juliana thought about it but not for long. "Sure. Why not? I'm willing to take a risk or two if the prize is worth it."

Travis shook his head in silent wonder. "So reckless."

"Only when I'm going after something important."

"I guess I should be flattered that you consider me a worthwhile prize."

"That remains to be seen. At this point, you're just a potentially worthwhile prize."

"Yeah. Well, as long as we're dealing in warnings, I guess I ought to inform you that you've had yours. No promises from me, Juliana, implied or otherwise. No commitments. We take things a day at a time. I won't be pushed into anything."

"I've had my warning," she agreed smoothly. "But you haven't had yours."

His brows rose. "What warning is that?"

"Since you are unable to see your way clear to make a commitment, I am unable to see my way clear to go to bed with you until we've resolved all the issues between us."

Travis's eyes narrowed coldly. "I didn't think you were the kind of woman who used sex to get what you want."

"I'm not. Just as you're not the kind of man who could be manipulated with sex." She smiled brilliantly. "Therefore, I wouldn't dream of trying to hold you that way."

"Very thoughtful of you," he muttered.

"By not going to bed with you I will leave your brain free of hormonal clutter," she added. "You'll be able to think much more clearly about our future."

"Juliana," Travis said with elaborate patience, "last night we discovered we happen to be very good together in bed. Remember?"

"Of course I remember. So what?"

"So why deny ourselves that element of the relationship?" he asked gently. He reached across the table and covered her long, copper tinted nails with his big palm.

"Simple. I happen to view the act of going to bed with a man as an act of commitment. And when it comes to this relationship of ours, I'm not making my commitment again until you've made yours and that's final. I have no intentions of sticking my neck out twice. Still want to use your month's grace period?"

He stared at her for a long, charged moment. "What the hell. Why not? Maybe it's better this way. This relationship doesn't stand a snowball's chance, anyway. I must have been crazy to think I could have my cake and eat it, too."

"What are you talking about? What's all this about a cake?"

"Nothing."

"But, Travis…"

He got to his feet. "I'd better get back to the office."

Juliana looked up at him anxiously. She reached out to catch hold of his arm. "Travis, wait. I don't understand what's going on. Do you want to see me again or not?"

He touched her hand as it rested on his sleeve. His gaze was diamond hard in the sunlight. "Yes, Juliana. I want to see you again."

She relaxed. "Even under my terms? You don't look too thrilled about the prospect."

He looked down at the bright copper-colored nails on his sleeve. Then his eyes met hers. "I thought you knew what I wanted better than I did."

Juliana gnawed on her lower lip. "Once in a while I guess wrong, just like everyone else. I can make mistakes. It's happened before."

"With the fiancé who ran off with the petite blonde a few years ago?"

"Like I said, I'm not infallible. Up until last night, I was very sure about you and me. As you said, things clicked between us and not just in bed. But if I'm wrong, I'd rather call it quits right now."

"Would you?"

Juliana drew a deep breath. "You're a very hard man, aren't you?"

"And you are a very volatile woman."

"Maybe that's not such a good combination after all. Maybe all we'll ever succeed in doing is striking sparks off each other. That's not enough, Travis."

"Getting cold feet already, Juliana?"

She reacted to that instinctively. "No. I'll give you your month."

"Thanks." Travis leaned down to brush her mouth with his own. "I'll pick you up for dinner tonight. Six o'clock okay?"

"Yes. Fine." She smiled again, pushing aside the dark second thoughts that had crept into her mind. "I'll be ready. How about the new Thai place on Paloma Street?"

"It's a date." He walked out to where the tan Buick was parked and got inside.

Juliana sprang to her feet and hurried after him. "And do you still want to go with me to my cousin's birthday party next Saturday?" she asked anxiously. "It will mean meeting a lot of my family, including Uncle Tony."

Travis looked up at her through the open window, his expression so startlingly, unexpectedly harsh that Juliana instinctively stepped back a pace.

"Wouldn't miss it," Travis said and turned the key in the ignition.

Juliana smiled uncertainly and waved as he drove off. It was nice to know Travis was the kind of man who didn't mind getting involved with family, she told herself. And immediately wondered why she was not particularly reassured by that information.

The following Saturday evening Juliana sat in the passenger seat of her snappy, fire-engine-red two-seater sports coupé and reveled in the balmy sea air coming through the open sun roof. Travis was at the wheel, and under his guidance the little car hugged the twists and turns of the coast road with easy grace. The blackness of the ocean filled the horizon, merging with the night. Far below the highway, moonlit breakers seethed against the rocks. It was a perfect Southern California evening, Juliana reflected, feeling happy and content. The past few days had been good with Travis, even if there were a lot of uncertainties hovering in the air between them.

"You're wasting your talents behind the wheel of that Buick," Juliana declared as Travis accelerated cleanly out of a turn. "One of these days you'll have to get yourself a real car."

"The Buick suits me. We understand each other."

"Don't you like driving?"

"Not particularly."

"But you do it well," Juliana observed.

"It's just something that has to be done and I try to do it efficiently so that I don't get myself or anyone else killed in the process. That's the extent of my interest in the matter."

Juliana sighed in exasperation. "You've been in a rather strange mood ever since you appeared at Charisma to tell me you wanted your month. And tonight you're acting downright weird. Are you sure you want to go to Elly's birthday party?"

"I've been planning on it for weeks." He braked gently for another curve.

"Yes, I know, but I don't want to force you into this. I mean, a lot of men are not real big on family get-togethers."

"It's a little late to change my mind now, isn't it? We'll be at the resort in fifteen minutes."

"True. You'll like my family, Travis. I would have introduced you to Elly and David before this but Elly's been out of town for the past three weeks. She's been visiting other resorts to get some ideas for Flame Valley. My folks flew into San Diego earlier today to pick up Uncle Tony and drive up the coast to the resort. They should be there by the time we arrive and I know they'll want to meet you. David is—"

"Juliana?"

It worried her more and more lately when he spoke in that particular tone, she was discovering. She did not understand him when he was in this mood. "Yes, Travis?"

"You don't have to sell your family to me."

"Okay, okay. Not another word on the subject. I promise."

He smiled fleetingly, with visible reluctance. "And if I believe that, I ought to have my head examined."

"Hey. I can keep a promise."

"Yeah, but I'm not sure you can keep your mouth shut."

"You got any serious objections to my mouth?" she demanded.

"No, ma'am," he said fervently. "None." He paused. "Has your cousin been married to this David Kirkwood long?"

"Almost three years. They make a wonderful couple. Perfect together. Elly was involved once with someone else about five years ago. I never met the man and she refuses to talk about him, but I know he traumatized her. For a while I was worried she wouldn't let herself love anyone again. And then along came David."

"And they're happily running this resort?"

Juliana smiled. "Flame Valley Inn. One of the most posh on the coast. Wait until you see it, Travis. It's beautiful and it's got everything. Golf course, tennis courts, spa, fantastic ocean view, first-class luxury rooms and a wonderful restaurant. My father and my uncle Tony, that's Elly's father, built it over twenty years ago. They wanted to cash in on the spa craze."

"And now your cousin and her husband run it." It was a statement, not a question.

Juliana slanted Travis a quizzical glance. "That's right. My father sold a lot of his stock in it to Uncle Tony four years ago but he still holds a minority interest. Uncle Tony was supposed to take over running the place full-time but about three years ago he developed some heart problems and the doctors insisted he start taking it easy. Elly and David took over and they've been running the place ever since. They love it."

"So your cousin's husband has been making most of the decisions about Flame Valley?"

"For the past couple of years, yes. David has a lot of big plans for Flame Valley." Juliana propped her elbow on the door sill and lodged her chin in her hand. "Unfortunately I think he moved a little too quickly on some of those plans, though."

"Too quickly?"

The small show of interest was all Juliana needed. Her brows snapped together as she frowned intently. "David and Elly have a lot of ambitious plans for Flame Valley. If they work out, the place will be one of the premier resorts in the whole world. But if they don't, Flame Valley could be in real financial trouble."

"I see."

"Travis, I've been meaning to ask you something. I know your company consults for a wide variety of businesses. Do you know anything about the resort business?"

There was a beat of silence. Then Travis said softly, "Yes. I know a little something about resorts and hotels."

"Hmmm." Juliana mulled that over. "I wonder if I could get David and Elly to talk to you. I've been a little worried about them lately."

"How much trouble are they in?"

Juliana drew a breath and settled back in her seat. "I really shouldn't say anything more until I've talked to them first. David is very touchy on the subject of his business ability, and Elly gets defensive. But if I could talk them into hiring you for some consultation, would you be willing to take them on as clients?"

"I've got my hands full at the moment, Juliana. I

managed to squeeze Charisma into my schedule but I'm afraid that's the limit. Taking on a project the size of Flame Valley would be impossible."

"Oh." Juliana swallowed her disappointment. "Well, in that case, I guess I'd better not say anything to David or Elly."

"That would probably be best."

Juliana brightened. "But maybe you'd have room in your schedule in another month or two?"

Travis gave her a brief, sharp glance. "You never give up, do you?"

She grinned. "Only when the situation is clearly hopeless."

"The question is, would you recognize a hopeless situation when you saw it?"

"Of course I would. I'm not an idiot. Slow down. There's the sign for Flame Valley. Turn right toward the ocean at the next intersection."

Travis obeyed. He was silent as he navigated the narrow strip of road that wound its way toward a glittering array of lights perched on a hill overlooking the ocean.

He continued to say nothing as he parked the red coupé in the lot below the resort. Then he switched off the ignition and sat quietly as Juliana unbuckled her seat belt. He watched as she turned quickly, kneeling on the seat to reach into the back of the car to retrieve a bundle of brightly wrapped gifts.

"Juliana?"

"Yes, Travis?"

"I want you to know something."

"What's that?" She was bent over the back of the seat, fumbling with the biggest of the presents and wondering if she'd made a mistake buying Elly the huge

Italian flower vase. Not everyone liked two-foot-tall pillars of aerodynamically shaped black glass.

"When it's all over tonight, try to remember that I never meant to hurt you."

Juliana froze, the packages forgotten. She whipped around in the seat, eyes widening quickly. "My fiancé said exactly those words three years ago just before he announced his engagement to someone else. What are you trying to tell me, Travis?"

"Forget it. Some things cannot be changed once they've been set in motion." He cupped her face quickly between his strong hands and kissed her with a fierce possessiveness. Then he released her. "Let's go." He opened the car door and got out.

"Travis, wait a minute. What's going on here?" Juliana scrambled out of the car, clutching the gifts. The glass beads that trimmed the scoop-necked black velvet chemise she was wearing sparkled in the parking lot lights. "You owe me an explanation. You can't just go around making bizarre statements like that and expect me to overlook them."

"You're going to drop that if you're not careful." He put out a hand and took the biggest package, the one containing the vase, out of her arms. Then he turned and started walking resolutely toward the main entrance to the resort.

Juliana hurried after him, hampered by the remaining presents, the tight chemise skirt and the two-inch heels of her black and fuchsia evening sandals. "You can't get away with this sort of behavior, Travis. I want to know what you meant. If you're seeing someone else, you'd damn well better tell me up front. I won't be two-timed. Do you hear me?"

"There is no one else." He walked under the dazzling lights that illuminated the entrance.

The massive glass doors were opened by a young man uniformed in buff and gold. "You must be here for the owners' private party," the doorman said with an engaging grin. "Right straight through the main lobby and out to the swimming pool terrace. Can't miss it." He nodded at Juliana. "Good evening, Miss Grant."

"Hi, Rick. How's everything going?"

"Just fine. You should enjoy yourself tonight. The kitchen's been working overtime for the past three days getting ready. A real blowout."

"I believe it. See you later." Juliana smiled distractedly and dashed ahead to catch up with Travis who was still moving forward with the purposeful air of a man heading into battle.

"Honestly, Travis, you're getting weirder by the minute."

He stopped at the doors at the far end of the elegant lobby and paused to hold one open for her with a mocking gallantry.

Juliana scowled at him and then peered through the glass at the throng of people gathered around the turquoise swimming pool. She caught sight of her mother and father, her uncle Tony and then she spotted her cousin, Elly.

As Juliana looked at her cousin, a tall, fair-haired, good-looking man moved up behind Elly and draped an arm around her shoulders. They made a handsome couple, no doubt about it. Elly, petite, blond and delicate looking, was a perfect foil for her tall, charming husband. When Elly glanced up at David and smiled, it was easy to see the love in her eyes.

Juliana jerked her gaze away from the sight of Elly and David just in time to catch Travis staring intently at the couple. There was something in his expression that sent a frisson of genuine alarm through her veins.

"Travis?"

"We'd better go out and join the others, hadn't we? Wouldn't want to keep them waiting. It's been long enough as it is."

Confused, Juliana walked through the door, conscious of Travis right behind her. Several faces in the crowd turned to smile in a friendly fashion. Juliana paused to say hello a few times before she reached the small group composed of Elly and David and three of their acquaintances.

Elly turned, David's arm still resting affectionately on her shoulders. She smiled with genuine pleasure when she saw her cousin. Her short, silvery hair gleamed in the light.

"Juliana, you're here at last. Uncle Roy and Aunt Beth got here with my father a couple of hours ago. We've been waiting for you."

"How did the spa survey go?" Juliana asked.

"Great. I picked up all sorts of terrific ideas. Now, who is this mysterious date you told me you were bringing tonight?" Elly's gaze switched to the man standing behind Juliana. Her blue eyes widened with shock and the words of greeting died on her lips.

*She looks as if she's just seen a ghost,* Juliana thought. She watched in sick fascination as her cousin struggled to conceal the panic that had so clearly blossomed at the sight of Travis Sawyer.

Travis did not move but Juliana felt the tension in the atmosphere between him and her cousin. It was the kind of tension that signals powerful emotions and danger-ous secrets.

In that moment Juliana's parents came forward with her uncle Tony, and Juliana saw Elly's shock mirrored on the faces of the other three Grants.

And suddenly Juliana understood it all. Travis was the man from Elly's past, the one she'd been engaged to five years ago, the one no one talked about.

# *Three*

"The most amazing thing is how calm, cool and collected everyone is behaving," Juliana muttered to Elly twenty minutes later when she finally managed to corner her cousin in a remote section of the terrace. "I thought you were going to faint from shock when you first saw him, but then, two seconds later, there you were, greeting him as if he were just another casual acquaintance. Uncle Tony was just as cool. Just an old business associate. And Mom and Dad acted as if they could barely remember him."

"Well? What did you expect us to do?" Elly demanded. "Scream hysterically and fling ourselves over the balcony? It's been five years, after all."

"Yeah, but we both know his showing up here at this point is not just one of those strange little coincidences that sometimes happen in life. Nothing that man does is a coincidence. Believe me."

"You know him that well, do you?" Elly gripped the railing and faced the sea. The evening breeze ruffled her graceful white skirts.

"Let's say I'm getting to know him better by the minute. He's the one, isn't he? The one you were going to marry five years ago. The one who saved Flame Valley Inn from bankruptcy."

Elly bowed her head. "Yes. He wanted me and he wanted the resort, and Dad and Uncle Roy needed his help desperately."

"Nobody ever told me the whole story. All I knew was that you'd been shaken to the core by the whole incident. I thought he'd seduced and abandoned you or something, but it wasn't like that, was it?"

"No." Elly sounded thoroughly miserable. "I'm the one who broke the engagement."

"But not before you'd played the role of Judas Goat, right? You led him on, making him think that you were going to marry him and that he would get a share of the inn that way? But first he had to do everyone the little favor of saving Flame Valley from its creditors."

Elly turned to Juliana, her expression anguished. "It wasn't like that. I honestly thought I was in love with him at first. And everyone encouraged me to think that way, including Travis. It was only as time went on that I began to realize I was not in love with him, that what I had felt was just a sort of fascination, a crush. You ought to understand crushes. Men are always having them on you."

"Sure. And they last all of a day, if that. Within forty-eight hours they always come to their senses and back off as fast as they can. But this was more than a crush, Elly. You got engaged to the man."

"It was a mistake," Elly cried.

"What brought about that great realization?"

"You don't know what it was like. He…he frightened me in some ways, Juliana. He was always one step ahead of everyone else. Always plotting and scheming. Always had his eye on the main goal. Always willing to do whatever it took to reach that goal. I decided he was just using me to get a share of Flame Valley. I didn't think he could really be in love with me. A man like that never really falls in love with a woman."

"So you used him? You didn't tell him the engagement was off until after he'd accomplished the job of saving Flame Valley, did you?"

"I didn't use him," Elly protested. "Or if I did, you'd have to say I was evenly matched, because he certainly used me, too. In any event, the reason I didn't tell him the engagement was off was because Dad wouldn't let me."

"Oh, come on, Elly." But Juliana believed her. Anthony Grant had his faults but he had been a good father and utterly devoted to Elly, having raised her alone since the death of his beloved wife years ago. Elly returned that devotion in full measure. She was fiercely loyal to Tony Grant. It would have taken a great deal to make her go against her father's wishes. Obviously whatever she had felt for Travis had not been enough to counter the loyalty she felt toward her father.

Elly swallowed heavily, slanting an uneasy sideways glance at Juliana's angry expression. "It was wrong, I know it was, but I was afraid. I couldn't bring myself to tell Travis the truth and wind up being the reason the inn went into bankruptcy. And make no mistake about it, Travis would have walked out and let the whole place go under if he'd found out the wedding wasn't going to take place. Dad explained to me that Travis had only taken the job in the first place because he wanted a piece of Flame Valley Inn. They had an understanding. A sort of gentleman's agreement. Travis would collect his fee—a partnership in Flame Valley—the day he married me."

"So you continued to wear Travis's ring until he'd pulled Flame Valley out of the red."

"I had to wait until Dad and Uncle Roy were sure everything was stable financially. I felt a responsibility to the family. You should understand that. They'd all worked so hard to build this place. It was a part of them. It still is. I couldn't let them down in the crunch."

"You must have felt something for Travis. You've never wanted to talk about the time you were engaged to him. You've never even mentioned his name to me since I moved here four years ago."

"No one in the family talks about him. No one wants to remember the whole mess, least of all me. It was embarrassing and traumatic and painful. And rather scary, to be perfectly honest. Especially at the end when Travis found out I was calling off the engagement."

"How did he react?"

"Like a chunk of stone. I'd never seen anyone look so cold. It was terrifying, Juliana. I'd expected him to yell or fly into a rage or threaten a lawsuit. But instead he was utterly quiet. No emotion at all. He stood there in the middle of the lobby and just looked at me for what had to be the longest minute of my life. Finally he said that someday he'd be back to collect his fee. Only next time, he said, he wouldn't take just a share in the inn, he'd take the whole damned place. Those were his exact words. Then he turned around and walked out the door. We never saw him again."

"Until tonight. Oh, Elly, what a mess."

"I know." Elly closed her eyes. Teardrops squeezed through her lashes.

"Why do you think you were in love with him in the first place? Why did you develop the crush, as you call it? He's not your usual type."

"I know. But please try to remember that I was a lot younger then. Only twenty-four years old. Travis was older, successful, powerful. It was exciting to realize he was attracted to me. And everyone kept saying what a wonderful match it would be. Dad and Uncle Roy and Aunt Beth all wanted him in the family because they knew they could safely turn Flame Valley over to him. He'd know how to run it. It was easy to think I was in love with him at first and by the time I realized I wasn't, it was too late. Everything was very complicated."

"I'll bet." Juliana went to stand beside her cousin. "Too bad I wasn't here at the time. I could have told you instantly that you and Travis were all wrong for each other." She hesitated and then added, "Does David know who he is?"

"No." Elly shook her head quickly, her eyes shadowed with worry. "I've never told him about Travis. I'd rather he didn't know. He might not understand. Juliana, what are we going to do?"

"We?"

"Don't torment me. You have to help us."

Juliana shrugged. "I don't see that there's anything we can do. At least not until we find out why Travis has gone to all this effort to stage his big return scene."

"There's only one reason why he'd appear like this out of the blue," Elly hissed. "He's here to get his revenge. He must have found a way to take Flame Valley away from us. Or ruin the place."

"Elly, be reasonable. How's he going to do that?"

The soft sound of shoe leather on flagstone made both women turn their heads.

"I'll tell you how I'm going to do it," Travis said, materializing out of the pool of darkness cast by a clump of oleander bushes. "In the simplest way possible. I'm going to watch Flame Valley Inn go straight into the hands of its biggest creditor."

Elly's hand flew to her throat. "Oh, my God."

Juliana glared at Travis. "Must you creep up on people like that?" But she didn't think he even heard her. His whole attention was on Elly. Juliana felt very much a fifth wheel and she did not like the sensation at all. She'd felt this way once before when she'd stood near her beautiful cousin and another man.

Elly stared at Travis's harshly shadowed features. "You know, don't you? You know everything."

He moved his hand, and ice clinked in the glass he was holding. "I know. I've known from the beginning."

Juliana's gaze flicked from one face to the other. "What are you two talking about?"

"Don't you see, Juliana?" Elly's voice was thick with unshed tears. "He's here because he knows Flame Valley is having financial problems again. He's here to watch everything fall apart the way it would have five years ago if he hadn't rescued it."

"You and your husband have certainly managed to make a hash of things with your big expansion plans, haven't you?" Travis observed. "If Tony and Roy Grant had kept their hands on the reins, they might have been able to pull it off. But once they turned things over to you and David Kirkwood, it was just a matter of time."

Juliana was incensed. "What do you plan to do,

Travis? Sit around like a vulture watching the inn collapse under a mountain of debt? Is that your idea of revenge? If you can't have it, nobody else can, either?"

He glanced at her. "Who says I can't have it?"

"What do you mean?" Elly demanded, sounding even more panicked than she had a moment ago.

Travis took a slow swallow of his drink and then smiled a grim, humorless smile. "I'll spell it out for you, Elly. Five years ago I was promised a one-third interest in Flame Valley Inn. I was cheated out of my share, as I'm sure you recall. So this time around, I'm going to take it all."

"But how?" Elly's voice was no more than a faint whisper of distress.

"You and Kirkwood, in your eagerness to get on with your grand plans for remodeling and expanding Flame Valley, have been borrowing from a lot of sources, but you're in debt most heavily to a consortium of investors called Fast Forward Properties, Inc."

"But what does that have to do with you?" Elly asked.

"I am Fast Forward," Travis said softly.

*"You."* Elly looked stricken.

"I put together that group of investors and I make all the major investment decisions for them," Travis explained coldly. "When Flame Valley falls, as it surely will sometime during the next six months, it will fall right into my hands. I timed things so that I'd be here to step in and manage everything from the new Jewel Harbor headquarters of Sawyer Management Systems."

"Travis, you can't do this," Elly pleaded.

"You're wrong, Elly. It's as good as done. Everything is in place and all the fuses have been lit. It's too late for anyone to do anything about it. Nothing can stop what's going to happen to Flame Valley."

"Oh, my God." Elly burst into tears. They streamed down her face, sparkling like jewels in the moonlight. She made no effort to brush them away. "I should have known that sooner or later you would come back. I should have known."

"You knew. I told you I'd be back, remember?" Travis took another swallow of his drink.

Elly's tears flowed more heavily.

Juliana had had enough. She scowled at her beautiful cousin. "For pity's sake, Elly, are you just going to stand there crying? Haven't you got any backbone? Don't let him bully you like this."

Travis snapped another quick look at Juliana. "Stay out of this," he said. "It's got nothing to do with you now."

"I've already played my part, right? I helped the big bad wolf stage his grand entrance. Now I know what you meant that morning you left my apartment saying I was just icing on the cake. You wanted the entire Grant family to pay for what happened five years ago, didn't you? Even me, the one member who hadn't been around when you got aced out of your share of the Inn."

"That's enough, Juliana," Travis said, so cold, so quiet.

"Enough?" she yelped furiously. "I've got news for you, Travis. I haven't even started. If you think you're going to get away with destroying Flame Valley as an act of revenge, you're crazy. I'll fight you tooth and claw."

Travis's eyes glinted. "The inn belongs to the other members of the Grant family, not to you. Stay out of it."

"The hell I will. This is a family matter and I'm family. We'll find a way to fight you, won't we, Elly?"

Elly shook her head mournfully, the tears still flowing copiously. "It's hopeless," she whispered.

"Don't say that, Elly." Exasperated, Juliana caught

her cousin by the shoulders and shook her gently. "This
is your inheritance we're talking about. It belongs to you
and David. Surely you're not going to just give up and
surrender like this. You've got to fight back."

Travis wandered over to the edge of the terrace and
leaned one elbow on the teak railing. "You're wasting
your time, Juliana. Elly's not like you. She doesn't know
how to fight for what she wants. She's used to having
someone else hand it to her on a silver platter."

Elly's head came up abruptly. "You…you bastard.
Thank heaven I didn't marry you five years ago. I would
have been married to a…an inhuman monster." Elly
choked audibly on her tears and broke free of Juliana's
grip. Without a backward glance she ran toward the
relative safety of the crowd near the pool.

Juliana gritted her teeth in disgust as she watched her
cousin dash away like a graceful gazelle fleeing the
hunter. Then she whirled to confront Travis. "Satisfied?
Are you proud of yourself? Do you enjoy hurting things
that are softer and weaker than you are?"

"There's nothing all that soft or weak about your
cousin. She may not know how to fight a fair fight, but
that doesn't mean she's not very good at getting what
she wants. She uses her softness, trades on it."

"She's a gentle, loving creature by nature. And you've
got a lot of nerve talking about a fair fight. Is that what
you call this nasty bit of vengeance you're after? A fair
fight? So far all I've seen is a lot of low-down, sneaky,
underhanded, manipulative, back-stabbing tactics."

"Believe me, everything I know about that kind of
fighting, I learned from your family."

"Don't you dare use them as an excuse. My guess is
you were born knowing about that kind of fighting."

"It's not an excuse. After what they did to me five years ago, I've got every right to fight as dirty as I have to in order to get even."

"You make it sound like you're involved in some sort of vendetta."

"I guess you could call it that," Travis agreed. "I told Elly the day she called off the engagement that I would come back and when I did, I'd take the whole damned place out of Grant hands. I always follow through on my promises, Juliana."

"Really?" She lifted her chin. "Is that why you were so very careful not to make any promises of marriage to me? You wanted to feel you'd maintained your high standard of business ethics even in bed? How very noble of you."

"I know you won't believe this, but I'm sorry that you got caught in the cross fire. You're different from the others. I should have left you out of it. I can see that now."

"You couldn't have left me out of it. I'm family, remember? I'm a Grant."

"I remember. And that automatically puts you on the other side. I've known how it would be from the beginning. But, like I said, I'm sorry, all the same."

"Stop saying you're sorry. I don't believe that for a minute."

He swirled the contents of his glass. "No, I don't suppose you do." His gaze was on the darkness of the sea.

"If you were truly sorry," Juliana said suddenly, knowing she was clutching at straws, "you'd call the whole thing off, walk out of here tonight and never bother my cousin and her husband and the rest of the family again."

His teeth were revealed in a brief, macabre grin that vanished as quickly as it had appeared. "Not a chance in hell of that happening, Juliana. I've come too far, waited too long and planned too carefully. Nobody gets away with making a fool out of me the way your family did five years ago."

"Sounds to me like you made a fool out of yourself."

"It's true I made a few mistakes. I let the personal side of my life get mixed up with the business side. I don't make that kind of mistake these days."

"Yes, you made a few mistakes." For an instant Juliana was overwhelmed by the sense of loss that swept through her. "Damn it, Travis, how could you be so blind? We could have had something wonderful together, you and I. I was so sure of us. So certain we were meant for each other. But you're going to throw all the possibilities away for the sake of your revenge. You are a fool."

His face was a taut mask of controlled anger. "You know something, Juliana? I don't expect you to accept the situation and I don't expect you to forgive me. I knew from the start that you'd have to end up on your family's side of this thing. But I think that, given your own talent for straightforward action, you might at least understand my side."

"If you're talking about your desire for revenge," she said, impatient with him now, "I might be able to understand it. But I don't approve of it. How can I? This is my family you're going to hurt."

"Yeah, I know," he said, watching her with what looked like resigned regret. "That's the way the chips had to fall."

"Just for the record," Juliana said, "it isn't your notion of vengeance that has convinced me you're a fool and a muddle-brained, stubborn idiot." She turned on her heel and started toward the crowd near the pool.

"Juliana, wait." The words came roughly through the darkness, as if they had been wrenched out of him.

She refused to turn around. Head high, two-inch heels clicking furiously on the terrace stones, she walked swiftly away from the man she loved.

"Juliana." Travis came up behind her. "Look, I know you're angry and I know you probably won't ever be able to forgive me. But I had my reasons and I did what I had to do. Maybe if I were confronted with the same situation today, I'd handle it differently."

"Don't give me that bull." Juliana didn't pause. She was nearing the long buffet table.

"Okay, so I'd probably do it the same way a second time if I had to do it all over again. That doesn't mean I'm not sorry about involving you the way I did."

"Stop whining. I don't want your apologies. Things are bad enough as it is."

"Damn it, I am not whining. And I'm not apologizing. I'm just trying to explain—" He broke off with a muttered oath, moving quickly to keep up with her. "Juliana, what did you mean a minute ago when you said it wasn't my plans for revenge that convinced you I'm a fool?"

Juliana paused beside the buffet table long enough to pick up a huge glass bowl full of guacamole. She swung around, the bowl held in both hands. "Revenge I can comprehend. Being the magnanimous, liberal person that I am, I could even understand your using me to further your scheme. I don't condone it, mind you, but I can understand your doing it. Given a similar situation, I might have been tempted to do something very much like what you're doing."

"I knew you'd be able to see my side of it." Travis

looked bleakly satisfied. "I realize you can't side with me, but at least you understand why I'm doing it."

"What I cannot and will not forgive," Juliana continued fiercely, "is the fact that this whole mess occurred because you thought you were in love with my cousin."

"Now, Juliana, listen to me. That was a long time ago. I was a lot younger then."

"Oh, shut up. I don't intend to ever listen to you again. Why should I listen to a fool? How could you have been so dumb, Travis? She's too young for you. Too soft. You would have run roughshod over her and then gotten angry because she didn't stand her ground. You would have been climbing the walls after six months of marriage. Can't you see that?"

"Uh, Juliana, why don't you put down that bowl?" Travis eyed the guacamole uneasily.

"She's not your type. I'm your type."

"Juliana," Travis said very firmly. "The bowl. Put it down."

"I'll put down the bowl when I'm good and ready. You asked me why I thought you were a fool. I'm telling you. You're a fool because you fell in love with the wrong woman. You still don't even realize that I'm the right one. I could forgive just about anything but that kind of sheer, unadulterated masculine stupidity."

"Juliana." He put out his hand, as if to catch hold of her.

"Don't touch me."

"Damn it, Juliana. *Juliana.*"

Travis released her and leaped back but it was too late. The avocado-green contents of the bowl were already sailing through the air toward him. He held up a hand and instinctively ducked but the guacamole was faster than he was. It spattered across his white shirt and jacket, a good deal of it hitting him squarely on his striped tie.

Juliana surveyed her handiwork with some satisfaction and put the bowl back down on the table. "Now, at least, you're the right color for a frog."

She swept away from the buffet table, moving through the stunned onlookers like a queen through a crowd of stupefied courtiers. She had never been this infuriated, this hurt before in her life. Not even when her fiancé had told her he wanted to marry another woman.

She had been so sure of herself this time; so sure of Travis. How could she have been so certain and yet be so wrong? It wasn't fair.

Her mother, petite, silver-haired and quite lovely at fifty-nine, was suddenly hovering anxiously in front of her. "Juliana, dear, what's going on? Are you all right?"

"I'm fine, Mom."

"Your father and Tony are worried. That man…" Beth Grant's voice trailed off as she glanced helplessly past her daughter to where Travis stood covered in guacamole.

"I know all about it, Mom. Excuse me, please. I'm going home."

"But, Juliana…"

Juliana patted her mother reassuringly on the shoulder and hurried around her. She took several deep breaths as she went through the lobby and out into the parking lot. She would have to calm down a little before she got behind the wheel of her car.

Travis stood staring after her, as riveted in place as everyone else around him. He could not quite bring himself to believe what had happened. No one he knew did things like this. Not in front of a hundred people.

"Welcome to the dangerous hobby of escorting

Juliana Grant." Like the good host he was, David Kirkwood waded through the shocked crowd toward Travis. He grinned wryly and picked up a napkin off the buffet table. "If you plan to hang around her very long, you'd better get used to being taken by surprise," he advised as he handed Travis the napkin. "She's got a way of keeping a man off balance."

Travis snatched the napkin from his host and took several furious swipes at the guacamole. He could tell instantly that the tie was ruined. "You sound as if you speak from experience. I take it you've seen other men buried under guacamole?"

"Oh, no. Juliana rarely repeats herself. She's too creative for that. But I've sure seen more than one man with that particular expression on his face."

"What expression?"

"That of a poleaxed steer. If it's any consolation, I know exactly how you feel."

"How would you know?" Travis looked with disgust at the avocado stained napkin.

"I was engaged to Juliana for a short but very memorable month almost four years ago."

Travis crushed the napkin in his fist, his gaze slamming into David Kirkwood's amused eyes. Sympathetic, lively hazel eyes. Six foot three, at least, Travis estimated. Fair-haired. Smile like something out of a toothpaste commercial. An expensive Italian pullover sweater over a designer sport shirt and pleated slacks. A massive gold ring on one hand that went with the massive gold watch on his wrist. Travis's instincts warned him of the truth. No doubt about it, this was Juliana's golden god, the one who'd left her for the petite blonde. The blonde was Elly.

"You were engaged to her?" Travis wiped off more guacamole.

"I know what you mean. Hard to believe, isn't it? She's definitely not my type. I'm not quite sure how it happened, myself. She sure dazzled me for a while, though. Something about her makes a man look twice. Then run."

"What do you mean, she dazzled you?"

"Hey, give me a break. You've been around her long enough to know what I mean. She's a lot of woman. But maybe a little too much woman for most of us poor mortal males. Who wants to marry Diana the Huntress? You always get the feeling you're one step behind Juliana. Say, you want to wash the rest of that stuff off in the men's room?"

Travis shook his head, feeling oddly numb. Before he could think of what to do next, Juliana's father and uncle hove into view, planting themselves squarely in front of him. Just what he needed, he thought. They'd been coolly ignoring him for the most part until now. Apparently Juliana's exit scene had prodded them into staging a confrontation.

"What the hell do you think you're doing, Sawyer?" Roy Grant demanded. He glared hostilely at Travis through the lenses of his bifocals. "What did you say to my daughter to upset her that way?"

"Why don't you ask her? I'm the one wearing the guacamole," Travis muttered. Roy Grant hadn't changed much, he reflected briefly. The younger of the two Grant brothers by two years, he was still in good shape for his age. He'd always been the quieter, calmer one but he wasn't playing that role tonight.

"The real question," Tony Grant interrupted, his florid face turning red with anger, "is what are you doing here tonight, Sawyer? I know you. You've got something up your sleeve. Whatever it is, you'd better watch your step, mister. Roy and I are going to keep an eye on you."

"I'll bear that in mind." Travis wondered if his tie was salvageable. Then a sudden thought struck him, galvanizing him back into action. Juliana was in a mood to walk out of here tonight and effectively strand him thirty miles from his apartment. "Oh, hell. The car."

"If she's got the keys, she's probably long gone by now," David assured him cheerfully.

"I've got the keys." Travis shoved his hand into his pocket and found them. "But I don't know if she's one of those women who keeps a spare in her purse."

"She always did when I dated her," David remarked. "Like I said, she's usually one step ahead of a man. That's our Juliana. Gets on the nerves sometimes, doesn't it?"

"The *car*." At the thought of being left without transport, Travis launched himself toward the lobby doors.

"Now hold on just one damned minute," Roy Grant called after him.

Travis ignored the warning. He flew through the lobby doors, raced past a startled desk clerk and dashed outside to the resort's brightly lit entrance.

The roar of an angry sports car engine was already reverberating through the night air. Travis came to an abrupt halt in the drive and watched in furious dismay as Juliana's red coupé hurtled toward the main road.

"That blasted, redheaded witch." Travis stood with his hands bunched into fists on his hips and watched the coupé headlights disappear around a curve in the highway. "She did it. She went and left me here."

"The thing you have to keep in mind about Juliana," David said as he ambled casually over to stand beside Travis, "is that she tends to be a mite impulsive even under normal circumstances. The only thing she's ever really levelheaded about is business. On the other hand, she's generous to a fault. Can't stand to see someone suffering. There's a chance she'll get ten miles, remember you don't have a ride home and come racing back to rescue you."

"Sure there's a chance of that happening. A fat chance."

David nodded. "You're probably right. She did look a little annoyed with you. Hey, but not to worry, mate." He clapped Travis familiarly on the shoulder. "I'll run you back to Jewel Harbor. No problem."

Travis cursed softly, fluently, and with great depth of feeling. The thought of accepting a friendly lift from the man he fully intended to ruin was enough to make him a little crazy. And on top of everything else, Kirkwood was Juliana's ex-fiancé—her golden god.

Travis wondered if Juliana had deliberately abandoned him just so he'd be faced with this bizarre social situation. He was certain the awkward irony of the whole thing would appeal to her warped sense of humor. The woman was a menace.

"Maybe one of your other guests is going to be returning to Jewel Harbor later this evening," Travis suggested tightly.

David frowned consideringly. "Can't think of anyone right off."

"Maybe I can rent a car from your front desk."

"We don't have any car rental service."

"An airport van service?" Travis tried, feeling desperate.

"The kid who drives the airport run has gone home for the night." David grinned. "Afraid you're stuck with me."

Travis flipped another puddle of guacamole off his sleeve and said very carefully, "I think I'd better tell you who I am."

"Why don't you do that?" David said quietly. "I've been wondering just who you are since you walked onto the terrace and caused my wife to nearly faint. And Roy and Tony have been looking as if they'd seen a ghost."

Travis looked at him with a tinge of reluctant respect as it sank in that there was more to David Kirkwood than appeared on the surface. He should have been prepared to find the man had hidden depths, Travis reminded himself. After all, Juliana had once thought herself in love with him.

"I'm the head of Fast Forward Properties, Inc.," Travis said.

David exhaled slowly. "So my time has run out, has it?"

"That's about it. I'm running a business, Kirkwood, not a charitable foundation."

David ran his fingers through his hair. "No, you don't look like the charitable type. But that doesn't answer my question. What else are you besides the big, bad wolf come to blow the house down?"

Travis sighed, not particularly enthusiastic about telling him the rest but knowing it would all be coming out eventually. "I'm the guy who saved this place five years ago when Tony and Roy Grant were teetering on the brink of bankruptcy."

David's gaze sharpened. "The consultant they stiffed? The one who thought he was going to get a third of the resort as his fee for services rendered?"

"You know about that deal?"

"Not all of it. No one talks about that incident. No

one talks about you or what happened five years ago. But there were some papers and records left in the office when I took over after my marriage. I think I pieced most of the story together. Including the fact that you were once engaged to my wife."

"Yeah, well, if it's any consolation, I'm not here to claim her. All I want is Flame Valley."

"You don't just want your fee. You're here to get revenge, aren't you?"

Travis shrugged. "I just want what's due me."

"Juliana wasn't a part of what happened five years ago, was she?"

"No." Travis stared out into the darkness. "I shouldn't have involved her."

"No way you could avoid it." David fished a set of keys out of his pocket. "Come on, Sawyer. I'll drive you back to Jewel Harbor."

"Why would you want to do me any favors?"

"I don't see it as a favor," David said as he led the way toward a white Mercedes. "I see it as a final, desperate struggle of a drowning man. I intend to use the time between here and Jewel Harbor to get you to listen to my side of this thing."

"You might as well save your breath, Kirkwood. I've already told you, I'm not running a charity." But Travis reluctantly walked toward the Mercedes. He wasn't going to argue with a free ride at this time of night.

"And you've already told me you wished you hadn't involved Juliana." David opened the door of his car.

"That's right. As far as I'm concerned, she's out of it now. Financially, at least."

David smiled coolly. "I've got news for you, wolf. Juliana is in this up to her big, beautiful eyes."

Travis looked at him sharply over the roof of the car. "How?"

"A year ago she loaned Flame Valley Inn a sizable sum of money."

"She did *what?*" Travis felt as if he'd been punched in the stomach.

"You heard me. It was a very large loan. I was planning to repay her at the end of this year. That won't be possible if you foreclose, of course. If the inn goes under, all Juliana's big plans for Charisma Espresso will probably go with it."

# *Four*

Juliana was in bed, but she was far from being asleep when someone began leaning on her doorbell and did not let up. The famous notes of the opening passage of the William Tell Overture clamored throughout the condo, over and over, endlessly repeating themselves until Juliana's head was ringing. She wondered when the Lone Ranger would arrive.

It didn't take her intuitive mind long to figure out who among her acquaintances was most likely to be standing on her doorstep making a nuisance of himself tonight. It also did not require great mental endowment to figure out that the offender was probably not going to give up and go away anytime soon.

Travis Sawyer was not the type who gave up easily, as he had already demonstrated by waiting five years for his vengeance.

Juliana got out of bed and reached for her peach satin robe. She ignored the dueling chimes long enough to pause beside her dressing table mirror and gloss her lips with a shade of lipstick she thought went well with the robe. She was considering adding blusher when the endless chimes finally got to her. Unable to stand the torture any longer, she stepped into a pair of silver high-heeled lounge slippers and stalked into the living room and threw open the door.

"Whatever you're selling, I'm not buying," she announced. "But you can try."

Travis, who was leaning against the chime button, straightened slowly, his eyes chips of ice. "Why didn't you tell me you had dropped a chunk of your personal savings into Flame Valley Inn?"

"Why should I have told you? It was family business and I only hired you to consult on Charisma. Besides, I had no idea of your deep, personal concern for the inn until a few hours ago."

His gaze swept over her and his cold expression grew even harsher. "You can't stand around out here dressed like that. Someone's likely to drive past any minute. Let's go inside."

"I don't think I want you inside my apartment. Maybe you secretly hold the mortgage on this whole building or something. Maybe you're getting ready to foreclose on the condominium association and kick all us poor owners out into the street."

"Stop talking nonsense. I am not in the mood for any more of your warped humor tonight. Stranding me at Flame Valley was the last straw." He shouldered his way past her, heading for the living room.

"How did you get back to Jewel Harbor?" Juliana

closed the door slowly and followed Travis. She noticed that he had removed his tie and there were several green splotches on his white shirt. A niggling sense of guilt shot through her. She quelled it quickly.

By the time she caught up with Travis he had already lodged himself on the salmon-colored leather sofa. He sprawled there with negligent ease, one foot prodded on the black and chrome coffee table.

"What do you care how I got back?"

"It wasn't a question of caring exactly," Juliana explained as she sank into a turquoise chair and crossed her legs. The silver slippers gleamed in the light from a nearby Italian style lamp. "I asked out of simple curiosity."

"I flew."

"On your broomstick?"

"No, you used the broomstick, remember?"

"Ah," said Juliana. "Feeling peevish, are we? I'll bet David gave you a lift home. He would. David's always the perfect host. Did you tell him who you were before or after he went out of his way for you?"

"Before."

"How very upright of you. Your sense of business ethics is certainly an inspiration to the rest of us." The silver sandals winked again as Juliana recrossed her legs and smiled blandly.

"Don't give me that superior look, Juliana. My temper is hanging by a thread tonight."

"Shall I fetch a pair of scissors?"

Travis closed his eyes and leaned his head back against the leather cushion. "No, you can fetch me a shot of brandy. Lord knows I need it."

"Brandy is expensive. Why should I waste any of my precious supply on you?" Juliana asked.

Travis's eyes opened and he looked straight at her. "One of these days you're going to learn when to stop pushing," he said very softly.

"Who's going to teach me?"

"It's beginning to look like I'm stuck with the job. It's obvious there aren't a lot of other candidates and one can certainly understand why. Go and get the brandy, Juliana. I want to talk to you."

She hesitated a few seconds and then, hiding a smile, got to her feet and went into the kitchen. She opened a cupboard, found the expensive French brandy she saved for special occasions and carefully poured two glasses.

"Thank you," Travis said with mocking courtesy as she returned to the living room with the balloon glasses balanced on a clear acrylic tray. He picked up one of the glasses.

"Okay," Juliana said as she sat down again. "What do you and I have to talk about?"

"How the hell could you get yourself engaged to David Kirkwood?"

Juliana had thought she was prepared for whatever bomb Travis dropped, but this salvo took her by surprise. "My, you and David certainly got chummy on the drive back to Jewel Harbor, didn't you? The old male bonding routine, I suppose."

Travis scowled. "Answer me, Juliana."

"How did I get engaged to him? Well, let me think a minute. It's been nearly four years now and my memory isn't totally clear on the subject, but as I recall it was in the usual manner. He took me out to dinner at The Treasure House, the same place you and I ate the night you tricked me into going to bed with you, as a matter of fact, and…"

"I didn't trick you into bed and you know it. Stop trying to sidetrack me with a guilt trip. It won't work. And I don't give a damn about where Kirkwood put an engagement ring on your finger. I want to know why in the world you manipulated the guy into asking you to marry him in the first place. Anyone with half a brain can see he's all wrong for you."

Juliana's temper flared at the accusation. "I didn't manipulate him. He asked me and I accepted for all the usual reasons."

"Don't give me that. Nothing happens around you for the *usual reasons*. Damn it, Juliana. How could you even think of marrying a guy like that?"

"David is a very nice man as you witnessed tonight. There aren't a lot of other people in his position who'd give you a lift knowing you planned to ruin them."

"You don't need a very nice man," Travis said through his teeth. "You need someone who can hold his own with you. Someone who won't let you get away with murder. Someone as strong or stronger than you are."

"You may be right." Juliana smiled and gave him a pointed look. "But a woman can't afford to be too choosy these days. Sometimes we have to lower our standards a trifle."

Travis's smile was as well chilled as hers. "Meaning you lowered your standards when you picked me for your second fiancé?"

"You said it, not me. But now that you mention it—"

"Juliana, that's enough. I've already told you I'm not in the mood for your backchat. All I want tonight are a few straightforward answers. I always thought straightforwardness was your specialty. You once told me you like everyone to know exactly where he stands with you and you like to know where you stand with others."

"I've answered your questions. I got engaged to David because we had a lot in common and because I thought I loved him and he thought he loved me. We both realized our mistake within a month. Actually, to be perfectly truthful, I realized it within a couple of days. At any rate we ended the engagement. No hard feelings."

"You mean David ended things when he realized he would drive himself crazy trying to keep up with you. Elly probably looked like a restful, sweet, golden-haired angel to him after a month of being engaged to you."

"Are you implying I'm a witch?"

"No, ma'am, although I'll admit I called you that earlier tonight when I watched you drive out of that resort parking lot. You're what Kirkwood said you are, a lot of woman. Not every man wants that much woman. Kirkwood sensed he couldn't handle you. You'd have run him ragged and then gotten irritated with him for letting you do it."

"Rather like you and Elly." Juliana felt goaded and warned herself not to let Travis trap her into losing her self-control.

"Like Elly and me? Possible." Travis took a swallow of the brandy and gazed broodingly at the black stone gas fireplace. "You're probably right, as a matter of fact. It doesn't matter anymore, though. Whatever was between Elly and me five years ago is nothing but ashes now."

"I'm not so sure of that," Juliana said coolly. "I saw the way you two looked at each other tonight. There was a lot of old emotion in the air."

Travis waved that observation aside with an impatient movement of his hand. "Old anger on my part. Old fear on hers, probably. Five years have passed and she

had convinced herself I'd forgotten all about Flame
Valley Inn. She practically had an anxiety attack tonight
when she realized that I hadn't forgotten anything."

"Revenge is powerful stuff, isn't it, Travis?"

"It'll keep you warm when you haven't got much
else," he agreed. His gaze switched back to her face.
"Tell me what happened when you found out Kirkwood
was calling off your engagement because he was in love
with your cousin."

"That's personal. Why should I tell you?"

"I'll bet there was a hell of a scene. Fireworks and
mayhem. Blood and guts everywhere. You wouldn't
easily surrender something you wanted. Did you fight
like a she-cat to hold on to your handsome tin god?"

Juliana wrinkled her nose. "Golden god, not tin god."

"Let's compromise on papier-mâché god. Did you
fight for him, Juliana?"

"Why do you care?"

"I want to know, damn it. I want to know if you
fought for him. I want to know how hard you fought for
him. Maybe I want to know if you're still fighting for
him. Just answer the question."

"I don't owe you any answers. Did you fight for
Elly? How hard? Are you still fighting for her? Is taking
over Flame Valley your way of trying to reclaim her?"

That appeared to startle him for an instant. Travis
looked honestly taken aback. "I don't do things the
way you do."

"You just turned around and walked out, huh?
Vowing revenge, of course."

"I think," Travis said, "that we had better change
the subject."

"You started this conversation."

"Your logic is irrefutable, madam." He saluted her with his glass. "You're right. I started it."

"I love it when you use big words. So professionally macho."

He shook his head. "You're in a real prickly mood tonight, aren't you?"

"I have good cause."

"You're not the one who found himself stranded in the middle of nowhere without a ride home." Travis's crystal cold gaze locked on hers. "Why in hell did you sink your personal cash into Flame Valley, Juliana? You're a better businesswoman than that. You must have realized it was a high-risk investment."

She blinked at the quick shift of topic. "We're back to that, are we?"

"Yes, we're back to that and we're not letting go of it until I get some answers."

Juliana sighed and sipped her brandy. "I've already given you the answer. It was a family thing. I knew David and Elly were in trouble. I made them a loan. So did my parents, for that matter. And Uncle Tony. Everyone in the family has tried to help David and Elly save the inn. We've all got a stake in it."

Travis set the brandy glass down on the table with a snap. "Damn it, Juliana, you're too smart to have let yourself get sucked into that mess. I've been working with you long enough to know you're anything but a fool when it comes to business. You must have known how bad things were with the inn." He slanted her a quick, assessing glance. "Or did Kirkwood lie to you about how precarious the situation was?"

"No, he did not lie. I knew exactly how bad things were."

"And you loaned him the money, anyway."

"He and Elly are fighting to save the resort. I wanted to give them a chance. Of course, the one thing I didn't know at the time was that you and Fast Forward Properties, Inc. were waiting to pounce on the wounded victim at the first sign of blood. We all assumed Fast Forward would be reasonable when David approached them in a month or so and asked for an extension. Obviously that was a false assumption."

"Obviously," Travis agreed dryly. "You're going to lose a hell of a lot of money because of David and Elly Kirkwood."

"If I lose my money, Travis, it will be because of you, not David and Elly."

Travis swore and surged to his feet. "Oh, no, you don't. You're not going to blame this on me." He began to pace the length of the gray carpet. "Don't you dare try to blame this on me," he repeated huskily. "You should never have put money into Flame Valley and you know it."

In a way he was right and Juliana did know it. She lifted one shoulder carelessly. "Win some, lose some."

Travis swung around at the far end of the room and leveled his finger at her. "You can't afford to lose that much cash, Juliana. Not if you want to expand Charisma Espresso. No one knows your financial situation better than me, and I'm telling you that you can't take this kind of loss. All your plans for Charisma will be set back three or four years at the very least."

"Okay, okay. You've made your point. I can't afford the loss. Not much I can do about it now."

Travis shoved his hands into his back pockets. "Is that all you can say?"

"No point crying over spilt espresso."

"You're looking at the end of all your plans to finance Charisma's expansion this year, and that's your reaction?" Travis asked, staring at her in disbelief. "'No point crying over spilt espresso'? I don't believe I'm hearing this."

"Be reasonable, Travis. There's not much I can do now, is there? The damage is done." She took a swallow of brandy and gazed forlornly into the dark fireplace. "I'm ruined."

"Let's not get melodramatic. We've got enough problems as it is."

"You don't have any problems. I have the problems. And frankly, Travis, if you can't offer anything helpful to the discussion, I'd just as soon stop talking about my dismal business future. It's depressing."

"Helpful?" he snarled. "What kind of help do you expect from me?"

She slanted him a sidelong glance. "Well, Travis, you are the problem, in case you've forgotten. That means you're also the solution."

"I didn't get Flame Valley Inn into this mess," he growled furiously. "Kirkwood and Elly did it all on their own. With a little help from you and your parents and good old Uncle Tony, of course. Don't expect me to solve everything by paying you back after I take over the resort. I've got investors to pay off first, remember? A half dozen of them, and they'll all be standing in line waiting for their money. I've made commitments to them. And I can personally guarantee that none of them are going to be feeling charitable."

"You're right. I don't expect you to pay me off when you and your investors take over the inn."

"Well, what do you expect out of me?" Travis roared.

She pursed her lips primly. "You're my personal business consultant," she reminded him. "You are paid to keep me out of hot financial waters. You are paid to guide and advise me. I'm putting my complete faith, total trust and all my hopes for the future in your hands. I feel certain you'll save my hide."

"Juliana, what the hell am I supposed to do?"

"Save Flame Valley Inn from the clutches of Fast Forward Properties, Inc."

Travis looked thunderstruck. For a moment he just stood there in towering silence, staring at her as if she'd lost her mind. Juliana held her breath.

"Save the inn?" Travis finally repeated blankly. "From myself?"

"From yourself and that pack of hungry wolves you're leading."

"Am I supposed to do this for you?" He looked as if he was having trouble following the conversation.

"I'm one of your clients, aren't I? I hired you to help me put together a workable plan to expand Charisma. As far as I'm concerned, we still have a valid consulting contract. And the bottom line is that we can't expand my firm unless you rescue Flame Valley from Fast Forward Properties. Therefore, yes, I'm expecting you to do this for me."

"You," Travis announced softly, dangerously, "are crazy."

"No. Desperate." If only he knew how desperate, Juliana thought. She wasn't fighting to save the inn or Charisma's future. She was fighting to save the love of her life. But she did not think now was the time to point that out to him. "Will you help me, Travis? Will you salvage the resort from bankruptcy?"

"I already did that once, remember? And I didn't get paid for my efforts. What makes you think I'd repeat that mistake?"

"This time I'll be paying your fee. And you already know I pay my debts."

"Lady, you can't afford my fee."

She frowned. "I'm paying you already, remember? For the consulting work on Charisma. And so far I haven't had any trouble meeting the tab. I paid your retainer right on time and I'll meet the monthly fees, no sweat."

"Oh, Lord. What an innocent." Travis rubbed the back of his neck in a gesture of pure exasperation. He stalked to the end of the room and back again. "Juliana, let me make this crystal clear. The fee you are paying me for consulting work on Charisma is only a fraction of what I would normally charge for that kind of job. In fact, under normal circumstances, I would never even agree to take on a job the size of Charisma. Your operation is far too small for Sawyer Management Systems. Do I make myself plain?"

"You're telling me I got a special deal?"

"You got a hell of a deal."

She caught her lower lip thoughtfully between her teeth. "Why? Because I was a Grant and you were out to punish all the Grants? You wanted to get close to me so that you could hurt me by destroying Charisma?"

"No, damn it, I never intended to destroy Charisma. I don't know what happened. Not exactly. All I know is that I walked into your shop that day last month because I was curious to meet the one member of the Grant family who hadn't been around five years ago." Travis's palms came up in a gesture of total incomprehension. "The next thing I knew I was having a cup of coffee and agreeing to consult on your expansion plans."

"You mean you took on my project out of the kindness of your heart?"

"I don't do business out of the kindness of my heart," he said grimly.

"Well, that's neither here nor there now, is it? We've got a contract. You're my business consultant and I am facing a financial disaster. It seems to me you're duty bound to save me."

"Is that right?" His gaze was unreadable.

"Looks that way to me."

"Since you've got all the answers," he said, "maybe you'll be kind enough to tell me just how I'm supposed to save you?"

"I don't know. That's your business, isn't it?"

Travis shook his head. "You are really something else, you know that?"

"So I've been told. Well? Will you do it?"

He sighed. "It can't be done. I'm too good at what I do, Juliana, and I've set this up so that there aren't any loopholes. Even if I thought I might be able to save the inn and even if I was idiotic enough to agree to try, there's still the little matter of my fee for the job."

"Name it. I'll tell you whether or not I can afford it," she challenged softly.

He looked at her through dangerously narrowed eyes. His gaze moved from the toe of her silver lounge sandals to the top of her red mane. "What if I told you my fee was an all-out affair with you? What if I said that the price of my services, win, lose or draw, no guarantees on saving the resort, was access rights to your bed?"

Juliana stopped breathing for a few seconds. Then she

sucked in a dose of air and sat very still to conceal the fact that she was trembling. "My fabulous body in exchange for your services as a consultant? Don't play games with me, Travis. If you don't do business out of the kindness of your heart, you certainly wouldn't do it for sex."

He didn't move. When he spoke his voice was very, very soft. "But what if I said that was the fee, Juliana?"

She shivered, aware that he was deliberately tormenting her. "I'd tell you to take a long walk off a short pier."

He turned away and stood looking out the window into the darkness. "Yeah, I figured that's what you'd say. All right, smart lady, I'll tell you what my fee for trying to salvage Flame Valley Inn and Charisma's future would be. It would be the same as it was five years ago, a piece of the action."

Juliana gasped, not in shock this time but in outrage. "You expect David and Elly to make you a partner in the business if you save it from your own investors? Talk about gall." She thought quickly. "Still, I suppose something along those lines might be worked out. It would have to be a very small piece of the action, however. You simply can't expect David and Elly to give you a half interest or anything like that."

Travis slanted her an assessing look over his shoulder. "No. You don't understand, Juliana. I don't want a piece of Flame Valley Inn. If, by some miracle, I do manage to save the resort, it's going to need a lot of cash and a lot of work and even then there's a good chance it will still go under within a couple of years. I want a piece of a sure thing this time."

She watched him closely, the way she would a predator, and felt her stomach tighten. "What sure thing?"

"Charisma."

Juliana nearly dropped her brandy glass. Her mouth fell open in amazement. She sat staring at him, unable to comprehend what he was saying. "A piece of Charisma? You want a piece of my business? But, Travis, Charisma is mine. All mine. I built it from scratch. No one else in the family is even involved with it. You can't be serious."

"Welcome to the real world. I am very serious. I told you my usual fees are always very high, Juliana. And if you agree to the deal, you'd better understand going in that there's a big possibility I won't be able to save the resort. But I'll expect to be paid, even if I fail to salvage Flame Valley."

Juliana was reeling. She struggled frantically to collect her thoughts. She hadn't been expecting this, although looking back on things, she probably ought to have expected it or something equally outrageous. Travis Sawyer was a formidable opponent. "But Charisma is mine," she repeated, dazed. "I made it what it is all by myself. I learned the ropes managing an espresso chain in San Francisco for years while I saved my money to buy my first machines and find a good location. I've done it all, all by myself."

"And all by yourself you put Charisma's future at risk by making that loan to Kirkwood and your cousin." Travis started for the door. "Think about it, Juliana. I'll drop by your shop Monday morning to get your decision."

"Travis, wait, let's talk about this. I'm sure we can find some reasonable compromise if we just—"

"I don't make compromises when it comes to insuring my fee. I learned my lesson on that five years ago. And I learned it from dealing with people named Grant."

"But, Travis…" Juliana leaped to her feet but the

door was already closing behind him. She raced to the window in time to see him get into the Buick he'd left parked in front of the apartment earlier in the evening. The headlights came on, blinding her. In another moment he was gone.

"You sneaky, conniving, hard-hearted, son of a... Charisma is mine, damn it. *Mine*. And I'm not going to let you or anyone else have a piece of it." Juliana halted in the middle of her tirade as a thought struck her with the force of a lightning bolt.

If she gave him a chunk of Charisma Espresso Travis would be financially bound to her for what might be years. Their lives would inevitably be deeply entangled. It was easier to get rid of a spouse these days than it was a business partner.

And if she had him around to work on all that time, Juliana told herself, spirits soaring, she just knew she could convince him to see that they were meant for each other.

Travis was aware of the tension that gripped his insides as he parked the Buick in front of Charisma Espresso on Monday. He should be used to the unpleasant sensation, he told himself. He'd been awake two nights in a row because of it.

He could see the lights on inside the espresso bar, and he thought he caught a glimpse of Juliana's red hair as she ducked into the back room. His hands tightened on the steering wheel. He still could not quite believe he was doing this. But he supposed he shouldn't be too surprised. This whole deal had been skewed from the moment he had met Juliana. Nothing had happened the way he had planned it since then, so why should anything straighten out now?

He forced himself to get out of the car and walk toward the shop. He had to be prepared for whatever answer he got. Juliana was nothing if not unpredictable. And Charisma was very, very important to her.

He wondered if she would realize what he was doing and why. The whole, crazy scheme had come to him in a flash in the heat of the argument Saturday night and he still was not certain where it would all lead. He had been acting on instinct, trying to buy himself some time.

Would Juliana guess that he was using this bizarre deal to hold on to her for a while longer? And if she did, would she be furious or secretly glad?

Even if she did agree, he would have no way of knowing for certain just why she was doing so. She might be doing it because she was desperate to help her cousin and David Kirkwood. Or she might agree because he had made her aware of just how precarious Charisma's future was because of that foolish loan she had made to the Kirkwoods.

Or she might agree because she still cared a little for him and was willing to take the risk of being snared in financial bonds until they could work out the rest of their muddled relationship.

Then, again, she might simply hurl a cup of espresso in his face and tell him to get lost.

The lady or the tiger? Travis wondered as he pushed open the door. Life with Juliana was never dull.

"He's here, Juliana." Sandy Oakes, her multiple earrings clashing merrily, turned toward the door as Travis entered. Her hair was gelled into a slick 1950s ducktail and her eyes were bright with speculative interest. "Come and get him, boss."

Matt Linton looked up from where he was stacking

espresso cups. "Yup. There he is. Poor devil. Look at him standing there, so naive and unsuspecting."

"Kinda breaks your heart, doesn't it?" Sandy observed. "I mean, the poor man doesn't even know what he's in for yet."

"If I were him, I'd run for it," Matt added with a grin.

Travis groaned silently, wishing Juliana would show a little more discretion at times. "You know, the plans for the expansion of Charisma Espresso don't necessarily have to include you two," he muttered.

"Oooh," said Sandy. "I think I detect a threat."

"Juliana," Matt called more loudly. "Come and rescue us. We're being threatened out here."

Travis lifted his eyes beseechingly toward the ceiling and set his back teeth. An instant later Juliana came out of the back room, wiping her hand on a towel. She was wearing a black jumpsuit trimmed with fringe and a pair of black leather high-heeled boots. Her hair was pulled back with two silver combs.

"What's going on out here?" she demanded, brows snapping together. "Oh, it's you, Travis. It's about time you got here."

He shoved his hands into his back pockets. "I didn't realize you'd be waiting so eagerly for my arrival."

"Of course I've been eager for you to get here," she informed him waspishly. "We've got a ton of things to do before this evening, and I won't have time to do them all. You'll have to help out." She ducked into her tiny, cluttered office and reemerged with a piece of paper. "Here. This is what you have to pick up from the grocery store. And on the back are some things I want from the cheese shop three doors down. You might as well pick those up, too. And while you're at it, get some champagne, will you?"

Travis stared blankly at the list in his hand, a conviction growing within him that he had once again lost the upper hand. "Why am I buying all this stuff, Juliana?"

"For the party we're having tonight, of course. Now run along. I'm busy. Got a lot to do here. It's Monday morning, you know. Melvin is late with my shipment of Colombian and I just got word one of the coffee roasters has broken down. I'm swamped."

Travis refused to be budged. "Why are we having a party?" he asked with forced patience.

"Don't worry, it's not a big deal. I've just invited David and Elly over tonight to announce that you'll be going to work to save Flame Valley Inn." She looked straight into his eyes and silently defied him to argue.

Travis returned the challenging look, his fingers tightening on the paper in his hand. His gamble had paid off. "We have a deal, I take it?"

"We have a deal."

"You understand I can't give you any guarantees? I can't promise to save the resort. Things have gone too far for me to make any promises."

She smiled fleetingly. "If anyone can save it, you can."

"But if I can't, Juliana, I'll still expect to be paid."

"Stop carping. You'll get your fee."

Travis glanced around the interior of Charisma, aware of an almost light-headed sensation of relief. "I've always wanted to own part interest in an espresso bar."

"Since when?"

"Since Saturday night. See you later, *partner*."

# Five

"There's just one more thing about tonight," Juliana said, tossing a handful of chillies into the Asian-style noodles she was stir-frying. "I don't want anyone to know about our little, uh, arrangement."

The knife Travis had been using to slice mushrooms paused in midstroke. He glanced sideways at Juliana. "Why not?"

"Why not?" she echoed, exasperated. "Isn't it obvious? Because David and Elly will feel terrible if they think I'm paying your fee by making you a partner in Charisma. I don't want to put any more of a guilt trip on them than they're already under."

"Why should it bother them to know you're paying the fee? They didn't have any qualms about taking your money in the form of a loan."

"That was before things got so bad." Juliana concentrated on the noodles. "At the time it looked as if David really was going to be able to pull it off. Travis, have things really gone too far?"

"Probably. I told you, I set the whole thing up so that there wouldn't be any room for Kirkwood to maneuver. I won't know for certain until I get a good look at the books, but if I were you, I wouldn't hold my breath."

Juliana was undaunted. "It'll all work out. I know it will. Hand me those little tart shells, will you?"

"What kind of meal is this going to be, anyway? Just about everything here qualifies as an hors d'oeuvre in my book."

"Stop grumbling. Everyone knows the hors d'oeuvres are always the best part of a meal. I say why bother with the entrée? We'll just graze on the good stuff. When you've finished with the mushrooms, you can help me fill these shells with the cheese mixture."

"You like giving me orders, don't you?"

"It's just that you look cute in that apron. There's a glass platter in that cupboard to your right. Use it for the sliced vegetables. Hurry, David and Elly will be here any minute."

"How do I get myself into these situations with you?" Travis asked so softly Juliana barely heard him. "Every time I think I've got things back under control, I find out I'm barely keeping up with the new detour you're taking." He finished slicing mushrooms with sharp, fast strokes of the knife.

"About our partnership, Travis…"

"What about it?" His head came up warily.

"Well, I think we ought to establish right from the outset that you're more or less a silent partner. Know what I mean?" She smiled brilliantly. "I'll consult you, of course, before making major decisions. And heaven knows you're already involved in the planning process for Charisma's future. But in the final analysis, I'm the senior partner in Charisma. I just want to be sure we understand that little point."

"You can call yourself anything you like," Travis said easily, "just so long as you understand you can't make any major decisions without consulting me."

"Just what is your definition of a major decision?" Juliana retorted.

"We'll figure that out when we come across one. Where do you want this tray of vegetables?"

"On the end table near the sofa." Juliana glanced out the window and saw a familiar white Mercedes sliding into the space next to her coupé. "Good grief, they're here already. I'll bet David and Elly are dying of curiosity."

"Why? What did you tell them?"

"That you're going to save everyone's bacon, naturally." Juliana carried the tray of tiny cheese tarts into the living room.

"Don't make too many rash promises, Juliana. I've said I'll do what I can. I can't guarantee anything."

"I'm not worried, Travis. I have complete faith in you."

"You're too smart a businesswoman to have blind faith in any consultant."

"You're not the usual sort of consultant." Juliana swept toward the door, the skirts of her liquid silk hostess pajamas shimmering around her. "Open the champagne, Travis. David and Elly are going to be thrilled."

"I'll just bet they are."

David and Elly were not precisely thrilled. They regarded Travis with great caution as they walked into the living room and sat down. And they greeted Juliana's grand announcement initially with stunned surprise. The astonishment turned only gradually to careful, cautious concern, and all the questions soon developed a single focus.

"Why are you doing this?" David finally asked point-blank.

"Believe me, I've been asking myself the same question," Travis said dryly, helping himself to one of the mushrooms he'd sliced earlier.

"I mean, what's in it for you?" David persisted, brows drawn together in one of his rare, serious frowns. "Don't think we're not grateful, but I'd like to know what we're getting into here."

Juliana felt Travis's eyes switch to her face, obviously leaving the answer to that one up to her. She smiled at David. "Don't you see, David? He's doing it as a favor to me."

"A favor," Elly repeated, her eyes widening.

"A business favor," Juliana clarified. "Would anyone like another cheese tart?"

"But, Juliana," Elly persisted, "why would he do you any favors?"

"Yeah, why?" David echoed, but he looked thoughtful as he regarded Travis's unreadable expression.

"An interesting and timely question," Travis said. "Why would I want to do you any favors, Juliana?"

Juliana smiled fondly at him. "Why, to save Charisma's future, of course." She turned to David and Elly. "You have to understand something here. Travis had already committed himself to doing consulting work for Charisma before he realized the extent of my financial involvement with Flame Valley Inn. It set up a conflict of interest for him, you see. Once he discovered how much money Charisma stood to lose, he immediately insisted on trying to salvage the Flame Valley situation. He felt ethically bound to help Charisma. Travis is very big on business ethics, you know."

"Is that right?" David murmured. "I believe I will have another cheese tart, Juliana. And another glass of champagne."

"Certainly." Juliana reached for the tray of tarts. It was all going to work out just fine, she told herself as David plied Travis with further questions. Things were falling into place nicely. She ignored Elly's anxious glances.

Twenty minutes later, however, David cornered her in the kitchen where Juliana had gone to whip up another batch of stir-fried noodles.

"Just what the devil is going on?" David demanded in low tones.

Juliana glanced up from the wok. "What do you mean?"

"You know damn well what I mean. Juliana, I don't for one minute believe all that nonsense about Travis Sawyer suddenly being stricken with a severe case of business ethics. It's just you and me out here in the kitchen, kiddo, and we've been friends a long time. Now tell me the truth. Why is he galloping to Flame Valley's rescue? The real reason this time. What's in it for him?"

"David, really." Juliana switched off the electric wok and busied herself piling noodles onto a platter. "Keep your voice down. Elly and Travis will hear you."

"Are you the fee this time around, Juliana?"

David took a step closer, towering over her in the way Juliana used to find so exciting. She realized now she found it annoying.

"Don't be silly, David."

"I'm serious, Juliana. What's going on between the two of you? Are you sleeping with him in exchange for his help? Is that the deal? Because if so, I won't let you do it and that's final. God knows I'll take all the help I can get up to a point. But I sure as hell won't let you sell yourself to Sawyer as payment for saving Flame Valley."

Juliana opened her mouth to order him out of her kitchen but before the words could be uttered, Travis interrupted from the doorway. His voice was cold and hard.

"Leave her alone, Kirkwood. Juliana doesn't need your protection. The deal she and I have made is a private one, and you don't have any need to know the details."

"He's right," Juliana said briskly. "The arrangement is strictly between Travis and myself. We're both satisfied with the details so you need not concern yourself. Here, take these extra napkins out to Elly. We'll need them for the next round of noodles."

"But, Juliana…"

"Go. Shoo. Get out of my kitchen. The noodles are getting cold. And stop worrying about me, David. You know perfectly well I can take care of myself. I always have."

"I know, but I'm not sure I like the setup here."

"You may not like it but you'll go along with it, won't you?" Travis asked softly. "Because it's the only chance you've got to save the resort."

David met his eyes for a few seconds and then, without another word, walked back into the living room with the napkins.

Travis turned back to Juliana. "You do realize that's how everyone's going to interpret this crazy deal we've made? Your folks, your uncle Tony, David and Elly, they'll all come to the conclusion you're sleeping with me in exchange for my help."

"But you and I know the truth, don't we? This is a business arrangement. Nothing more."

"Oh, sure. Right. A business arrangement. Get real, Juliana."

"Look at it this way," Juliana said as she shoved a plate of noodles into his hands. "Since we know that the business side of this deal is just that, strictly business, we're free to continue working on our relationship without worrying about each other's motives." She started briskly for the door, heedless of the shock in Travis's eyes.

"Juliana. Damn it, come back here. What did you mean by that?"

Juliana ignored him, sailing into the living room with a warm smile for David and Elly. "Everyone ready for another round of noodles? Don't be shy. I've got plenty of hot sauce."

Travis closed in on Juliana the instant the Kirkwoods' Mercedes pulled out of the lot.

"About our relationship," he began darkly.

Juliana had been feeling very confident earlier, but now that she was alone with Travis she wasn't quite so sure of herself. So she compensated by acting more sure of herself than ever. It was an old habit. When people assumed you could take care of yourself, you learned to do it. "What about it?" she asked as she began picking up napkins and plates.

Travis paced toward her very deliberately. "The last time I inquired into the subject, you had sworn off sleeping with me until I had made a commitment to marry you. As I recall, I was given one month to come to my senses. Then you said very specifically that all we had was a business arrangement. Now you're talking about a relationship. Are you changing the rules on me again, Juliana?"

"You want the truth? All right, I'll give you the truth. We're going to be seeing a lot of each other from now on, and I've been in love with you since the day I met you. To be perfectly blunt, I don't think I'll be able to resist you for much longer. Not if you put your mind to seducing me, that is." She picked up an empty tray and carried it into the kitchen.

"What the hell does that mean?" Travis stormed into the kitchen behind her and caught her in his arms as she set down her burden. "Tell me exactly what it means. No more cute games, Juliana."

"It means just what it sounds like. Are you going to put your mind to seducing me?" She twined her arms around his neck and brushed his hard mouth lightly with her own soft lips.

"Juliana." Travis breathed her name on a hoarse, urgent groan. He caught her head between his hands and crushed her mouth hungrily beneath his own.

Juliana responded instinctively, willingly and with all the pent-up eagerness that she had been fighting to keep in check.

"Hold it," Travis ordered, although his arms were already tight around her waist. "I've got to figure out what's going on here. You say our business arrangement is separate. That is has nothing to do with this end of things. And you claim you still love me. So what is all this? You think that if you let me back into your bed I'll suddenly decide I have to offer marriage, after all?"

"Who knows? You might, you being such an ethical type and all."

He shook his head in slow wonder. "You never give up, do you?"

"No. But I don't want to talk about marriage right now."

"Good. Neither do I."

Travis kissed her hard and then took her hand firmly in his and started toward the bedroom. He turned out lights en route and by the time they reached the end of the hall they were deep in the never-never land of night and shadow.

"Travis?" She smiled up at him as he drew her to a halt near the bed. She trailed her fingertips along his shoulder, enjoying the strength she found there.

"I've been going out of my mind wondering when it would happen with you again." Travis caught her earlobe between his teeth as he began to unbutton the top of Juliana's silky hostess outfit.

"I should never have set that month deadline the first time around," Juliana confided, leaning into his vital warmth. "I should have known I'd never last that long."

"We agreed after that first night together that what we have between us is very special." Travis finished unbuttoning the yellow silk top and eased it off her shoulders.

Juliana felt the whisper softness of the fine material on her skin and shivered with anticipation. Travis looked down at her bare breasts and his crystal eyes glinted in the darkness. His palm closed gently over one budding nipple and Juliana inhaled deeply.

"You feel so good." Travis's mouth found the curve of her throat. "So right."

"So do you." She tugged at his tie and tossed it aside. Then she unbuttoned his shirt with fingers that trembled.

As soon as she had freed him of the shirt, she locked her arms around his waist and leaned her head against his bare shoulder. The crisp mat of hair on his chest grazed her nipples. She wriggled against him experimentally, enjoying the teasing sensation.

Travis laughed softly, the sound husky and very sexy in the darkness. He slid his palms beneath the waistband of Juliana's silk pants and pushed them down over her hips. A moment later she stood nude in his arms.

"This is how it's supposed to be between us," Travis muttered as he picked her up and carried her to the bed. He settled her on the pillows and stood back to rid himself of the rest of his own clothing.

"I know." Juliana lay gazing up at him, glorying in the solid, hard shape of him. The strength in his shoulders and thighs appealed to all her senses and the boldness of his arousal pleased her on a deep, primitive level. But it was not simply the physical aspect of Travis that captivated her and made her so aware of him on a sensual plane, she realized. There were other men just as solidly masculine and far better looking.

"You look very serious all of a sudden," Travis observed as he came down beside her on the bed, a small foil packet in one hand. "What are you thinking?"

She looked up at him as he loomed over her. "I was just wondering what it is about you that makes you so sexy."

He grinned, teeth flashing in the darkness as he dealt with the contents of the packet. "You're trying to figure out why you couldn't resist me any longer?"

"Um-hm." She trailed her fingers through his hair and tangled one leg between his.

"Don't think about it too hard," Travis advised, leaning down to kiss the valley between her breasts.

"Some questions don't have any clear answers. Just accept it and go with it."

"Whatever you say, partner." Juliana arched invitingly as his hand stroked down the length of her to her hip. When his fingers squeezed the curve of her thigh she sighed, feeling her own response deep within her body. He had such good, strong, knowing hands, she thought. The barest touch of his rough fingertips aroused her, and when he kissed her breast, she almost cried out. She could feel herself growing warm and damp already.

Turning slightly in his arms, Juliana snuggled more closely against Travis. She began to explore him intimately, rediscovering the secrets she had first learned during their one previous night together.

She could feel the sexual tension in him as her hand slipped over his body. The muscles of his back and shoulders were taut with the desire he held in check. Travis's obvious need elicited a fierce reaction within Juliana. She stirred restlessly against him. When his fingers slid between her thighs into the dampening heat of her she parted her legs and whispered his name softly. Her nails grazed his shoulders.

"The kind of woman who leaves her mark," Travis muttered, rolling her onto her back.

"What?"

"Never mind. Wrap your legs around me, sweetheart. Tight. Take me inside and hold me close."

Juliana gathered him to her, aware of his hard shaft pressing against her softness. She was aching for him, her body throbbing with need.

"Now," Juliana whispered, her eyes closed as she clung to him and tightened her legs around his lean hips. "Come to me now. I love you, Travis."

"I couldn't wait any longer if I tried."

Travis eased himself into her carefully, filling her completely, stretching her gently until she felt the spiraling tension begin to build to unbearable heights.

She lifted her hips and Travis responded by driving more deeply into her and then withdrawing with excruciating slowness. Juliana clung more fiercely, urging him closer. He stroked into her again and again withdrew.

"Travis," she hissed, clutching at him.

"I'm not going anywhere without you."

He surged into her again, more deeply than before and Juliana gasped as the delicious tension within her went out of control. She gave herself up to the release, Travis's name on her lips as she felt him plunge into her one last time. The muscles of his back went rigid beneath her palms and she was crushed into the bedding beneath his solid weight.

For a time there was nothing else of importance in the entire universe.

A long while later Travis stirred on top of Juliana and looked down at her, his gaze intent in the shadows. She smiled sleepily, her fingers sliding slickly through the traces of perspiration on his shoulders.

"Don't worry," she said, yawning delicately. "I'm not going to bring up the subject."

"What subject?"

"Marriage."

"You just brought it up," Travis pointed out, kissing the tip of her nose.

"Well, I'll change it to a more pressing issue."

"Such as?"

"Such as which of us gets up first in the morning to make the tea."

"I'll do it this time," Travis said.

"Such an accommodating man." Juliana yawned again and drifted off to sleep.

Three days later, at ten-thirty in the morning, Travis sat at his desk in the new Jewel Harbor offices of Sawyer Management Systems and tried to decide if he really needed to take a coffee break. Charisma Espresso was only a few blocks away. He could walk over, say hello to Juliana, grab some coffee to go and be back at the office within twenty minutes.

Or he could save fifteen minutes by helping himself to the office pot. Lord knew he needed every spare minute he could salvage to work on the Flame Valley Inn problem.

Travis eyed the stack of papers on his desk with a brooding eye. He and Fast Forward Properties had certainly done a very thorough job of setting the inn up for a takeover. The grim truth was that he was not at all certain he could save it now. A lot of creditors, including his own group of investors would have to be put on indefinite hold and a big infusion of cash would be required to get the inn back on its feet financially. It was a nightmare of a task.

Every time he thought of Juliana's blithe faith in his ability to pull the fat back out of the fire, he swore silently. Lately he found himself trying very hard not to think about what would happen if he failed.

The intercom on his desk murmured gently. "Mr. Sawyer, there's a Mrs. Kirkwood here to see you."

Travis gritted his teeth. The last thing he needed right now was a visit from Elly, but there wasn't much he could do about it. "Send her in, Mrs. Bannerman."

A few seconds later Elly came through the door, her fragile features accentuated by her short gamine haircut, her delicate figure set off by close-fitting white pants and a white silk blouse. The big blue eyes that had once seemed so clear and guileless to Travis were filled with an irritating apprehension. Had he ever really been in love with this woman, he wondered fleetingly. She was a sweet, pale azalea next to the vibrant orchid that was Juliana.

"Hello, Elly. Have a seat." Travis got reluctantly to his feet and waved her casually to a chair.

"Thank you." Elly sat down, never taking her eyes off him. She crossed her feet at the ankles and folded her hands in her lap. She looked very nervous but very determined. "I had to come here today, Travis. I had to talk to you."

"Fine. Talk." Travis sat down again and leaned back in his chair. He wished he'd made up his mind about going over to Charisma five minutes earlier. He would have missed this little heart-to-heart chat. It went to show that he who hesitated was definitely lost.

Elly took a deep breath. "You're sleeping with Juliana. You're having an affair with her."

Travis glanced out the window. He had a pleasant view of the harbor from here. He could even see The Treasure House restaurant down at the marina. "That's none of your business and you know it, Elly."

"It is if you're using her. She's my cousin, Travis. I won't have her hurt by you."

Travis looked at her. "Did you worry a lot about hurting Juliana when you lured Kirkwood away from her?"

"That's not fair," Elly cried. "I didn't lure him away. We fought our feelings for each other until…until…"

"Until Juliana finally noticed and let Kirkwood go?"

"Damn it, Travis. You don't know what you're talking about. Juliana didn't just let David go."

"Did she fight for him?" He waited tensely for the answer. He wanted to know how important Kirkwood had once been to Juliana.

Elly looked shocked at the question. "There was no fighting involved. They both realized they had made a mistake and they ended the engagement by mutual agreement. It was all very calm and civilized. Ask her. She'll tell you the truth. Travis, I don't want to talk about the past."

"Not even our own past?" he asked with mild interest.

"Especially not our own past." Her gaze slid away from his.

He nodded and tossed his pen down onto the desk. "You're right. It's a rather boring subject, isn't it?"

Elly leaned forward anxiously. "Travis, I must know if you're blackmailing Juliana into sleeping with you."

"Why?"

"Because if that's the price you've put on saving Flame Valley for us, it's too high. I won't let Juliana pay it."

"You think your cousin would let herself get blackmailed into sleeping with a man, regardless of the reason?"

Elly frowned, looking momentarily confused. "Not under normal circumstances, but this is different."

"How is it different?"

"She's very attracted to you. In fact, I think she's in love with you. I don't think it would be very difficult for her to convince herself that it was all right to sleep with you in exchange for your help. But she would be hurt when the end came, and I don't want her to pay that kind of price."

Travis was suddenly impatient. "Don't worry about it, Elly."

"She's my cousin. I can't help but worry. You've thrown everything into such chaos by coming back this way, Travis. You're a very dangerous man and I'm the only one who seems to fully comprehend that fact. David refuses to look below the surface to see what you're really up to, and Juliana is blinded by her emotions. My father and aunt and uncle are totally confused by the whole situation. They want desperately to believe the inn can be saved, and although they all love Juliana, they're used to letting her take care of herself."

"So you've decided you're the only one left to sound the warning? Save your breath, Elly. Juliana won't listen to you."

Elly got to her feet and walked nervously over to the window. She stood there, clutching her leather purse, her back toward Travis. "You're doing this to punish me, aren't you?" she whispered.

Travis thought about that for perhaps twenty seconds. "No," he said.

"You didn't come back just because you felt you hadn't been paid for saving the inn five years ago. You came back because of what happened between us."

Travis studied Elly's slender back and shook his head. Juliana had been right: this fragile, delicate, easily startled doe of a woman was not for him, had never been right for him. "I came back because I'd been cheated out of my fee, Elly. That's the only reason I came back."

Elly swallowed a sob. "I'm sorry about what happened five years ago. I was sorry at the time. I didn't want to do it. I wanted to tell you the truth, about how I wanted to end the engagement, and I wanted to tell you just as soon as I realized we weren't right for each other. But Dad was sure you would walk out, and he said if you did, we would lose Flame Valley. He said things had gone too far and that you were the only one who could save it. He said I had to make you think I was going to marry you, and that you would get the partnership in the inn as a wedding present."

"So you went along with the lie. I'll have to admit you were very convincing, Elly."

She swung around, an anguished expression in her damp eyes. "What was I supposed to do? I had to make a choice between my family and you."

"And your family won."

"Yes, damn you. There was no other option. But I won't have Juliana hurt because of what I had to do five years ago."

"You make a charming martyr, Elly. But you can relax. I am not hurting Juliana."

"You're using her. She's a stand-in for me. I know that's what it is. If you can't have one Grant woman, you'll take another, is that it? Your revenge wouldn't be complete unless you got one of us into bed."

Travis stared at her, real anger gathering in him for the first time. He stood up. "That's enough, Elly. You don't know what you're talking about. Just for the record, I will tell you that there is no way in hell Juliana could ever be a stand-in for you. Juliana is totally unique. She's not a stand-in for anybody. She could never be that. Now, I suggest you leave before you say another word."

"I haven't finished." Elly lifted her chin, defying him with all the boldness of a traumatized deer. "I want you to know I'm on to your tricks. I don't trust you one inch, regardless of what the others think."

"Is that right? Well, I'll certainly have to watch my step, won't I?"

Travis took a menacing step forward and Elly stifled a small shriek. "Don't touch me, you big brute." She leaped back, turned and ran for the door.

Travis watched with mild disgust as his former fiancée fled his evil clutches. Juliana would never have run like that, he reflected. She would have stood her ground.

Travis sat back down at his desk and picked up the stack of papers he'd been wading through a few minutes earlier. Elly's words flickered through his head.

*I had to make a choice between my family and you.*

Travis knew he'd been wrong when he had told Elly that Juliana was totally unique. She had one very important thing in common with Elly. She was fiercely loyal to her family.

Travis prayed he would never be in the same situation with Juliana that he'd been in five years ago with Elly—one where the lady was forced to choose between him and her family. He always seemed to lose in those situations.

That realization made him wonder again what would happen if he failed to save Flame Valley Inn.

The door burst open in the middle of that thought, and Juliana swept into the room bearing a paper sack with the Charisma logo emblazoned on the side.

"All right, what did you do to my cousin, you big brute?" She smiled sunnily as she set the sack down on the desk and removed an extra-large Styrofoam cup of coffee.

Travis studied her, a smile playing around the edge of his mouth. She looked very chic today in a full, pleated menswear style skirt, a tight fitting vest and a wide-sleeved shirt.

"Big brute?" Travis repeated, eyeing the cup of coffee with enthusiasm.

"I believe those were her very words." Juliana uncapped a second cup and sat down in the chair her cousin had just vacated. "The two of you had a little scene up here, I take it?"

"It's hard to have more than a small scene with Elly. She always takes off running just when things start getting interesting." Travis popped the lid on his cup and inhaled gratefully. "Just what I needed."

"I figured you'd be ready for your midmorning coffee break about now. Thought I'd save you the hike over to Charisma. Besides, I needed a break myself. Melvin and I are feuding again. So what did you and Elly argue about?"

"She thinks I'm blackmailing you into sleeping with me." Travis watched Juliana over the rim of the cup as he took a swallow of the rich, dark-roasted coffee.

"Her, too, huh?"

"I wouldn't be surprised if Sandy and Matt, your parents and Tony Grant suspected the same thing. Which would make the opinion practically unanimous."

"Too bad it's not true," Juliana remarked. "It's certainly an exciting thought."

Travis was irritated. "You weren't very excited the other night when I came up with the suggestion. As I recall you turned me down flat when I offered to take your fair body as my fee for saving Flame Valley."

"Well, of course I turned you down. I had to, for your sake."

"My sake?"

"Sure. If I'd agreed to let you blackmail me into sleeping with you, you would have worried yourself to a frazzle in no time."

Travis set down his cup cautiously. "About what?"

"About the real reason I was having an affair with you. Every time I kissed you or told you I loved you, a part of you would have wondered if I really meant it or if I was just saying it to keep you working like a dog on behalf of the resort. This way we keep business completely separate from our personal relationship."

Travis swore wryly. "Always one step ahead, aren't you?"

"I can't help it. It's my nature. I confess it was for your own good that I had to put my foot down on your thrilling blackmail attempt." Juliana got to her feet and came around to his side of the desk. Her eyes were filled with seductive, mischievous humor. "But never think for a moment that I didn't find the offer wonderfully exciting."

Travis grinned, set aside his cup and reached for her. He tumbled her down across his thighs, cradling her in his arms. "For your information, if you had accepted my blackmail offer, I wouldn't have worried about it all that much."

"No?" She kissed his throat.

"No. Next time you do something for my own good, consult with me first, okay?"

"Okay." She nuzzled his neck invitingly. "When's your next appointment?"

"I have no scheduled appointments this morning." Travis slid his hand up along her thigh, aware of the growing tautness in his lower body. Everything about this woman aroused him, he thought in wonder. He crushed a thick handful of red curls in his fist.

Juliana giggled. "Have you ever done it on the job, so to speak?"

"No." He grinned. "You?"

"Never."

"Sounds like we have some catching up to do."

He gently eased her up onto the desk so that she perched on the edge, facing him. Then he pushed the gray flannel skirt slowly up to her thighs. His fingers closed around her knees. Juliana had very nice knees, he thought. Beautifully rounded knees. Funny, he had never realized how attractive a woman's knees could be.

"Travis?" Her hand rested on his shoulders. Her topaz eyes gleamed.

"Yeah?"

"It wouldn't hurt once in a while if we sort of pretended you were blackmailing me into this, would it?"

He grinned wickedly and slowly spread her gorgeous knees apart. "I'm always willing to oblige a fantasy for you, sweetheart."

# *Six*

"Juliana, this is a very serious situation. We are all gravely concerned about the implications. That's why we all decided to hold this family conference. We need to understand just what is going on."

"Sure, Mom. I understand. But everything's under control. Trust me." Juliana confronted the three serious faces around the table, sighed inwardly and then dug a spoon into her bowl of zesty black bean soup. Not a lot of trust in this little family group; just a lot of anxiety, she decided. The excellent California-style Mexican food provided here at the colorful shopping mall restaurant would have to serve as compensation for the doleful company she was obliged to endure.

When the invitation to lunch had come that morning, Juliana had tried to think of a polite excuse to refuse but there simply was no acceptable way to turn down her parents and Uncle Tony. Lunch this afternoon had been more or less a command performance.

"Tony and I have been over this whole thing a number of times," Roy Grant informed his daughter. He watched her closely through his bifocals, concern etched in the lines of his face. "We can't figure out what Sawyer is up to but there's no question but that it's got to be bad news for all of us."

"Damn right," Tony Grant chimed in, scowling at his plate, which was overflowing with a sour cream and chicken enchilada. "Sawyer is nothing but trouble. We all know that. He's after Flame Valley and he's going to take it one way or another. Spent five years setting us up. Can you believe it? *Five years*. Christ, the man holds a mean grudge, doesn't he?"

"We knew five years ago the situation could get dicey when he found out Elly didn't want to marry him," Roy said. "Tried to pay him off then, but he wouldn't have any of it."

Juliana looked up. "As I understand it, the fee was supposed to have been a one-third interest in Flame Valley. Did you offer him that after Elly turned him down?"

"Hell, no," Tony exploded. "Couldn't go givin' away one-third of the place to someone outside of the family. For pity's sake, girl, where's your common sense? Flame Valley is a family thing. When the marriage was called off, that meant the deal was off, too. But Roy and I tried to compensate Sawyer. Wasn't like we just stiffed him completely."

"Uh-huh." Juliana helped herself to a handful of tortilla chips, dipping them into the salsa. "Did you actually offer him the cash equivalent of one-third of Flame Valley?"

Her mother's mouth tightened. "Of course not, dear. That would have meant giving him something in the neighborhood of close to a million dollars. We couldn't possibly have paid him or any other consultant that much in cash. But we did offer him a very reasonable consulting fee."

"The only thing wrong with the fee you offered was that it wasn't the fee that had been agreed to when he took the job."

Tony Grant turned red in the face. "It was just an understanding, not a signed contract, and it all hinged on his marrying Elly. That didn't work out, thank the good Lord. Whenever I think of how unhappy she would have been married to Sawyer, I get sick to my stomach. Hell, my stomach's upset right now."

Juliana rolled her eyes and munched chips. "I think that's the green chili sauce on your enchilada. You know it always upsets your stomach, Uncle Tony."

"Look, this is getting us nowhere," her father said brusquely. "Honey, we're not here to rehash the past. Right or wrong, what's done is done. It's the present we've got to worry about."

"But there's nothing to worry about, Dad." Juliana smiled soothingly. "I told you, it's all under control. Travis is working for me now. Because of his obligation to Charisma, he's agreed to try to salvage Flame Valley. He knows that if the resort goes under, I stand to lose a chunk of dough."

"Darling, it makes no sense," Beth Grant said anxiously. "Why should Travis Sawyer do you any favors?"

"I told you why. Charisma is a client of Sawyer Management Systems. It's not a favor, it's a business arrangement."

"All those bloody investors in Fast Forward Properties are clients of his, too," Uncle Tony rumbled. "Bigger clients than Charisma, believe me. They'll come first and don't you forget it."

Juliana blushed. "All right, so maybe there's more to it than just Travis's sense of commitment to Charisma. Maybe he's doing it for me."

Her parents and Uncle Tony all stared at her, their mouths open. Beth Grant recovered first.

"For you? What do you mean, Juliana? What is going on here?"

"Well, if you must know, Mom, I'm hoping to marry the man one of these days. And I think he's kind of fond of me, too, although he's still shy about admitting it."

Her father looked appalled and then outraged. "Has that bastard led you down the garden path?"

"We're getting there," Juliana assured him.

"Damn it, girl, has he proposed to you?" Tony Grant blustered. "Is that what this is all about? Is he trying to make you a substitute for Elly in this blasted revenge business?"

"Well, no, Uncle Tony, he hasn't actually proposed yet, but I have great hopes."

Her mother leaned forward, topaz eyes deeply concerned. "Darling, surely you wouldn't be taken in by a proposal of marriage from that man? You're an old hand at dealing with proposals. Men propose to you all the time. They're never serious for long."

Juliana winced. "Thanks, Mom."

"Oh, dear, I didn't mean to hurt your feelings, but you know it's the truth. You've been collecting proposals since you were in college. Men are always asking you to marry them within about twenty-four hours of meeting you and then, about twenty-four hours after that, they change their minds."

"And start looking for the nearest exit. Yeah, I know, Mom. A sad but true phenomenon. No doubt about it, I have a curious effect on men. I overpower them. But Travis is different. Nothing overpowers him." Juliana brightened. "To tell you the truth, I consider it a good sign that he hasn't rushed into a proposal."

"Why?" Her father looked suspicious.

"Well, as Mom said, the others all do it within about twenty-four hours of meeting me. Travis is apparently giving the matter much thought, which means that when he does ask me, he'll be sure of what he's doing." Juliana smiled. "But, then, Travis always knows what he's doing. He's always one step ahead."

Uncle Tony pointed his fork at her from the other side of the table. "You remember that, my girl. That man is always one step ahead of everyone. That's what makes him so dangerous."

Juliana shook her head in exasperation. "Just because he's fast and smart doesn't mean you can't trust him. I, for one, trust him completely. If anyone can save Flame Valley, he will."

A sudden thrill of awareness caused Juliana to glance around. Travis was there behind her. She smiled in welcome as his large hand settled on her shoulder.

"Thanks for the vote of confidence, honey," Travis said.

"*Travis*. What are you doing here?"

"I called Charisma to see if you could get away for lunch. Sandy said you'd already been kidnapped and were being held for ransom here at the mall." Travis surveyed the glowering expressions of the other three people at the table. "Thought I'd stop by and rescue you."

"She don't need rescuing," Tony Grant muttered.

"Damn right," Roy Grant added grimly. "My daughter can take care of herself."

"She certainly can," Beth Grant said with maternal pride.

"Everybody needs rescuing once in a while," Travis said easily as he sat down next to Juliana and picked up a menu. "I'm starving. Working on Flame Valley finances all morning is enough to give a man an appetite. Either that or make him slightly nauseous, depending on his point of view. Fortunately I've got a strong stomach. The resort's in a hell of a mess again, isn't it?"

Tony Grant blanched and then turned red. "Pardon me," he muttered, pushing his chair back from the table. "Got to get going if we're going to make it to San Diego this evening. Roy, you and Beth have a plane to catch."

Beth rose to her feet and nodded at her husband. "Yes, dear, we must run along." She frowned at Juliana. "You will remember what we talked about?"

"Sure, Mom. Have a good trip back to San Francisco."

With one last uncertain glance at Travis, Beth turned to follow her husband and brother-in-law out of the restaurant.

"Don't look now," Juliana said, "but I think I just got stuck with the tab."

"You can afford it. You've been making money hand over fist since the day you opened Charisma."

"Does that mean I'm going to get to pay for your lunch, too?"

Travis closed the menu, looking thoughtful. "It's customary for the client to pick up the consultant's expenses."

"Oh."

"Just how many marriage proposals have you collected since college, Juliana?"

Juliana blinked. "Did a bit of eavesdropping, did you?"

"Couldn't help it. Everyone was so wrapped up in that little intimate family conversation, I hated to interrupt."

"Forget my long and sordid history of collecting marriage proposals. None of them meant anything."

"If you say so."

Two days later Juliana again sat down to eat in a restaurant. This time she was alone with Travis.

"So how did the meeting with David go today?" Juliana speared one of the pan-fried oysters on her plate and chewed with enthusiasm. The Treasure House always did this dish particularly well, she thought. When there was no immediate response from the other side of the table, her brows came together in a firm line. "Not good?"

"Let's just say that Kirkwood is not a happy camper at the moment." Travis ate his swordfish in a methodical fashion that did not indicate great enjoyment.

"You know, Travis, you've been in a rather difficult mood for the past couple of days," Juliana pointed out.

"I'm working eighteen hours a day trying to save that bloody resort, get my new office up and running, keep a lot of important clients happy and find some time to spend with you. What kind of mood do you expect me to be in?"

"Maybe going out to dinner tonight wasn't such a hot idea."

"It wasn't. I've got a pile of papers back at the office I should be going through even as we speak. But since eating out was my idea, I suppose I ought to keep my mouth shut."

"So how did the meeting with David go?"

"Like I said, he's not happy. I pointed out one possible way out of the mess and he didn't like it."

"What was that?"

"Find a buyer for Flame Valley. Maybe one of the big hotel chains. An outfit that will agree to pay off the resort's creditors and agree to let Kirkwood stay on as manager."

Juliana winced. "I can see why he didn't jump at that. The last thing he wants to do is sell the place. The whole point is to hang on to it." She paused, thinking of what her Uncle Roy had said at lunch two days earlier. "It's a family thing."

"He reminded me of that. Juliana, I have to tell you, there's a chance, a very real chance, that I won't be able to pull this off."

"You'll do it." She smiled at him with all the confidence she felt.

"Damn it, I wish you weren't so irrationally sure I can save the resort." Travis's impatience blazed in his eyes. "Oh, hell. Look, I don't really want to talk about Flame Valley tonight."

"All right. Want to talk about Charisma instead?" Juliana helped herself to the last oyster on her plate. "I've been thinking about adding a new line of mugs with the store logo on them. Subliminal advertising, you see. Every time a customer uses one of them at home, he'd think of Charisma."

"It's probably not a bad idea but right now I don't want to talk about it or anything else to do with Charisma."

"Well, what do you want to talk about?" she asked patiently as she forked up the remainder of her anchovy and garlic spiked salad.

"Us."

"Us?" She paused in midchew and eyed him intently. He definitely was in a strange mood tonight. "What about us?"

She watched Travis glance around the casually chic dining room. The place was filled with casually chic diners, casually chic ferns and a lot of waitpersons who could have modeled for magazine covers. Classic California restaurant style.

"Did you say Kirkwood brought you here the night he asked you to marry him?" Travis asked.

"Yup. So did most of the others who have proposed since I arrived in Jewel Harbor."

"How many would that be?"

She scowled at him. "Still after a number, hmm? Well, there really weren't that many. Two or three, at the most. I mean, you can hardly count the real estate agent who got me the lease for Charisma or the hunk who sold me my first espresso machine. They were very nice men, but extremely superficial. Salesmen types."

"Uh-huh."

"Look, Travis, I'm sorry about the fact that several men have asked me to marry them. I've explained before that none of them were serious for long."

Travis smiled wryly. "You terrorized them all, didn't you?" He reached for his wallet. "Come on, let's get out of here."

"Where are we going?"

"For a walk."

"At this time of night?"

"This isn't downtown L.A. It's Jewel Harbor, remember? I want to talk to you and I don't want to do it in here." Travis caught the waiter's eye and the young man came hurrying over to present the check.

Five minutes later Juliana allowed herself to be led outside the restaurant and down to the marina. For a while Travis strolled beside her in silence. It was a lovely evening, filled with soft breezes and the scent of the sea. Beneath Juliana's feet water slapped the wooden slats of the docks. The boats bobbed in their slips, and here and there cabin lights indicated owners who lived on board.

Travis took a seemingly aimless path that led them to the farthest row of slips. He paused finally and stood in brooding silence, staring out over the water.

Juliana tolerated the silence for a moment or two before her curiosity overcame her. "Why did you bring me out here, Travis?"

"To ask you to marry me." He didn't look at her. He seemed mesmerized by the dark horizon.

Juliana couldn't believe her ears. *"What?"*

"You said I had a month to come to my senses. I don't need a month. I've known for quite a while that I want to marry you. It was just that everything was so damned complicated. It still is, for that matter. Nothing has changed. But I'm tired of waiting for the right time. At the rate things are going with the resort, there may not be a right time."

"Travis, turn around and look at me. Are you serious? You want to marry me?"

He turned his head slowly, a faint smile curving his mouth. "I'm serious. I haven't had time to buy a ring, but I'm very serious."

"You're not going to change your mind within twenty-four hours like the others, are you?" In spite of her confidence in him, old habits died hard, Juliana discovered. She was instinctively cautious when it came to receiving marriage proposals.

"Juliana, I guarantee I'm not going to change my mind about wanting to marry you. Trust me."

She smiled tremulously. "I do."

"Do I get an answer tonight or are you going to make me suffer awhile?"

"Oh, Travis, how can you even ask such a silly question? Of course I'll marry you. I practically asked you first, remember?"

"I remember."

Elation seized Juliana as she studied his face in the soft light. She couldn't recall a happier moment in her whole life.

"I'm sorry about the anchovy and garlic on the salad," she said as she hurtled toward him, her face raised for his kiss.

"Juliana, no, wait…"

It was too late. Normally there would have been no problem. Travis was getting used to catching Juliana's full weight against his body. But tonight the dock under his feet was bobbing precariously and he was caught off balance when she went flying into his arms.

At the last possible instant Juliana realized that disaster loomed. She clutched at Travis, her eyes widening in startled dismay as she felt him stagger back a step. She tried to catch her own balance but one of her two-inch heels got caught between the dock slats.

Travis groaned in resignation as they both went over the edge of the walkway, landing with a splash in the waters of the marina.

Juliana surfaced a few seconds later, spitting salt water out of her mouth. Her hair had been instantly transformed into a wet, tangled mop. She could feel the weight of her clothing dragging at her.

"Travis? Where are you?" She turned quickly, searching for him.

"Right here," he said from behind her, splashing softly as he made his way back toward the dock.

Juliana whipped around in time to see him plant both hands on the edge of the dock and haul himself out of the water. Juliana smiled up at him, vastly relieved. "Thank goodness. Are you all right?"

"I'll survive." Sitting on the edge of the dock he reached down to grab her hand. "I should have known that the simple task of asking you to marry me would turn into an adventure in Wonderland. By rights I ought to charge you hazardous duty pay."

"Just add it on to your usual fee, Mr. Sawyer."

His usual fee. Much later that night as he lay awake in bed beside Juliana, Travis reflected that for his usual fee, he usually produced results. This time he was not at all certain he could satisfy the client.

And he wondered if an engagement ring would be strong enough to hold Juliana if he failed to save Flame Valley Inn.

He couldn't seem to escape the premonition of disaster that hovered over him these days. In an effort to fight it off he turned on his side and gathered Juliana more tightly into his arms. She came to him willingly, fitting herself instinctively against him. After a while Travis was able to find sleep.

Juliana lounged back in her squeaking desk chair, her booted feet propped on the edge of her desk and cheerfully chewed out her supplier who was late on a delivery.

"No, Melvin, I do not want a double shipment of the

regular Sumatra. I want the aged stuff. I can tell the difference, so don't try to con me. I've got standards to uphold, remember?"

"You don't even like coffee," the man on the other side of the line complained good-naturedly.

"That doesn't mean I don't know how to taste it. By the way, how are you doing getting me another batch of those good Guatemalan beans? I'm using them in my new house blend."

"I'm trying, Juliana, I'm trying. The two estates I usually buy from have cut back shipments for a while. Weather problems. How are you doing with the decaffeinated blends?"

"Going like hotcakes. Although why anyone would want to drink decaffeinated coffee defeats me. Seems sort of pointless. I mean, why drink the stuff at all if you're not going for the caffeine jolt? Say, Melvin?"

"Yeah?"

"You know anything about buying tea?"

"Sure. Tea is a staple sideline in my business. Why? You interested in adding a line of tea there at the shop?"

"I'm thinking about it. Actually, I was thinking about opening a whole shop devoted to tea."

"Forget it. There aren't enough tea drinkers around here to keep you in business. Try adding tea there at Charisma as a sideline before you go off the deep end."

"I'll discuss it with my new business partner."

"Partner? You've got a partner now? That's a surprise. I thought you liked owning Charisma lock, stock and barrel."

"The new partner is my fiancé," Juliana confided, feeling smug. She studied the toe of her lizard skin boots. The exotic footwear went nicely with the yoked and pleated pastel jeans and the snappy little bolero jacket she had on today.

There was silence on the other end of the line. "I don't know, Juliana. I'm not so sure it's a good idea to mix business and marriage. Just look at me. I've been through three wives. Gave them all a piece of my business. Every time I got a divorce I got wiped out financially and had to start over again."

"You should have paid as much attention to your wives as you do to your coffee-importing business," Juliana chided. She glanced out the door of her office and spotted a familiar dark-haired woman entering the shop. "Look, I've got to run. See what you can do about the aged Sumatra, okay? And the Guatemalan stuff. As a favor to me, Melvin."

"Juliana, if I do you any more favors I'll probably go out of business."

"Just be sure you leave me a list of other coffee importers I can go to if you go under."

"You're a hard-hearted woman, Juliana Grant."

"I'm a businesswoman, Melvin. Just trying to make a living and keep the customer satisfied. Talk to you later."

Juliana slid her feet off the desk and recradled the phone as she stood up. She hurried out of the office and hailed the woman who had just come into the shop.

"Angelina. Just the person I want to see."

Angelina Cavanaugh smiled from the other side of the counter. Her aristocratic Spanish ancestry was evident in her fine dark eyes and the sleek brown hair she wore in a classic chignon. "Good morning, Juliana. How are you today?"

"Great."

Sandy grinned. "Be careful, Angelina. She's finally

cornered her man. She's brought him to his knees and she's still wallowing in her victory."

Angelina laughed in delight as Sandy handed her a small cup of intense, dark espresso. "Is that true, Juliana? You got a proposal out of your business consultant?"

Matt leaned over the counter conspiratorially. "It wasn't easy. Sawyer told me this morning just how it happened. She tripped the poor guy, got him off balance and threw him into the marina. He said that by the time he surfaced, he knew he was finished. He decided to surrender before she tried something more drastic."

"That," proclaimed Juliana, "is a gross distortion of events."

"Hey," said Matt, "I got the story from the victim, himself."

"Never mind him, Angelina. Come over here and sit down. I want to talk to you about the engagement party and wedding plans. Have you got room for me on your client list?"

Angelina's bright red lips curved in a smile. "Angelina's Perfect Weddings always has room for one more client, not that we aren't quite busy, what with repeat clients."

"This wedding will be a one-time event," Juliana declared.

"That's what they all say until the divorce. Have you set a date?"

Juliana frowned. "Not for the wedding. Travis is very busy right now with, uh, other matters. But I don't see any reason why I can't go ahead and schedule the engagement party on my own. Travis won't mind."

"Are you thinking of a major event?"

"Are you kidding?" Juliana chuckled in anticipation.

"I'm pulling out all the stops. I want Travis to have the wedding of his dreams, and that includes the perfect engagement party."

"I see," Angelina drawled. "And have you checked with Travis to find out just exactly what his dreams entail?"

Juliana waved that aside. "I told you, he's very busy these days. I'll take care of the wedding and engagement party details for him."

Matt, eavesdropping unabashedly, nearly choked. "Poor Travis. And he thought getting dunked in the marina was the end of his problems."

"Ignore him, Angelina. How do you like the espresso?"

"It's wonderful. Full-bodied and distinctive flavor. Very rich and strong."

"Yeah, it'll put hair on your chest, all right," Juliana agreed. "Have another cup while I start making some notes on the engagement party. Sandy," she called across the room, "fix me a cup of tea, will you, please? I hid a tin of English Breakfast behind the counter this morning."

Travis, his sleeves rolled up to the elbows, his tie loosened and his shirt rumpled, regarded the man who sat across the overflowing desk.

"There just aren't a lot of options, Kirkwood. You've been teetering on the edge of bankruptcy for months and you know it. I'm telling you, the best I can do is try to find a buyer for the inn."

"No, damn it." David leaped to his feet and paced to the window. His expression was haggard. "I told you selling out is not an option. I can't sell the inn. Just call off your wolves and buy me some breathing space."

"Breathing space isn't going to do you any good."

Travis flicked a pile of papers that all spelled impending disaster. "I might be able to stall my investors but that still leaves the banks you've been dealing with. It also leaves you needing cash. A lot of it. Even if I can get my group to hold off for a few months, which is unlikely, there's no way in hell I can ask them to pour more money into your operation."

"Fast Forward is your company. You told me yourself, you make the investment decisions."

"I do. But I've got obligations to my backers. I've made certain commitments that have to be met."

David looked back over his shoulder, his eyes intent. "I can't sell the inn, Sawyer. Even if you can dig up a buyer at this late date, I just can't sell out."

Travis studied him in silence for a minute. "Because of Elly?" he finally asked quietly.

David turned back to the view of the harbor. A deep sigh escaped his chest. "Yes. Because of Elly. I've made a lot of commitments, too, Sawyer. Told her I was going to make the resort the biggest and best on the coast. Told her I'd keep it in the family, just like her Daddy wanted. Told her she'd always be proud of it. I don't think she'll ever forgive me if I lose it."

"What will Elly do if you can't keep your promises?"

"I don't know."

"You think she'll leave you? Is that what you're afraid of?"

"Shut up, Sawyer. You worry about saving the inn. I'll worry about my marriage, okay?"

"Whatever you say. But you'd better get it through your head that I may not be able to save the inn."

David hesitated and then said under his breath, "And I may not be able to save my marriage."

There was another moment of silence. "It looks like we'd better get back to work," Travis said eventually.

Fifteen minutes later he looked up again. "Did I tell you I'm engaged to Juliana?"

David reluctantly dragged his gaze away from an accounts journal he had been studying. "What's that?"

"I said, I've asked Juliana to marry me."

David smiled slowly. "Are you sure that's the way it happened? You asked her? She didn't ask you?"

"As I recall, she told me I had a month to ask her properly. I did so last night and she rewarded me by pushing me into the water at the marina."

"Very romantic. I hope you know what you're getting into."

"So do I." Travis smiled to himself as he remembered Juliana sending them both into the harbor the previous night.

"You're doing this for Juliana, aren't you?" David asked. "Not because you're her business consultant, but because you want her to marry you and you know that if you destroy the inn, you'll lose her."

Travis shrugged and went back to his papers.

"Be a little weird if this turns out to be an instant replay of five years ago. Maybe Juliana is leading you on, getting you to save the inn and planning to dump you once Flame Valley is in the clear."

"That's enough, Kirkwood."

"You know, it's obvious to me that you would have been all wrong for Elly and she would have been wrong for you," David said conversationally.

Travis put down his pencil and folded his elbows on the desk. "Yeah?"

"Yeah." David waited, his eyes full of challenge.

"I'll tell you something, Kirkwood. You're right. Elly and I would have been all wrong for each other. And I'll tell you something else."

"What's that?"

"You and Juliana would have been a damned bad mismatch, too." Travis picked up his pencil and then reached out for the phone.

"Who are you calling?"

"An eccentric old venture capitalist I know. Tough as nails. Got money coming out his ears and no one to spend it on. Thrives on a challenge. Sometimes he'll go for something off the wall that no one else will touch."

"I told you, I don't want to sell the inn," David said angrily.

"I'm not going to try to sell this to him," Travis explained. "I'm going to see if I can talk him into paying off your biggest creditors and pour some cash into the resort."

David's expression lightened. "Think he'll go for it?"

"No, but it can't hurt to ask. We're running out of options." Travis concentrated on the phone. "This is Travis Sawyer," he said when a pleasant voice came on the line. "Tell Sam Bickerstaff I'd like to talk to him for a few minutes, please…. Yeah, I'll wait."

Elly flew through the door of Charisma Espresso shortly after lunch. She plowed through the standing-room-only crowd of coffee aficionados, searching the place until she spotted Juliana.

Juliana saw her cousin approaching and knew immediately she had heard about the engagement. Elly looked stricken.

"*Juliana*. Juliana, I just heard. Oh, my God, how could you do it? You don't know what you're doing."

"I always know what I'm doing, Elly, you know that. Everybody knows that. Now calm down. Here, I'll have Sandy make you a nice latte. You like her lattes. You can drink it in my office."

Five minutes later with Elly cradling the cup of steamed milk and coffee in her hands, the two women shut the door of Juliana's office and sat down.

"All right," Elly said tensely. "Tell me first of all if it's true. Are you engaged to Travis?"

"It's true," Juliana said cheerfully. "How did you hear about it? I was going to call you this evening. In fact, what are you doing here in Jewel Harbor? Surely you didn't feel compelled to race all the way into town just because you got the word about my engagement."

"David has an appointment with Travis today. I came with him into town. I just saw him at lunch a few minutes ago and he told me Travis is claiming he's engaged to you. Juliana, how did that happen?"

"Well, it wasn't easy, I can tell you that. Travis has been so busy what with all this business with the resort. But last night…"

"I knew it, he coerced you into sleeping with him but that wasn't enough to satisfy his ego, was it? Oh, no. He had to go all the way and trick you into an engagement." Elly shook her head sadly. "He really is trying to duplicate the past except that this time around he's using you instead of me."

Juliana smiled a little grimly. "You know me well enough to realize I wouldn't have gotten engaged to a man unless I was in love with him. Look how much practice I've had gracefully declining marriage proposals. Now stop carrying on about how I'm being suckered in a revenge plot and let's get on to a more interesting subject."

"Like what?"

"My wedding." Juliana scrabbled around on her desk, uncovering two hefty tomes she had picked up at the Jewel Harbor Library.

Elly blanched at the sight of the books on wedding etiquette. "You can't. Juliana, please. Think about this. Don't rush into anything. You mustn't set yourself up like this. He's only using you. He has no intention of marrying you."

"I talked to Angelina Cavanaugh this morning. Remember her? She has that wedding business in town. She gave me a booklet to read and recommended these books. The first step is the engagement party. I was thinking of something spiffy at The Treasure House. They have a special room they rent out for catered events."

"Juliana, this is insane. Listen to me, he won't go through with it. He just wants revenge and he'll get it by leading you on and then dumping you when he finally takes over Flame Valley."

Juliana opened one of the etiquette guides. "He's working to save the inn, remember?"

"I don't believe it," Elly whispered. "I know David believes him, but I don't. It's all a game with Travis. A game of vengeance. Neither of you know him. Ask your folks or my father. They know Travis for what he is. They know how dangerous he can be. They heard him vow revenge five years ago."

"People change," Juliana said easily.

"God. I feel like Cassandra calling out a warning that no one will heed."

Juliana nodded in commiseration. "Always a frustrating role."

"It's not funny," Elly flared. "This is serious. Very

serious. Right now Travis is feeding David all sorts of nonsense about getting another investor involved in the inn. Somebody named Bickerstaff. That's all we need. Another creditor. Oh, Juliana, what are we going to do? It's such a mess."

"Travis will straighten things out. Now about my engagement party. I think I want a buffet affair with lots of yummy goodies rather than a sit-down dinner. And it would be fun to have a band, don't you think? I wonder if Travis knows how to dance."

"I can't stand it. Nobody will listen to me." Elly put aside her cup of latte, covered her eyes with her fingers and wept. Juliana sighed and reached for a tissue. She handed the tissue to her cousin as she got to her feet.

"Here, Elly. Dry your eyes. I'll be right back."

"Where are you going?" Elly asked, lifting her tear-stained face.

"To get you a cup of tea. When the chips are down, a good cup of tea is infinitely better for the nerves than a cup of coffee."

Juliana walked back into the office a few minutes later, tea in hand and found that Elly had, indeed, managed to stop the flow of tears.

"Thank you," Elly mumbled as she took the tea.

"Feel better?"

Elly nodded, sipping daintily at the brew. "I'm sorry to be so emotional but I'm frightened, Juliana."

"I can see that. But you're worrying yourself sick over nothing. Everything's going to be all right. Travis is going to save the inn and give you and David a second chance with it. You'll see."

"But what if he doesn't? Even if he's not deliberately plotting against us, he might not be able to save it. David hinted at that much today. Juliana, I'm scared about what will happen if we lose Flame Valley."

Juliana drummed her nails on the desk. "It would be unfortunate, but it would not be the end of the world, Elly."

"It might be the end of my marriage."

"Oh, come on now."

"I mean it, Juliana. David's been acting tense lately. Not like his usual self at all."

"He's worried about the inn. We all are."

"It's more than that." Elly looked up from the steaming tea. "If we lose the Flame Valley, I might lose David."

Juliana sat very still. "That's ridiculous. Why do you say that?"

"He wanted the resort very badly back in the beginning. You know that, Juliana." Elly's voice was a mere thread of sound.

"I know he's been interested in it right from the start. He's thoroughly enjoyed running the place and planning for its future," Juliana agreed carefully. "But…"

"Sometimes I think that he married me to get Flame Valley…."

"Elly. How can you say such a thing? It's not true. It's absolutely not possible. I was there when you two met, and I was there when you realized you were in love, remember? In fact, I realized the two of you were in love before either one of you admitted it to each other."

"We tried so hard to hide our feelings, didn't we? Even from ourselves," Elly recalled wistfully. "We didn't want to hurt you, Juliana."

"I'm well aware of that. Now pay attention. David cares very deeply about you. One of the reasons he cares so much about Flame Valley is because he knows how important it is to you. It's the legacy your father wants you to have, and David feels obliged to hold on to it for you at all costs."

"I tell myself that over and over again, but lately I've begun to wonder. And now I realize that a part of me has always wondered. Ever since…"

"Ever since what, Elly?"

"You have to remember that I just narrowly escaped being married once before because of the inn. To Travis Sawyer. I guess I'm sensitive on the subject."

Juliana narrowed her eyes and studied her cousin. "It's no wonder women occasionally question the motives of the male of the species," she observed. "We've all been burned a few times. But women are born to take risks. You know what they say—no guts, no glory."

Elly smiled mistily. "Juliana, you're incredible."

Juliana smiled and picked up another piece of paper she'd been studying earlier. "Now, about the engagement party menu. What do you think about having those little rounds of marinated goat cheese wrapped in grape leaves?"

"Nobody actually likes goat cheese, Juliana. They just eat it because it's trendy."

"Being trendy is an excellent reason for including goat cheese. Besides, believe it or not, I like it."

Elly's brows rose. "And it is your party, isn't it?"

"Right."

# *Seven*

That evening Travis turned the key in the lock of Juliana's front door and was amazed at the quiet sense of pleasure he experienced in the small, mundane act. Another day was over and he felt as if he were home. It was true he had not yet officially moved in with Juliana, but he was spending so many nights here, he might as well do so. He could smell something savory in the oven, and he knew his redheaded lady would be waiting on the other side of the door with a glass of wine in her hand.

What more could a man ask, he wondered as he stepped into the white-tiled hall and set down his heavy briefcase. If only he didn't have to worry about how long he would be able to claim these small, vital treasures.

"I'm home." Travis listened carefully to the words as he said them. Not quite the whole truth and they might never be the whole truth, but he liked the sound of them anyway.

"Be right there," Juliana called from the kitchen.

Travis walked through the living room, picking up the evening paper that was lying on the coffee table. He scanned the headlines and then glanced up as Juliana appeared in the kitchen doorway. He smiled slowly.

She was holding a glass of wine in one hand and a spatula in the other. Her hair was caught up in a high shower of curls and she was wearing a Charisma Espresso apron over her pastel jeans. He saw that she had removed the lizard-skin boots she had put on that morning and replaced them with a pair of fluffy pink slippers. The slippers had bunny faces in front and a pouf of a bunny tale at the ankles. Juliana had once carefully explained to him that the silly looking slippers had something called "a charming wittiness." Whatever it was, they still looked like dead rabbits to Travis.

"You seem exhausted," Juliana announced. She came forward, and because she wasn't wearing heels, had to go up on her toes to give him a kiss as she put the wine-glass in his hand.

Travis felt her tongue tease his bottom lip and he groaned as his body reacted immediately. "I am exhausted. But I know my duty and I'm sure that, with the right stimulus, I can manage to get in a quickie with you before dinner."

"Absolutely not," Juliana said with mock horror. "Married people save it until after dinner."

"We're not married yet," he complained, following her into the warm, fragrant kitchen.

"We have to start practicing. Besides, I don't dare leave this walnut and blue-cheese sauce just now, and the corn bread would certainly burn if I surrendered to your lecherous ways."

"I take it back. Maybe I am too exhausted. What a day." Travis, newspaper still in hand, sat down at the cozy little breakfast table and took a sip of wine.

"Another meeting with David, right?"

"If you can call it that. I have to tell you, Juliana, I can see now why Flame Valley is on the brink of collapse. Even I didn't realize how easy it was going to be to take over the inn. Kirkwood is pigheaded stubborn in some areas. No wonder he's in trouble."

"He's stubborn in areas that have to do with Elly, and the resort has a lot to do with Elly."

"Yeah, I'm beginning to see the problem. Any man who lets his business decisions be dictated by his need to please a woman is setting himself up for a—" Travis broke off abruptly as he realized what he was saying.

Juliana batted her eyelashes outrageously. "Yes, dear? What was that about basing one's business decisions on the need to please a woman?"

Travis felt a rueful smile tug at his lips. "All right, so the poor jerk and I have something in common besides the fact that we both proposed to you."

"You'd better not have too much in common. I don't want to catch you running off with a petite blonde."

"Not a chance. I'm only interested in redheads these days. Tall redheads who know how to cook." Travis paused, eyeing her thoughtfully as he remembered Kirkwood's fear of losing his wife as well as the inn. "Did it hurt a lot?"

"Did what hurt a lot?" Juliana asked, concentrating on the sauce.

"When Kirkwood left you for Elly?"

"Well, it wasn't the high point of my emotional life, I'll say that much. But by the time it happened, I was more or less prepared for it. I'd seen it coming before either of them did. Whenever they were in the same room together there was a certain electrical charge in the air. They both just sort of hummed with it. I envied the force of the attraction but I knew from the beginning I couldn't duplicate it. Not with David, at any rate."

"So you just let him go and wished them well?"

"That's me. Gracious, even in defeat," she agreed brightly.

"Is that so? Funny, the word *gracious* never came to mind the night you threw guacamole dip all over me." Travis smiled at the memory.

"That was different," she retorted.

"Was it?"

"Darn right. I could see early on I'd made a mistake thinking David was the right man for me. But I learn from my mistakes, and this time around I was sure I had picked the right man. It really annoyed me when I discovered you hadn't had the same blinding realization."

"Oh, I'd had it. Sort of," Travis mused, thinking about it. "But there was the business with Flame Valley and a big chunk of the past in the way. Blinding realizations sometimes take a while to clarify themselves. Juliana?"

"Umm?" She frowned over the cheese sauce and stirred ferociously.

"If things turned sour again between us, would you fight for me a little harder than you fought for Kirkwood? I don't think I want you being gracious in defeat in my case."

She didn't look up from the thickening sauce. As she stirred frantically with one hand, she tossed a huge handful of pasta into a pan of boiling water with the other. "If I ever catch you hanging out with petite blondes, I'll nail your hide to the office door. There. How's that for feminine machismo?"

"Very reassuring," Travis murmured and wished the situation with Flame Valley Inn was as simple and straightforward as dealing with a petite blonde would have been.

"Did you and David make any progress today?" Juliana asked, changing the subject as she scooped the pot of cheese sauce off the burner.

"Not much. He's in worse shape than I thought and that's saying something. I played a long shot and called a guy named Bickerstaff. Offered him the wonderful opportunity of paying off the inn's creditors and pouring a ton of cash into the place. In exchange, I promised to guide the restructuring of Flame Valley and personally guarantee to get the present owner back on his feet."

Juliana smiled, looked very pleased. "Good idea. I knew you were the resourceful type. Did this Bickerstaff go for it?"

"He said he'd consider it and get back to me."

"What does that mean?"

"Knowing Bickerstaff, it means he'll consider it and get back to me."

"Oh." Juliana chewed on her lower lip as she emptied the cheese sauce into a bowl. "It sounds like a good idea to me. And you can be very convincing. I'll bet he goes for it."

Travis shook his head, sighing to himself over Juliana's irrepressible faith in his business acumen. "Don't hold your breath. I'm not. Bickerstaff likes a calculated risk, but he didn't get where he is by playing real long shots."

"We'll see." Juliana opened the oven door and a tantalizing aroma wafted through the kitchen. She bent over to get the pan of golden corn bread out of the oven. "Ready to eat?"

Travis took another swallow of wine and studied the sight of Juliana's pastel jeans pulled taut over the full curve of her derriere.

"Starved," he said. "Let me know if you want me to do anything."

"No, not tonight. You've been working too hard lately as it is." She straightened with the pan of steaming corn bread in hand.

"You know, Juliana, I have to tell you that you really have a terrific gluteus maximus. World class, in fact."

"Why, thank you. That only goes to show you can find something nice to say about anyone if you try hard enough. To be honest, I think yours is rather cute, too." She busied herself getting dinner on the table. "Did I tell you I had a nice chat with the lady who's going to help me plan our engagement party and wedding?"

The wine slopped precariously in Travis's glass, and his stomach, which had been relaxing nicely, tightened abruptly. "No, you didn't tell me. Isn't that moving a little fast? You just agreed to marry me last night."

"No point waiting, is there?"

"Uh, no. I guess not." He felt dazed. What would happen if she actually married him before he found out if he could save the inn? Travis wondered.

"We'll need to start putting together a guest list. Start jotting down names as you think of them, okay?"

Travis reflected briefly, trying to catch up with her. "I don't have any names to jot down."

"Don't be silly. Of course you do."

"Can't think of anyone to invite. Well, maybe the staff here at the new office. That's about it."

"Just your staff?" Juliana gave him a severe glance as she sat down across from him and began slicing corn bread. "What about your parents, for heaven's sake?"

He shrugged, his mind on the corn bread as he watched her transfer a chunk to his plate. He hadn't had homemade corn bread in years. "I don't see any point in you going out of your way to invite my folks. They didn't bother to come to my last wedding."

Juliana's hand froze over the corn bread. Her gaze collided with his, her topaz eyes full of demanding questions. "You've been married before?" she got out in a throaty whisper.

"It was a long time ago." Travis massaged the back of his neck, aware he hadn't handled the announcement very well. He certainly hadn't meant to drop it on her like this. He wasn't thinking clearly tonight. Too tired, probably. Lord, he was exhausted. "Back in my early twenties. It was a mistake. Didn't last long."

"What happened? Who was she? Where is she now? Are there any kids? Exactly how long were you married? And why didn't your parents come to the wedding?"

Travis wondered why he hadn't kept his mouth shut. He really didn't feel like going into all this tonight. But it was too late now. "Jeannie and I were married less than a year. She was a secretary at the firm where I got my first job. There was a slight misunderstanding on both our parts. I thought she wanted to build a successful future with me. She thought I could make her forget her first husband."

"What happened?"

Travis took a big bite of corn bread. "She went back

to her first husband. I left the firm to go out on my own. Turned out we both made the right decision."

"Kids?"

"No kids. There's nothing more to the story than that, Juliana. It was over a long time ago."

"Why didn't your parents come to the wedding? Did you elope?"

"No."

"Didn't your folks approve of your intended bride?"

"They never even met her. Approval wasn't the problem. Neither Mom nor Dad showed up at the wedding because each knew I had invited the other."

Juliana frowned. "I don't get it."

Travis helped himself to more corn bread. "They divorced when I was fourteen. It was a very bitter separation and neither one has been able to say a civil word to or about the other since the legal proceedings were final. Not that they had too much to say to each other before the divorce, either. When I invited them to my wedding, each wanted to know if the other had been invited."

"Oh, dear." Juliana's eyes filled with sympathy.

"When I said yes, my mother made it clear she would not attend unless I promised to disinvite my father. And my father made the same stipulation. I refused to be put in the middle like that and they both got even by not attending the wedding."

"Oh, Travis, that's terrible. They put you in a terrible position. Of course you couldn't not invite one or the other. Didn't they realize that? Didn't they realize how that would make you feel?"

"I don't think my feelings came into the matter," Travis said dryly. "They were both too wrapped up in their own emotions. Always were. I hated the weekends

I spent with Dad because he always told me what a lousy mother I had and when I got back to Mom she always grilled me on what my father was doing and who he was dating."

Juliana grimaced. "How awful."

"Not that uncommon in this day and age, and we both know it. Frankly, it was easier on everyone not to have either of my parents show up at my first wedding, and I think I can safely promise the same thing this time around. Don't bother inviting my side of the family, honey."

"Do you have any brothers or sisters?"

"A couple of stepbrothers and two stepsisters. I don't know them very well. Mom and Dad both remarried soon after the divorce and started new families. But I left for college three and a half years after they split up, so I didn't spend much time with my new baby brothers and sisters. The only time I was invited to get involved in their lives was when each of my parents asked me to make a contribution toward their college funds."

Juliana wrinkled her nose. "Which you did, I bet."

"Sure. Why not? I can afford it and they all know it. I'm still picking up the tab on three of them. The oldest graduated last year and got a job at a company where I know a few people."

"And everyone just lets you do it? Lets you finance your stepbrothers' and sisters' educations and lets you help find them all jobs? Yet they can't be bothered to come to your weddings?"

"I believe picking up the college costs is seen as my contribution to the family. Everybody definitely agrees I'm the one in a position to handle it financially. And what the hell, they're right. Look, don't go wasting a lot of sympathy on this, okay? It's not worth it. Are you going to let that cheese sauce congeal or are you going to serve it over the pasta?"

Juliana gasped and leaped to her feet. "Good grief, the pasta. I forgot about it. It's going to be soggy mush. I can't stand overcooked pasta. It's no good if it isn't *al dente*."

"The cheese sauce isn't too bad over the corn bread," Travis said, running an experiment on his plate.

"Travis," Juliana said from the sink where she was dumping the pasta into a colander, "I want you to give me the addresses of your parents. I really think we should invite them, regardless of what they did the last time you got married. After all, that was a long time ago. They've probably mellowed by now."

"I doubt it, but do what you want."

"Do you ever see your parents?"

"Once in a while. I call them on their birthdays and they call me on mine, and I've managed a few short visits over the years. Which is sufficient for all concerned."

"Why do you say that?"

Travis helped himself to more corn bread and conducted another experiment with the cheese sauce. "After they remarried, my folks concentrated most of their attention on their new families. They both wanted to make fresh starts, I think."

Juliana's eyes widened as realization struck. "But you were a reminder of the past, weren't you? You were the living evidence of their failure. They probably felt guilty about the way they'd torn your world apart and made you witness their battles for so many years. It's easier not to have to face people who make you feel guilty."

"I think it was definitely a relief to all concerned when I left for college. The interesting thing," Travis said thoughtfully as he poured more cheese sauce over the corn bread, "was that they turned out to be fairly good parents the second time around, at least as far as I can tell. My stepbrothers and stepsisters seem happy and well adjusted. And my parents' second marriages seem to have worked out."

"Ouch. Darn it." Juliana turned on the cold water faucet and held a finger in the spray.

Travis glanced at her with concern. "What happened? Burn yourself?"

"Just a little. It's all right," Juliana said quickly. "I'll be over there in a minute. I think we lucked out. The pasta isn't too squishy after all."

*"After they remarried, they concentrated most of their attention on their new families."*

Travis's laconic explanation of why he wasn't very close to his parents echoed through Juliana's mind that night as she sat in bed waiting for him to emerge from the bathroom. It was clear to her that after the divorce and remarriage of his parents, Travis had been left out in the cold. He had not become a real part of either of the new families.

A few years later, his first marriage had ended in divorce when his wife had gone back to her first husband.

Five years ago his engagement had ended when his fiancée had used him to help her family and then called off the engagement.

All things considered, Juliana decided, Travis had not had a particularly good experience with family life. He'd always been the one left out. He was never the one chosen when choices had to be made—never a real member of a family. But people were quite willing to use him when it suited their purposes.

The bathroom door opened and Travis strolled out with a towel around his hips. He yawned and Juliana decided he was enormously sexy, even when he was yawning. He looked like a big, sleek wild animal that had somehow wandered into her very civilized white-on-white bedroom.

Travis saw her looking at him. His eyes glinted. "Still think I'm too short?"

"There are compensations," Juliana declared loftily. She put down the book she had been reading. "I called Melvin today."

"The guy who supplies your coffee?"

"Right. I asked him if he could supply the shop with tea, too. He said yes."

"Uh-huh." Travis did not look overly interested in the conversation. He rubbed the back of his neck as he walked toward the bed.

Juliana plunged ahead with enthusiasm. "I've been thinking about getting into tea in a big way. Travis, have you ever noticed that there are zillions of espresso shops and coffee houses opening all along the coast clear to the state of Washington, but no tea shops?"

"There's a reason for that," Travis explained as he slung the towel over a chair. "The money's in coffee, not tea. Nobody drinks tea."

"That's not true. I drink tea. Lots of people drink tea." Juliana was momentarily sidetracked by the sight of Travis's nude body. "And I'll bet there are thousands of people just like me."

"Closet tea drinkers? I doubt it." He pulled back the covers and slid into bed beside her.

"We aren't closet tea drinkers, we just tend not to drink a lot of tea in public because it's so hard to get it properly made in restaurants. Wimpy tea bags plopped into lukewarm water don't cut it for a real tea enthusiast. Most tea drinkers drink coffee when they're out rather than pay for bad tea."

"What's your point?" Travis plumped up his pillows and leaned back against them. He reached for a stack of papers he'd left on the nightstand.

"My point is that if tea drinkers knew they could get properly made tea at a certain place, they would go there and order it. Tons of it. They'd buy it in bulk to take home with them. They would experiment with different teas of the world and enjoy them the way coffee drinkers enjoy coffee."

Travis scanned the figures in front of him, frowning intently. "You want to add a tea option at Charisma? No problem. Go ahead and do it."

"Travis, you don't understand. I don't want to just put in a line of tea at Charisma. I'm going for the whole enchilada. I've been thinking about this for several months now and I've decided to open a shop devoted entirely to tea. The first in a chain."

"No, you're not." Travis didn't even bother to look up from his paperwork.

"Now, Travis, I'm serious about this. The tea shops would be a first around here."

"And a last because everyone around here drinks coffee. You'd lose your shirt, and right now, Juliana, you cannot afford to lose a single dime. Believe me, I'm in a position to know."

"We'd push for the upscale crowd, the same way we do at Charisma. We'd make tea drinking trendy. We'd serve power teas to business people and their clients, and we'd package a whole line of tea under our own label."

Travis grunted and finally raised his eyes from his paperwork as the enthusiastic determination in her voice
finally sank in. He glanced at her nightstand. "You've
been reading that book again, haven't you?"

Juliana looked at him innocently. "What book?"

"That book about the Boston tea heiress whose ancestor
was a witch. Leaves of something-or-other by Linda
What's-her-face. I saw it on your nightstand earlier."

"*Leaves of Fortune* by Linda Barlow," Juliana corrected automatically. "It's a great story and it's given me
all sorts of ideas, Travis."

"It's given you delusions of grandeur. You are not
going to make your fortune in tea, Juliana. Fancy coffee
is where the future is and you're perfectly positioned
with Charisma to take advantage of it. As your consultant and partner I'm not about to let you fritter away your
money and energy chasing an unrealistic business goal."

"I've been giving this a lot of thought," Juliana persisted. She broke off as Travis began rubbing the back
of his neck again. "What's wrong?"

"Nothing. I'm just a little stiff and sore from sitting
hunched over four years' worth of Kirkwood's income
tax forms all day." Travis eased himself into a slightly
different position on the pillows.

Juliana pushed back the covers. "Turn over on your
stomach and I'll rub your back for you."

He hesitated and then shrugged. "It's a deal."

Travis rolled onto his stomach, sighing heavily as
Juliana straddled his thighs. The long skirts of her frothy
French nightgown flowed around his lean hips.

The muscles of his back were sleek, strong and well
defined, she thought as she leaned forward to begin
working on his shoulders. Very sexy, very masculine.

She could feel the rough hair on his legs against her soft inner thighs. She adjusted her position, settling herself more firmly.

"No fair wriggling." Travis's voice was muffled in the pillow.

"Sorry." Juliana applied herself to the massage, easing the tension in Travis's shoulders and neck with smooth, deep movements.

"Lord, that feels good. If you'd told me you could give a massage like this I probably would have asked you to marry me the first day I met you."

"I wanted you to admire my brain, not my brawn. Now, about my tea shop idea. I've been going over a lot of different aspects of the project lately and I've come up with a basic plan. When you've got some free time I'll lay it out for you. It's going to work, Travis. I know it is."

Travis said nothing. Encouraged by the lack of a negative response, Juliana kept talking as she massaged. Slowly the hard muscles beneath her palms relaxed. As she stroked the strong contours of Travis's back she began to think of other things beside the future of her tea shops. She grew increasingly aware of the hardness of Travis's buttocks beneath her much softer shape and wondered just how tired he really was. Perhaps the massage would prove invigorating as well as relaxing. In the meantime, she kept talking about tea.

Fifteen minutes later when she finally came to a momentary halt in the middle of her monologue, Juliana realized that Travis had fallen asleep somewhere along the line. She groaned.

She was ruefully aware that while her efforts had apparently thoroughly relaxed Travis, they had had the opposite effect on her. Smiling wryly, Juliana dismounted from her sleeping stallion and crawled over to her side of the bed.

"Don't think that you can escape every discussion of my tea shop plans this easily," she whispered as she turned out the light.

Travis did not respond.

Two days later Sandy poked her head into Juliana's office. "Don't forget the coffee tasting at noon," she said. Then she frowned at the array of crumpled papers on the floor. "Hey, what's going on in here? You writing out a resignation or something? Going to turn Charisma over to me and Matt? I knew you'd see the light one of these days. We've already made plans to put in an ice-cream parlor out front."

Juliana didn't look up from where she was busily penning still another version of the letter she had been trying to write all morning. "The problem with owning your own business is that it's tough to resign. Forget the ice-cream empire. As it happens, I'm writing to Travis's parents."

"Introducing yourself?"

"Yes and inviting them to the wedding."

Sandy looked at all the aborted efforts. "What's so hard about writing a simple note telling them Travis is making a brilliant marriage to you?"

"I want to get just the right tone. They didn't come to Travis's first wedding and he doesn't think they'll come to this one. They're divorced and remarried, and apparently there was a lot of bitterness between them after they split. One won't be found dead in the same room with the other, not even at their son's wedding."

"Hmm. A messy situation, socially speaking."

Juliana sighed and leaned back in her chair. She tapped the tip of the pen on the desk. "Such childish behavior for adults. It's incredible. It's disgusting."

"It's also fairly common these days. Not much you can do about it."

"Travis's folks have been divorced for years and have raised second families. It's time they remembered their first-born son."

Sandy shrugged. "They'll probably remember him fast enough if and when he gives them a grandchild. It's been my observation that the older people get, the more interested they are in their descendants."

Juliana stared at her. "You know something, Sandy, you have just made a brilliant observation."

"I've been telling you since the day you hired me that I'm brilliant." Sandy folded her arms and leaned against the doorjamb. "How are you going to get Travis's parents to come to the wedding?"

"Well, I have been working on a pleasant, conciliatory approach." Juliana waved a hand at all the crumpled notes on the floor. "Something along the lines of what a really terrific daughter-in-law I'll be and how I want to get to know my husband's parents, et cetera, et cetera. But after talking to you, I think I'll try a different tactic."

"What's that?"

"Threats."

Sandy raised an eyebrow. "What sort of threats?"

"I don't know yet. I'll have to think about it." Juliana got to her feet. "Everything all set for the coffee tasting?"

"Yes. You wanted to do a comparison of Indonesian, Hawaiian and Mexican coffee today, right?"

Juliana wrinkled her nose. "Right."

Sandy laughed. "Your enthusiasm is overwhelming.

You should be looking forward to going out front in a few minutes. This series of comparative tastings you've been running the past month has really increased sales. The shop is already crowded."

"The problem with tasting days is that I have to actually drink the stuff." Juliana groaned. "The sacrifices I make for my business."

The phone rang just as Juliana was about to follow Sandy out of the office. She reached over and grabbed the receiver, hoping Travis would be on the other end of the line.

"Oh, hello, Melvin."

"You sound disappointed. And after all I've done for you."

Juliana chuckled. "You caught me on the way to my lunch-hour coffee tasting."

"I won't keep you. Just wanted to let you know I've got that aged Sumatra for you. I'll deliver it this afternoon."

"Great. I've got 'em standing in line for it. Customers seem to go for the word *aged*."

"Makes 'em think of fine wine, I guess," Melvin said absently. "Although there's no comparison between aged coffee and aged wine. Most aged coffee is kind of flat tasting. This Sumatra's not bad, though. Nice, heavy body. Should blend well. How are the plans for the tea shops going?"

"I'm still discussing the concept with my partner."

"Which, translated, means you still haven't sold him on the idea? I'm surprised at you, Juliana. What is it with this fiancé of yours? He must have a will of iron if you haven't managed to whip him into shape by now. Can't imagine any man holding out this long in an argument with you."

"We're not arguing about it, we're discussing the possibilities," Juliana snapped, irritated. "You make me sound like a shrew, Melvin. One of those tough, hard-edged, aggressive businesswomen men always dislike."

"Hey, don't put words in my mouth," Melvin said hastily. "I only meant that you're a very forceful lady and when you go after something, you usually get it, that's all. I'm just surprised this guy you're engaged to hasn't thrown in the towel and acknowledged the brilliance of your tea shop concept yet, that's all."

"Goodbye, Melvin," Juliana muttered. "Make sure that Sumatra gets here by three o'clock, or I'll find myself another supplier." She tossed the receiver into the cradle and stood glowering at Sandy.

"Something wrong?" Sandy asked politely.

"Tell me the truth. Do you find me forceful? Even a tad aggressive, perhaps? The sort of female who usually gets what she wants, no matter how many hapless males get in her way?"

Sandy grinned. "Definitely. And I want you to know I admire you tremendously. I consider you my mentor. When I grow up I want to be just like you."

Juliana smiled brilliantly. "Good. Glad I'm not losing my touch. For a while there I worried that being engaged might have softened my brain a bit. Let's go drink some coffee."

# *Eight*

Travis was poring over the papers he had spread out on the kitchen table when he heard the refrigerator door open and close in a stealthy fashion.

Out of the corner of his eye he watched Juliana pry the lid off the container she had just taken out of the freezer compartment. She had been working quietly at the kitchen counter for several minutes now, her back to him so that he could not see precisely what she was doing. All he knew was that it had something to do with a banana.

"I give up," he said, tossing down his pencil. "What are you doing over there?"

"Fixing you a little something special. I think it's about time you took a break. You've been working there since we finished dinner." She did not turn around but it was obvious she was very busy.

Travis exhaled heavily. "I think it's about time I took a break, too."

"Any word from Bickerstaff today?"

"No."

"Does that mean yes or no?"

"It means," said Travis, "that he's still considering it."

"Good. I'm sure he'll go for it."

Travis shook his head, awed, as usual, by her boundless faith in him. He could guess what would happen when that faith was shattered. Juliana was a businesswoman. She would expect him to live up to his end of the deal they had made, and if he didn't… "How are the engagement party plans going?"

"Great." Juliana opened a cupboard and removed a package of nuts. "Everything's all set for the fourteenth at The Treasure House. Be there or be square."

Travis groaned. "Why The Treasure House?"

"For sentimental reasons, of course. That's where you proposed."

"Not precisely. Unlike every other male who proposed to you in the restaurant, I showed some creativity. I took you down to the docks, remember?"

"Details, details. You're just irritable on the subject because you fell in the water that night." She reached for a jar of chocolate sauce.

"I did not fall in the water, I was thrown in. What are you making?"

"I told you, it's a surprise. Just be patient. I talked to Melvin again today."

"Yeah?" Travis mentally girded his loins for battle. He knew what was coming next.

"He wanted to know how the plans for the tea shops

were going. I explained you and I were still discussing the concept but that things are moving forward rapidly."

"The hell they are," Travis said mildly. "They haven't moved forward one inch and you know it. You are not opening a tea shop, Juliana, and that's final."

"You're just feeling a bit negative because you've got so many other things on your mind," she assured him. "We'll get down to details after this business with the resort is settled."

"We will never get down to details because there are no details to get down to. There will be no tea shops. I would be worse than a fool, I would be criminally negligent in my responsibilities if I allowed you to go ahead with your bizarre plan."

"You've said, yourself, I'm a very good businesswoman, Travis."

"You are. Very savvy and very realistic. A natural entrepreneur. Except when you get emotionally involved with something the way you did when you loaned money to Kirkwood and the way you're doing lately with the idea of a tea shop. When it comes to things like that, you let your personal feelings and emotions take over. That's a bad way to do business and we both know it." Just look at the situation he was in because of personal feelings and emotions, Travis thought as he glanced bleakly at the paperwork in front of him.

"I really think there's a wonderful potential for the tea shops," Juliana said resolutely, opening a jar of maraschino cherries.

"There is no potential for the tea shops."

"I can make them work."

"Nobody could make them work. You can add a

line of tea at Charisma but that's the end of the tea business for you."

"I appreciate your consulting expertise," Juliana said, an edge on her words. She opened a drawer with a jerk and snatched a spoon out of the silverware tray. "I assure you I will bear your comments on the subject in mind as I make my decision."

"You can't make any decisions of this magnitude without me," Travis reminded her quietly. "I'm not just your business consultant, I'm your partner. Remember?"

"I remember. Believe me, I remember." Juliana turned toward him, her culinary masterpiece held in both hands. Her eyes sparkled militantly. "But you're going to have to realize that I got where I am with Charisma all on my own. I know what I'm doing."

"Most of the time. But everyone's got a blind spot. Tea happens to be yours. Along with Flame Valley, of course."

"My, you are in a grouchy mood tonight. Maybe this will perk you up."

Travis's attention wavered from the argument as he studied the most spectacular banana split he'd ever seen. Three giant scoops of ice cream resided between halves of a plump banana in a large glass bowl. All three scoops and the banana were lavishly glazed with chocolate topping, nuts, whipped cream and three cherries. Travis's mouth watered.

"Maybe," he agreed.

"How does it look?" Juliana asked expectantly. She nudged aside some papers and put the concoction down on the table in front of him.

"I haven't seen anything like this since I was eight years old and the one I ordered then wasn't nearly this big." Travis picked up the spoon and wondered where to begin.

"I decided you needed some quick energy." Juliana reached across the table and dipped the edge of her own spoon into one of his scoops of ice cream. She popped the bite into her mouth. "Now, about the tea shops."

The lady was as tenacious as a terrier, Travis thought, not without a sense of grudging admiration. "I've told you before, forget the tea shops. You're fated to get rich as a coffee merchant." He carefully chose his first mouthful of ice cream and nuts.

"I want to try the tea shops, Travis."

"Look. When I've got some time, I'll sit down with you and show you just why you won't make any money with tea shops, okay? Right now I've got my hands full trying to save Kirkwood's rear."

"Damn it." Juliana jumped to her feet, eyes suddenly ablaze. "Talk about a blind spot. You won't even listen to me."

Travis scooped up another bite of ice cream. "I've listened to you. Your idea is lousy. As your partner, I'm not going to agree to allow you to go ahead with the plans. That's all there is to it."

"Well, I am going through with my plans and that's final," she hissed, her hands on her hips.

"You're not going to do a thing without my approval."

"You can't start giving me orders, Travis. As far as I'm concerned you haven't earned your fee yet. You haven't saved Flame Valley and until you do, you're not a real partner in Charisma."

"Yes, I am. We already agreed that the partnership was my fee and I would collect my fee regardless of how successful my efforts were with Flame Valley."

Juliana folded her arms under her breasts and stood defiantly, feet braced slightly apart, in the middle of the kitchen. "Charisma is mine. I created it and I made it what it is today. Even if you're a partner in it, you're the junior partner. Don't ever forget that, Travis. I make the decisions about the future of my business and that's the end of it. Don't think that just because you're going to marry me you can start telling me what to do."

Travis sighed. He had known this showdown was coming. He just wished it hadn't arrived tonight. He had too many other things on his mind. "And don't think that just because you got me to propose to you that you can lead me around like a bull with a ring through its nose," he said evenly.

"Why, you mule-headed, stubborn, hard-nosed son of a... You do remind me of a bull. A very thick-headed one." Juliana turned on her heel and stalked out of the kitchen.

A moment later the bedroom door slammed shut.

A fine example of high dudgeon, Travis decided as he reluctantly went back to work. He wished he'd gotten in a few more bites of the ice cream before Juliana had exploded. He hadn't even started on the banana. A slow grin edged his mouth. Juliana was the kind of woman who would keep a man young or wear him out. Either way, he would never be bored.

Juliana reappeared an hour later. Travis's eyes narrowed as he slowly became aware of her presence behind him. He turned his head and saw her lounging with sultry insouciance in the kitchen doorway. She was wearing what he privately considered her sexiest nightie, the black see-through one with the small lace flowers strategically placed over the relevant portions of her anatomy. Her mass of red hair frothed around her shoulders. Her feet were bare and her eyes were luminous.

"I've decided to forgive you," she said, her voice husky.

Travis felt desire seize his insides. "This must be my lucky day."

"I shouldn't have tried to discuss the tea shop idea with you tonight. You're much too involved with Flame Valley right now to be bothered with other business decisions."

Travis decided this was not the time to tell her that his opinion on the tea shops was not likely to alter regardless of how busy he was. "You're sure you're not just trying to use sex to get me to see the brilliance of your plan?"

She smiled with glowing innocence. "I would never stoop to that sort of tacky behavior."

"Too bad. I've always wondered what it would be like to be the victim of that sort of behavior."

Juliana held out her hand invitingly. "We could always pretend."

"Yeah. We could. We're pretty good at creating fantasies together." Travis got to his feet and went toward her. She was fantastic, he thought. He'd never before met anyone quite like her, and he knew deep inside he never would again. *He must not lose her.* He would cling to this fantasy with all his strength.

"Travis?" She was still looking at him with smoky sensuality, but there was a trace of concern in her gaze as she studied his face. "Is something wrong?"

"No," he muttered as he came to a halt directly in front of her. "Nothing's wrong."

But there was and he knew it. Every day that passed without a response from Bickerstaff or any of his other contacts meant losing one more piece of the small chunk of whatever hope he had of saving the inn. But he couldn't think about that tonight, Travis decided, not with Juliana standing here, inviting him to make love to her.

He kissed her, startling her a little with his sudden urgency. She hesitated a split second and then responded, as she always did, with everything that was in her. There was nothing like being wanted by this woman, Travis reflected, his hunger for her soaring.

"Do you feel yourself changing your mind about the tea shops yet?" Juliana whispered teasingly against his throat.

"No, but I definitely feel lucky." He was taut and heavy with his desire. He began nibbling on her ear. "Is this the way you're going to forgive me every time we argue?"

"Probably. I'm not the type to hold a grudge." She unbuttoned his shirt slowly until it hung open to reveal his chest. Then she ran her fingers through the crisp hair. Her eyes were soft with a woman's sweet need as her nails lightly circled his flat nipples.

"No," he acknowledged softly, "you won't hold grudges, will you? That's not your way. You'll yell at me for a while, slam a few doors and then put on a sexy nightgown and seduce me. I won't stand a chance."

"Putty in my hands," she agreed, pressing her breasts against him. "Does the thought make you nervous?" She unzipped his pants and unbuckled his belt.

"I'll take my chances." His hand slid down over her soft, curving belly. He found the small lace flower that barely concealed the triangle of red curls at the apex of her thighs. His palm closed over the flower and a glorious sense of satisfaction roared through him when Juliana moaned and melted against him.

He caressed her intimately through the filmy material of the gown until he felt her growing hot and damp. Her fingers slipped inside his pants and he groaned as she touched him. When he could take the subtle torture no longer, he picked Juliana up and carried her into the bedroom and put her down onto the bed.

A moment later, his own clothes in a heap on the floor, Travis slid into bed, gathered Juliana into his arms and rolled onto his back. She sat astride him, taking him deep within her warmth. Her legs pressed demandingly against his thighs.

Travis reached up to cup her breasts, coaxing the nipples into tight, sensitive buds. When he grazed the delicate peaks with his palms Juliana caught her breath and stiffened. Travis could feel her tightening around him and it was all he could do to muster some remnants of self-control.

Juliana began to breathe more quickly and her head tipped back. Her hair flowed in a silken wave around her shoulders. Travis waited until he couldn't stand it any longer and then he moved, easing Juliana down onto her back. When she reached for him, pulling him close once more, he slid all the way into her heat and surrendered to the fabulous oblivion.

A long time later Travis felt Juliana stir in the shadows beside him.

"Are you awake?" she asked softly.

"Umm." He had been unable to sleep, wondering if he should put in another call to Bickerstaff's office in the morning. But he didn't want to look too anxious, he told himself. Bickerstaff would get skittish.

"I shouldn't have lost my temper tonight just because you don't agree with me about opening a tea shop. The thing is, Charisma's always been mine. I've always made the decisions, all the decisions, about its future."

"I know." He let his hand drift over her curving thigh.

"I guess it's like having raised a kid all by yourself and then marrying and having to let someone else have a say in the kid's future."

Travis said nothing. As usual, he felt himself edging away from any topic that was even remotely concerned with children. One of these days he would have to deal with the subject, he told himself. But he intended to put it off as long as possible.

"Travis?"

"Yeah?"

"I know you mean well and I know you think you know what's best for Charisma but…"

"But you don't like having me tell you what's best for Charisma when it conflicts with what you want, right?"

"Right."

"Don't take it personally, Juliana. Don't let emotion enter into your decision-making process. Charisma is business. Keep it that way."

"Sometimes the two get mixed up, don't they?"

Travis thought about his current situation. Revenge, business and desire were irrevocably entwined into a knot he was not at all certain he could unravel.

"Yes," he said quietly. "Sometimes they get mixed up."

Juliana waited another two days before she introduced a subject that had not yet been discussed and which she had hoped Travis would bring up first. So far he had not done so and she was, as usual, too impatient to wait for things to happen in their own time.

She decided to do it very casually. Craftily she waited until she had coaxed him away from his desk for a walk on the beach. She led up to her topic slowly.

"You don't mind living in my condo until we decide where we're going to live permanently?" she asked.

"Your condo's fine." Travis's hand tightened around hers as he paced barefoot beside her on the damp, packed sand at the water's edge. "As far as I'm concerned, we can live there permanently."

"It's a little small."

"Plenty of space for two people." He sounded unconcerned. "I'm just about moved in now as it is and everything's working out fine."

That much was true. Juliana still found it something of a novelty to open the closet and discover a row of conservatively tailored men's white shirts hanging inside, but she was adjusting. She had complained briefly about Travis using up all the hot water during his morning showers but he had resolved the issue by making her share the shower with him. So far none of the problems of living together had been anything more than a minor challenge.

Obviously commenting on the small size of the condo was not going to open up the area of discussion that was foremost on her mind today. She would have to find another approach. *Subtle,* she told herself. *Keep it subtle.*

"Everything is all set for the engagement party," she reported. "Seven o'clock this Friday night. Just about everyone who was invited is coming. Even my parents are coming down from San Francisco. I've had several talks with the chef at The Treasure House, and the food is going to be fabulous."

"Fine."

The neutral tone of his voice disturbed her. Lately it seemed to Juliana she had been hearing that tone more and more from Travis. She sought for a way to ease the conversation from engagement party plans to the more important subject and gave up. So much for being subtle. She couldn't wait any longer to bring up the one undiscussed subject that remained. She would have to take the bull by the horns.

"So," Juliana said boldly, "what would you say if I told you I was pregnant?"

It didn't take long for her to sense she had made a mistake.

Travis came to an abrupt halt and spun halfway around to face her, his face rigid with anger. "You're *what?*"

It dawned on Juliana that she had obviously thrown the poor man into shock. "I was just wondering how you would feel if it turned out I was…"

"You're not pregnant," he cut in swiftly. "You can't be pregnant. We've been taking precautions. There haven't been any accidents."

"I know, but…"

"Are you telling me you are pregnant?" he asked through set teeth.

"No, no, it's okay, Travis. You're right. I'm not pregnant. It was just a hypothetical question."

"A hypothetical question? Are you nuts? You don't throw hypothetical questions like that around. What the hell got into you?"

"All right, so I didn't phrase it very well."

"No, you did not."

He stood looking at her with an expression that rocked her as nothing else had done since the moment she had watched him confront her cousin Elly that night on the terrace. Juliana pulled herself together quickly.

"I'm sorry, Travis," she said quietly. "I didn't mean to alarm you. I just thought it was time we talked about children. It's something we haven't discussed yet."

His unreadable gaze searched her face and then shifted to the ocean horizon over her left shoulder. "No, we haven't talked about children, have we? I somehow got the impression you weren't particularly interested in having kids. Ever since I've known you, you've seemed wrapped up with your plans for Charisma. You never said anything about wanting to have babies."

"I hadn't thought about babies very much before I met you," she admitted, realizing for the first time the truth of that statement. "There was never a time or a man that made me think about having kids. But now there's you and we're getting married and neither one of us is exactly young and, well…" The sentence trailed off.

"And you've decided you want children." Travis closed his eyes wearily and then opened them again. His crystal gaze was more unreadable than ever.

Juliana drew a deep breath. "Are you trying to tell me you don't?"

He began to massage the back of his neck. "This is a hell of a time to bring up the subject."

"What better time?" She studied him anxiously. "If you don't want children you should tell me now, Travis."

"Kids complicate things."

"Living is a complicated business. What sort of complications are you worried about?"

"Damn it, Juliana, you know what the complications are. Don't act naive. If things don't work out between us, we don't want to hurt anyone else, do we?"

She sucked in her breath. "You're already looking ahead to a divorce?"

"No, of course not. It's just that these days people have to be realistic. Half of all marriages fail, and there are probably a lot of others that would collapse if given a slight push."

"So what are you suggesting? That people stop having babies?" she snapped.

"I'm suggesting they give the matter a lot of thought before they go ahead with something as irrevocable as the decision to have a child," he muttered, resuming his pace.

Juliana hurried to catch up with him. "I agree with you, Travis. Babies should be planned and wanted. No question about it. But if two people are sure of their commitment to each other and if they both want children, then they shouldn't be afraid to go ahead and have them."

"Do we have to discuss this now, Juliana?"

Her palms were damp, Juliana realized vaguely. A sick feeling slashed through her. For the first time since she had met Travis she questioned her own judgment. Had she chosen the wrong man, after all?

"No," she said. "We don't have to discuss this now."

"Good." He glanced at his watch. "Because I've got to get back to the office. Bickerstaff still hasn't called and there are one or two other people I want to contact this afternoon."

"Sure. I understand. I'd better get back to Charisma, too. Lots to do today. I want to talk to my staff about trying a darker roast on some new beans I bought." She tried a bright smile on for size and thought it stayed put fairly well.

Travis slanted her a brief glance, nodded and turned back up the beach to where Juliana had parked her car. Little was said on the drive back into town.

Juliana dropped Travis off at his office and drove

very slowly back to her apartment. She would think
about trying a darker roast on the new coffee beans
some other time.

She parked the red coupé in front of her apartment
and went inside. The first thing she did was put a kettle
of water on the stove. The second thing she did was not
answer the phone when it rang two minutes later.

When the tea was ready she carried it over to the
kitchen table and sat down. She was still sitting there,
staring out the window, when she saw Elly's car pull
into the parking space beside the coupé.

The phone had been easy to ignore but there was no
point ignoring the knock on the front door. Juliana knew
there was no way she could pretend she wasn't inside.

"There you are," Elly said as Juliana opened the door.
"I stopped at Charisma but your staff said you hadn't
returned, and when you didn't answer the phone I
thought I'd just stop by on my way back to Flame Valley.
What's wrong?"

"Nothing's wrong. Why do you ask?"

"Don't give me that. You never come home in the
middle of the day." Elly stepped past her and went
straight into the kitchen. "And you're having a cup of
tea all by yourself. What's going on around here?"

"Elly, please, I'm just a little tired. I'm not feeling
very sociable."

Elly peered at her. "Something's wrong, isn't it?
Don't bother trying to lie, Juliana. We've known each
other too long."

"I've had a rough day." Juliana sat down at the table
and picked up her teacup.

"So have I. That's one of the reasons I wanted to talk
to you today. I'm getting very nervous about David and

what's going to happen if Travis doesn't pull off the deal with Bickerstaff."

Juliana nodded without much interest. "I know you're worried, Elly."

"But," Elly continued quietly as she sat down across from her cousin, "at the moment I am a lot more worried about you. You're not acting like yourself, Juliana."

"How can you tell? You just walked in the door."

"I can tell. You're normally as vivid as a neon sign. Right now you look as if someone has just unplugged you."

In spite of her morose mood, Juliana managed a flicker of a smile. "Not bad, Elly. A good analogy."

"It's Travis, isn't it? Tell me."

"There's not much to tell. I'm just wondering if I'm making a mistake. That's all."

Elly's brows rose. "I don't believe it. After all my ranting and raving failed to deter you, after the lectures from your parents and my father went unheeded, *now* you're suddenly wondering if you've made a mistake? That's a shock. All right, let's have it. What went wrong today?"

"I asked Travis how he'd feel if I got pregnant. He was furious."

"Are you?" Elly asked sharply.

"Pregnant? No. It was just a hypothetical question. I wanted to find a subtle way to introduce the subject of babies."

"Men aren't big on hypothetical questions," Elly observed with unexpected insight. "Or subtlety, either. You probably gave the guy the shock of his life. There he was, not thinking about anything except trying to salvage Flame Valley and you hit him up with something like that."

"He didn't calm down when I explained I just wanted to discuss the possibility of having children." Juliana met her cousin's eyes. "I don't think he wants kids, Elly. I think he wants to hedge his bets."

"What do you mean?"

"I get the feeling a part of him doesn't really expect our marriage to work. I think that deep down he doesn't want to have any loose ends around if things collapse. Probably because, as a kid, he was a loose end, himself."

"I think I'm beginning to see the problem. But, frankly, I'm surprised you're letting it get you down. You usually rise to a challenge the way a fish rises to bait. I've always envied your talent for self-confidence. Nothing really shakes it, not even when you lose once in a while. You just reorganize and bounce back. You're always so strong, Juliana. Everybody in the family says that, you know. We all see you as the strong one."

"I don't feel strong now. If you must know the truth, I feel scared. I was so sure of him, Elly. So sure he was the right one for me. I knew it the day he walked through the front door of Charisma. I practically jumped on him then and there and told him he was going to marry me. I knew I'd been waiting for him all my life. It was all I could do to control myself until the night he…we…the night we went to bed together for the first time."

Elly studied the table for a moment. "You were still sure of him even after he and I had staged that scene out on the terrace at Flame Valley, weren't you? You were mad at him, but still certain he was the right man for you."

Juliana nodded. "It's true. I was very annoyed with him that night. Furious that he'd tricked me about his past relationship with my family and even more upset to discover he'd once wanted to marry you. I mean, it's obvious you and he are all wrong for each other."

"Obvious."

"But I figure everyone's entitled to a mistake or two. Heck, I've made a few small ones, myself."

"Very understanding of you."

"And he soon saw the error of his ways," Juliana continued. "Didn't he turn right around and agree to try to save the inn and didn't he ask me to marry him?"

"True. That's just what he did."

"But this thing about the babies has shaken me, Elly. This is a different matter entirely."

"Not everyone wants to have children, Juliana. You've never shown much interest in them yourself until today."

"But I've always known that when the right man came along I would want to have them. There was never any question in my mind."

"It takes two to make an important decision like that."

"I know." Juliana sighed. "If it were a simple matter of Travis not wanting to be a father, I might be able to understand. But there's more to it than that. He talked about not wanting to see kids hurt in a divorce. He talked as though one went into a marriage planning for the worst possible case."

Elly sat back in her chair, frowning. "Whereas you, with your boundless certainty and enthusiasm are going into it prepared to give it your all."

Juliana looked up, feeling raw and very vulnerable. "Exactly. Elly, I can't marry a man who isn't as committed to making the marriage work as I am. I won't marry a man who feels he has to hedge his bets just in case things don't work out."

"Be reasonable. What do you expect from Travis? He's a businessman, Juliana. And I've told you from the very beginning there's a cold-blooded streak in him. He's not an emotional creature like you. If you ask me, it's perfectly in character for Travis to hedge his bets. Be grateful he's got enough integrity not to want to leave you holding the baby, so to speak."

Cold-blooded? Travis? Never. But it was true he was a businessman and he could be incredibly stubborn. Juliana reminded herself of how difficult he became every time she brought up the subject of the tea shops. Perhaps he was looking at marriage the same way he would look at a potential business investment.

The thought was enough to make her nauseous.

"Juliana? Would you like another cup of tea?" Elly got quickly to her feet. "Here, I'll make it for you."

At any other time the notion of Elly reversing roles with her and becoming the reassuring, bracing one would have made Juliana laugh. But when Elly put the fresh cup of tea down in front of her, she could only feel wanly grateful.

"Thank you," Juliana murmured.

Elly sighed. "I suppose I should be encouraging you to have these second thoughts. After all, I'm the one who's been warning you not to marry the man. But for some insane reason I can't bear to have you think you've made such a horrendous mistake. It's just not normal for you to be acting like this. You've got to get a grip on yourself, Juliana. Depression doesn't look good on you."

"I know." Juliana sipped her tea. It was too weak but that didn't seem to matter today. Nothing really mattered today except that she was staring at the possibility of having been totally wrong in her estimation of

Travis Sawyer. He was afraid to have kids because he was afraid the marriage would end. Which meant that he was not really committed to making it work.

"Juliana? Feeling any better?"

"No."

"Oh, Juliana, I'm so sorry."

Juliana stared unseeingly out the kitchen window. "What am I going to do, Elly?"

"I suppose you may have to consider calling off the wedding, if you're feeling this uncertain of the future."

Juliana gripped the teacup. "Heaven help me, Elly. I don't think I have the courage to do that."

## Nine

"Juliana? I'm sorry, but it looks like I'm not going to be able to get away from here in time for dinner tonight."

"That's two nights in a row, Travis. Is something happening with Flame Valley?"

"I'm not sure yet. Maybe."

"You don't sound encouraged."

Probably because I'm not, Travis thought. "I don't want anyone to get his hopes up. Look, I'd better get back to it. I don't know how long I'll be." He waited, praying she would tell him that it didn't matter how late he was, she would be expecting him when he was finished at the office.

"You'll probably be exhausted when you're done for the evening."

"Yeah. Probably." Travis's fingers tightened on the phone as he prepared himself for what he sensed was coming next. Juliana was going to say the same thing she had said last night when he'd called her to tell her he'd be late. *"You'll probably want to go straight home to your place and fall into bed."*

"Don't bother stopping by here. I know you're tired. You'll want to go straight home to your own apartment and collapse into bed," Juliana said with far too much calm understanding for Travis's taste.

"Yeah. I was just thinking that might be best. I'll see you tomorrow, honey."

"Fine."

"Everything on line for the party Friday night?"

There was a slight pause before Juliana spoke. "Yes. Everything's fine."

Travis could feel her sliding away. He gripped the phone harder, frantically searching for a way to keep her on the other end for just a bit longer. "Did you find a dress yet?"

"No. Elly insists I give it one more try tomorrow. She's going with me. I told her not to worry about it. If I don't find something new, I can always dig something out of my closet."

Travis closed his eyes in bleak despair as he heard the lack of enthusiasm in her voice. He knew that under normal circumstances Juliana would never have said such a thing. She would have been searching California from one end to the other for a new gown to wear to her engagement party.

"Good luck shopping," Travis finally said, knowing he was the one whose luck was running out faster than water through a sieve. "I'll try to stop by Charisma tomorrow for a cup of coffee."

"All right. See you tomorrow." Juliana hesitated. "Good night, Travis."

"Good night."

Travis slowly hung up the phone and watched as night enveloped Jewel Harbor on the other side of the floor-to-ceiling windows. The darkness looked cool and comforting—velvety soft. A place to hide. Inside his office everything was fluorescent bright and there was no place to hide from the failure he saw looming on the horizon.

That failure had been crouching there all along, of course. He had caught glimpses of it right from the start when he had first agreed to try to save the inn. But Juliana's indestructible faith in him had somehow obscured reality for a while. Even as her breezy confidence in him had irritated him, it had buoyed him.

Hell, for a while there, he had almost believed he could pull it off.

But Juliana hadn't expressed any of the familiar, serene assurance in his abilities for the past two days. There had been no bright, bracing lectures on how everything was going to work out.

There had also been no call from Bickerstaff.

But Travis knew the cold feeling in his gut tonight didn't come from facing the harsh business reality; it came from having to face the fact that Juliana was distancing herself from him before disaster even hit.

She had been growing cool and remote since that day they had walked on the beach, when she had asked him what he would do if she told him she was pregnant.

Since then, Travis reflected, she had stopped trying to pin him down to a wedding date. There had been no talk of the tea shops. And now Juliana seemed to have lost interest in shopping for a new dress for the engagement party. The signs couldn't get more ominous than that.

His bright, vibrant, enthusiastic Juliana was slipping out of his grasp even though nothing had happened to Flame Valley yet.

Travis reran the conversation on the beach in his mind for what had to be the hundredth time, trying to figure out what had happened to make Juliana grow cold.

His first thought this morning was that he had made a terrible mistake. Perhaps she had gotten pregnant accidentally and had tried to tell him, and his anger and refusal to believe her had hurt her deeply.

But that couldn't be it. He remembered he'd asked her point-blank if she was pregnant and she had denied it. She wouldn't have lied to him about a thing like that.

His second thought was that sometime during the past couple of days she had finally realized that the chances for saving the inn and the money she had in it, weren't good after all. Deep down, under all that flash and optimism, Juliana was still a realistic businesswoman. Maybe she was finally getting realistic about Flame Valley and its future.

And the bottom line was that if he couldn't rescue the inn, Travis knew he would automatically revert to the role of the bad guy. He had recognized that from the start. He was faced with only two options. He would be either the problem or the solution. There was no middle ground. If he didn't save Flame Valley, he would become the one who destroyed it.

Travis had tried to force himself to face that prospect from the beginning but somehow he had let himself believe some of the glowing press Juliana had insisted on giving him.

When he was with Juliana it was difficult not to get caught up in her enthusiasms, Travis reflected. But he had never had to deal with a Juliana who had lost her effervescent assurance.

It was beginning to look as if she had lost her faith in him.

Travis reminded himself that he had known from the start that if the chips were down, Juliana would side with her family. She would blame him for destroying Flame Valley and probably her cousin's marriage in the bargain.

The raw truth was that she would be right.

When it was all over, Travis knew he would be the outsider again. It was a role he had played often enough in the past and he recognized it immediately.

When choices had to be made, he got left out.

He tried to tell himself that maybe it was better this way. His relationship with Juliana had been on borrowed time from the start. Maybe it would be easier if she began to withdraw from him now.

But the idea of losing her before the final roll of the dice was more than Travis could endure. He would face the end when there was absolutely, positively no hope left of saving Flame Valley. Until then he was determined to grab what he could of Juliana's fire.

He loosened his tie and went back to work searching for the loophole that he knew didn't exist. It was ironic that he was going to walk away from this mess with the resort. After five years of being obsessed with the damned place, he now discovered he never wanted to see it again.

But one way or another, he decided, he would see that Juliana got her money back. It might take a while, but he would find a way to see she got paid off. He knew that wouldn't buy her back but it was the least he could do for her.

She had given him a great deal during the past few weeks and Travis prided himself on always paying his debts.

"Good grief, Juliana, you can't be serious about that outfit." Elly stared in shock as her cousin paraded forth from the dressing room.

"What's wrong with it?" Juliana glanced down the length of the demure winter-white crepe two-piece suit she was wearing. The long sleeves, high neckline and modest below-the-knee skirt were totally inoffensive as far as she could tell.

"What's wrong with it?" Elly's delicate brows snapped together in a severe frown. "Are you out of your mind? That dress is not you at all. It's got no spark, no sizzle, no color. It's plain, plain, plain. It might look fine on the sweet angelic type or a traditional preppy type, but it's definitely not you."

Juliana felt a momentary flash of annoyance. "Well, you suggest something, then. I'm getting tired of trying things on."

"You never get tired of shopping and trying on new clothes."

"I'm tired of it today, okay?"

"All right, calm down. You're not yourself today, Juliana. Just settle down and listen to me. Go back into the dressing room and try that green and gold number, the one with the V-back cut to the waist."

Juliana heaved a sigh as her irritation died and was replaced by the now familiar sensation of disinterest. She trooped back into the changing room and reached for the racy green evening dress Elly had selected earlier. As she smoothed the slender skirt down over her hips a part of her realized that the green and gold gown was done in the sort of dashing style that normally appealed to her. The deep V-back was at once elegant and daring. It ended in an outrageous bow at the small of her back. The snug outline of the skirt emphasized the curve of her hips and her long legs. For a moment or two Juliana almost got enthusiastic as she considered how a pair of rhinestone shoes she had recently spotted in a shop window would look with the dress.

But apathy set in again as she recalled exactly why she was buying the gown.

"Much better," Elly decreed as Juliana emerged from the dressing room. "In fact, perfect." She glanced at the hovering saleswoman. "She'll take it."

Juliana started to protest and then shrugged, not feeling up to arguing.

Twenty minutes later Elly led her out into the parking lot of the huge shopping center. The green dress was in a bag under Juliana's arm. A pair of rhinestone studded heels were in another sack.

"I've never seen you like this before, Juliana. You just aren't yourself today." Elly slid into the front seat of the Mercedes and turned the key in the ignition. "Things are really going bad in a hurry between you and Travis, aren't they?"

"How would I know? I haven't seen Travis in nearly three days. He's spent the last two nights at his old apartment."

"But he hasn't told you to cancel the engagement party, has he? He's a very assertive individual," Elly pointed out as she pulled away from the parking slot. "If he wanted to call off the party, he would do it. You, I presume, haven't changed your mind?"

Juliana stared out the window. "No. I've been telling myself things are terribly wrong and I should call it all off while I still can but I just can't get up the nerve to do it. I love him, Elly. What am I going to do if it turns out he doesn't love me enough?"

"I don't know." Elly eased the Mercedes onto the freeway, her expression sober. "I spend a lot of time asking myself the same question lately."

Juliana was instantly contrite. "You're still worrying about what David will do if you lose the inn, aren't you?"

"David and I haven't been communicating very well lately, to put it mildly. Not much better than you and Travis, as a matter of fact. He spends all his time either locked in his office or closeted with Travis. When he comes to bed at night, he falls asleep before I get out of the bathroom. The next morning he's gone before I get out of bed. I can't tell what he's thinking, but I know he's depressed and worried. I'm scared, Juliana."

"Join the club."


Travis was surprised at how hard he had to work to psych himself up to stop at Charisma Espresso on Friday. The fact that he had to work at the task at all alarmed him. He was accustomed to facing problems head-on but the problem of Juliana seemed to be unique.

It was noon, he reminded himself as he got out of his car. Only a few more hours to go until the engagement party. And no word yet from Bickerstaff. Time was running out on him fast. The closer Travis got to the bitter end, the more he perversely tried to believe Bickerstaff would call at the last minute and say he wanted in on the deal.

Talk about the irrational hope of the doomed.

Charisma was filled with people who were standing around with small cups and little notepads in their hands. Belatedly Travis remembered that this was one of the coffee-tasting days Juliana had inaugurated last month. Through the glass doors he could hear her behind the counter giving her lecture on coffee while Matt and Sandy poured sample cups.

Travis pushed open the door and stood quietly, listening to the windup of Juliana's talk.

"Always keep in mind that most of the coffee in your cup is water so you must pay attention to water quality. There's no point brewing a pot of coffee using water that doesn't taste fresh and good. Now, let's run through the three blends we tasted today. The first was the dark roasted Colombian. Remember that when you drink dark roasted coffees, you're tasting mostly the effect of the roasting process, not the specific characteristics of the beans used. The coffees taste stronger, but the caffeine level is actually about the same, sometimes even less than in lighter roasts."

Juliana looked a little wan today, Travis thought, frowning. As if she weren't feeling up to par. He wondered if she was coming down with a cold.

"The second cup we tasted was the Kona blend. The coffee grown in the Kona district of Hawaii is the only coffee grown in the United States. Production levels are small but the coffee, at its best, can be outstanding. Medium acidity, smooth, clear flavor."

She not only looked a little wan today, Travis decided; she looked a little preoccupied. Usually when she played to a crowd of customers, she was like a good actress onstage, full of presence and definitely *on*. Today she seemed to be just going through the motions. She was a professional, however, and she conducted the coffee tasting with all the panache of a wine-tasting event.

"The third sample was a blend using chiefly Tanzanian arabica beans from the slopes of Mount Kilimanjaro. Tanzanian coffee is known for its excellent balance. I hope you noted the intense flavor and full body." Juliana smiled at her customers. "And that wraps it up for today, folks. I hope to see you all next week when we'll be trying out several coffees brewed by a variety of methods. We'll also be discussing some more coffee history."

Travis watched Juliana smile one last time at her audience, a pleasant enough smile, but it lacked that extra measure of brilliance he was accustomed to seeing in it. Then she spotted him at the back of the room, and for just an instant he thought her smile bounced up to its usual dazzling wattage. He wasn't certain because the effect didn't last long. The smile slipped right back into the pleasant, polite level and stayed there as she came around from behind the counter.

"Hello, Travis. Taking a lunch break?"

"I want to talk to you."

Something that might have been fear flashed in her eyes but it disappeared instantly. "All right. I'm finished with the tasting. Let's go outside and sit at one of the courtyard tables."

He followed her as she wove her way through the milling crowd of people ordering freshly ground coffee at the counter. A minute later they emerged into the relative calm of the courtyard.

"Well? What is it, Travis? Having second thoughts about tonight?" Juliana asked with typical bluntness as they sat down.

"No. But I thought you might be having a few." Travis faced her across the table, willing the truth from her. He felt as if he were standing on the edge of a cliff.

"It's not as if we're getting married tonight," Juliana pointed out coolly. "It's just an engagement party. Nothing permanent. No reason to panic."

"Right. Are you sure you're not panicking?"

"I'm a little nervous, but I'm not panicked," she retorted with a burst of anger.

Travis nodded. "All right, calm down. I was just asking."

"Why?"

"Because you've been behaving a little strangely for the past few days," he said quietly. "Since that day we took a walk on the beach, in fact."

"Oh. Maybe it's nerves."

He waited but when there was no further explanation forthcoming, he tried again. "Juliana, did I say something to upset you that day? If you're hurt because I came down on you like a ton of bricks when you implied you might be pregnant, I'm sorry. It was just that I was so sure you couldn't be pregnant, I was stunned to hear that you might be and I..." He let the sentence wind down into nothing. "I overreacted, I guess."

"Don't worry about it. I didn't bring up the subject in a diplomatic fashion, did I?"

"Someday we'll talk about kids," Travis promised.

"Will we?"

He nodded, hastening to change the subject. "Is there anything else that's worrying you?"

She looked straight at him. "No."

"I thought maybe you were concerned about the situation with Flame Valley."

"No."

Of course she wouldn't come right out and tell him she was wavering in her faith in him, not after all the buildup she had given him for the past few weeks. She would keep her growing uncertainties to herself.

"It's not looking good, Juliana," Travis felt obliged to say one last time.

"You've already told me that several times," she said impatiently.

Travis felt his temper fray. He got to his feet abruptly. "Yeah, I have, haven't I? Maybe it's finally sinking in. See you tonight, Juliana. Shall I pick you up?"

"No. I'll drive myself. I want to go to the restaurant a couple of hours early to make certain everything's in order." She jumped to her feet. "Travis, I didn't mean to snap at you. It's just that I'm a little tense."

"Yeah. Me, too."

He stalked out of the sidewalk café into the sunlight. When he reached the Buick he glanced back and saw that she was still staring after him. He thought he saw pain in her eyes and he almost went back to her. But even as he hesitated, uncertain of what to do or how to handle her, she turned and walked back into Charisma without a backward glance. He saw her dab at her eyes with a napkin she had picked up off the table and his stomach twisted.

Travis looked down into the yawning chasm below the edge of the cliff and wondered how it was going to feel when he went over.

Hh found out exactly how it was going to feel when he hung up the phone after the final conversation with Bickerstaff. It felt rather as he'd expected it to feel—as if the ground had just dropped out from under his feet. There was nothing to hang on to, nothing he could use to save himself.

It was over.

Travis wondered at the unnatural sense of calm he was feeling. He rubbed the back of his neck and glanced at the clock. A few minutes past seven. The engagement party was already underway and he was late. He wondered if Juliana would guess the reason why.

Feeling more weary than he could ever remember feeling in his life, he got to his feet, went around the desk and retrieved his jacket. No point going back to the apartment to dress for the occasion. He wouldn't be staying long at his engagement party.

"If this is any indication of the future, Juliana, you'd better be prepared to find yourself standing alone at the altar."

"Not a good sign, friend, when the future groom is late to his own engagement party."

"I can't believe it, Juliana. How could you plan everything right down to the shrimp dip and then forget to make sure your fiancé got here on time? Not like you, pal. The prospect of marriage must have addled your brain."

Juliana managed a smile as she endured another round of good-natured teasing. It had been like this since shortly after seven when guests had begun arriving and discovered that Travis was not yet there. Most were treating it as a joke, fully expecting Travis to walk through the door at any moment.

The only ones who showed any real evidence of concern were Elly and the other members of Juliana's family. The Grants, as a group, looked decidedly grim.

"Do you think you should call his office? Or his apartment? Something may have happened, Juliana." Elly spoke from right behind her cousin.

"He'll be here when he's ready," Juliana said, wondering at the odd sense of resignation she was feeling. She felt almost anesthetized, she realized. It was something of a relief after all the painful anxiety and uncertainty she'd been experiencing most of the week.

She took another look around the room and saw that everything was running smoothly, if one overlooked the minor fact that the future groom was not present.

The large room The Treasure House rented out for special occasions was festively decorated with silver balloons, colorful streamers and a wealth of exotic hothouse flowers.

The centerpiece was a magnificent buffet table that stretched almost the entire length of the room. It was laden with a staggering array of delicacies that included everything from garlic toast to shrimp brochettes. In a moment of nostalgia, Juliana had even ordered a bowl of guacamole and had stipulated it be set in a place of honor in the middle of the table.

The room was filled with laughing, talking people decked out in typical California style, which meant that every conceivable variety of fashionable attire from silver jeans to elegant kimonos were represented.

David and Elly had arrived at six, volunteering last-minute services. It was the first time Juliana had seen David since the night she had invited him and Elly to dinner to tell them Travis was going to save the resort. One glance at his handsome face had warned her Elly was right; he did look worried. He tried to hide it behind his familiar genial smile, but Juliana knew David was deeply concerned. Elly was struggling just as hard to maintain a cheerful front.

Her parents and Uncle Tony were putting on a good front chatting with other guests but every so often one of them glanced toward the front door and scowled darkly.

Thank heavens she had decided to invite Travis's parents only to the wedding, not to the engagement party, Juliana thought.

She sighed to herself as she studied the crowd. How had she let things get this far? She ought to have called the whole thing off days ago, right after that fateful walk on the beach. She glanced at the clock for the fiftieth time. Seven-thirty. She wondered if Travis would bother to show at all.

Juliana was seriously considering the possibility of disappearing out the back door of the restaurant when she heard a murmur of awareness go through the crowded room. She swung around instantly, knowing Travis must have arrived. As she looked toward the door, her spirits lifted briefly. Hope died hard, she was discovering.

A roar of approval went up as Travis walked into the room. There was another round of teasing comments and congratulations and much laughter.

Travis ignored it all. He walked straight toward Juliana without glancing at anyone else in the room. He was wearing his familiar working uniform, a white shirt with the sleeves rolled up, a conservatively striped tie and dark trousers. He had his jacket hooked over his shoulder.

Juliana took one look at his grim, implacable face and knew that everything was lost.

She stood very still in the middle of the room as Travis paced toward her. She realized her hands were trembling. She folded them together in front of her. The crowd began to realize that something was wrong. The teasing became more muted and gradually disappeared. People stepped out of Travis's way and a hush descended.

Travis walked the last few steps in a charged silence. He seemed unaware of anyone else in the room except Juliana. His eyes never left her face as he came to a halt in front of her.

"I just got off the phone with Bickerstaff," Travis said in a terrifying cold, quiet voice. "It's all over. He doesn't want to get involved with Flame Valley. Too big a risk, he said. And he's right."

Juliana's mouth went dry. "Travis?"

"Sorry it went down to the wire like this. For a while it was close. You even had me thinking there was a chance, and I, of all people, should have known better. Bickerstaff was the last shot and he's out of it now."

"What are you trying to say?" Juliana demanded tightly.

"That I can't save Flame Valley from the wolf—can't save it from myself. Looks like I'll have my revenge, whether I want it or not. I just came here tonight to let you know that you don't have to call off our engagement. I'll do it for you and save you the trouble."

Travis turned on his heel and walked swiftly back out of the room.

Juliana stared after him, feeling as if she had just been kicked in the stomach. The layer of anesthetizing numbness that had been protecting her for the past few days began to crack. Underneath it lay a world of hurt.

Travis was walking out of her life.

"Juliana?" Elly came toward her quickly, keeping her voice low. "What's wrong? What did Travis say to you?"

"That Flame Valley's last chance just went down the

tubes so he's calling off the engagement. Saving me the trouble of doing it myself, he said."

"Oh, my God." Elly closed her eyes. "What will David do?" Then the rest of Juliana's words hit her. Elly's eyes flew open. "Travis is calling off the engagement? Now? Tonight? Just like that? In front of all these people?"

"You've got to hand it to the man, once in a while he displays a real flair for the dramatic."

"Juliana, I'm so sorry. So very sorry. I didn't think it would end like this. I really didn't. Do you know, during the last couple of weeks I'd decided he really did love you, that he wasn't using you for revenge. I'd actually decided we'd all been wrong about him and you'd been right."

"He never once told me he loved me, you know," Juliana said wistfully. "I thought he was working up to it, though. I really did."

"What are you going to do, Juliana? All these people. All this food. The music. What will you tell everyone?"

The last of the numb feeling fractured and disintegrated. The pain was there, just as she had known it would be. But so were a lot of other emotions, including anger.

"How dare he do this to me?" Juliana said through her teeth. "Who the hell does he think he is? He's engaged to me, by heaven. And if he thinks he can walk out on me like this, he's got another think coming."

She started through the crowd toward the door.

"Juliana," Elly hissed. "Where are you going? What shall I tell the guests?"

"Tell them to enjoy the food. It's paid for."

Juliana dashed through the startled crowd of guests and out the front door of the restaurant. She came to a brief halt on the sidewalk, scanning the parking lot for the familiar tan-colored Buick.

She heard the engine before she spotted the car. Travis was just pulling away from the curb.

"Come back here, you bastard…I said, come back here." Juliana hiked up her skirt and ran at top speed across the restaurant driveway, no easy feat in her glittering high heels.

She cut through two rows of parked cars and reached the Buick just as Travis paused to glance over his shoulder to check the traffic behind him.

He did not see her when she threw herself on the hood of the Buick but he certainly heard the resulting thud. His head came around very quickly, and he stared at the woman in green sprawled across the engine compartment as if he had just seen a ghost.

"Juliana!"

"You're engaged to me, you bastard," she yelled back through the windshield. "You can't walk out on me like this. I deserve an explanation and I'm warning you right now, whatever that explanation is, it won't be good enough. Because we aren't just engaged, we're partners, remember? You might be able to end an engagement like this, but you can't end a business relationship so easily."

Travis switched off the engine and opened the car door. "I don't believe this," he muttered as he got out. "On the other hand, maybe I do. Get down from there, Juliana."

She ignored the order and stood up on the tan-colored hood, balancing a little precariously. She paid no attention to the marks her heels were leaving in the paint. She folded her arms and gazed down at him with fire in her eyes. "I'm not going anywhere until I choose to do so. I want an explanation for the way you're trying to end our engagement. You owe me that much, Travis Sawyer."

He looked up at her, the lines of his face harshly

etched in the glare of the parking lot lights. "I gave you your explanation, Juliana."

"What? That business about not being able to save Flame Valley? That's no explanation, that's an excuse."

"Didn't you hear me? I can't salvage the damned inn for your precious cousin and your ex-fiancé and the rest of your family. Flame Valley is going to go under and there's nothing I can do to save it."

"Stop talking about that stupid resort. I don't care about it right now. Our engagement party is a hell of a lot more important."

"Is that right?" he demanded roughly. "Are you really trying to tell me you want to go through with marriage to the man who's going to be single-handedly responsible for destroying Flame Valley?"

"Yes!" she yelled back.

# Ten

The only thing that made it possible for Travis to hang on to his self-control was the sure and certain knowledge that if he lost it now, he would never be able to regain it. He looked up at the magnificent creature standing on the hood of his car and felt the blood pounding through his veins. Her hair was a wild, crazy shade of orange in the glare of the parking lot lights. Her shoes sparkled garishly as if they'd been coated with some sort of cheap glitter dust, and the huge satin bow at the back of her green dress had come undone.

Travis knew he had never in his life wanted a woman as badly as he wanted this one.

"Juliana, listen to me. I'm the Big Bad Wolf in this story, remember? That resort has been in the Grant family for over twenty years. I'm going to tear apart everything your father and his brother built. I'm going to ruin your cousin and Kirkwood. And you're going to lose a big chunk of your savings in the process. This is bottom-line time. You have to choose sides whether you like it or not and *I'm on the wrong side*."

"So you decided you'd make the choice for me? Forget it, Travis. I make my own decision."

His hand clenched into a fist. "You're going to hate my guts when you watch Elly and Kirkwood lose the resort."

"I could never hate you, although I might get madder than hell at you from time to time."

"Juliana, sometimes you have to make choices. You can't be on your family's side and my side, too, not in this. Don't you understand? You'll have to choose. I've already told you, I'm on the wrong side."

"I don't care which side you're on. That's the side I'm on and that's final. You can't get rid of me by telling me I have to choose between family and you. That's not how it is. Besides, I've already made my choices. I made them the day I met you. I chose you, Travis."

Travis took a step forward, coming up against the hard metal of the Buick's fender. He could have reached out and touched Juliana but he didn't dare. Not yet.

"Are you trying to tell me that you still want to get engaged to me? That you want to marry me? Even though I can't stop what's going to happen to Flame Valley?" he demanded. He could hear the rasp in his voice. His mouth was dry.

"Travis, for a reasonably intelligent man, you are sometimes awfully slow to catch on. Yes, that's what I'm trying to tell you. For crying out loud, I didn't fall in love with you because I thought you could save Flame Valley. I fell in love with you weeks before I knew anything about your connection to the inn."

"But after you found out about my connection to the inn things changed, didn't they?"

"I got mad but I didn't stop loving you. I've never stopped loving you. Besides, you offered to try to fix the damage. That was good enough for me. You made all the amends you needed to make."

"I didn't do a very good job of fixing things, did I?"

Her smile glowed. "That doesn't matter," she said, her voice suddenly husky. "You tried. If anyone could have saved Flame Valley, it would have been you."

Travis swore. "Trying isn't always good enough, Juliana."

"Yes it is. Most of the time, at any rate. And certainly this time it is."

"What makes it good enough this time?"

"Because you did it for me." She threw her arms open wide, and her smile was even more dazzling than usual. "And you did your best. You worked night and day to try to save the inn."

"But I didn't pull it off. Don't you understand?"

"You're the one who doesn't understand. You don't understand what your efforts meant to me. Nobody has ever even tried to do something on that scale for me before. They all think I can take care of myself. But you went to the wall for me, Travis. For *me*, not for Elly or David or my parents or Uncle Tony. You did it for me. It was for me, wasn't it?"

"Hell, yes, it was for you. If you hadn't been involved everything would have been a damned sight simpler, that's for sure. I'd have taken over Flame Valley without a second's hesitation and I would never have looked back."

"That's true. And you would have had every right. But you didn't do it because of me. Nobody does stuff like that for me, because I'm the strong one. Do you know how wonderful it is to have someone step in and try to save me?"

Travis was at a loss for words for a few seconds. All he could think about during that brief moment of charged silence was that until now no one had ever chosen him when a choice had to be made.

"Are you sure you want me?" was all he could manage to get out. "Your parents, Elly and David, Tony, they're all going to blame me for not being able to pull the fat out of the fire."

"They can blame anyone they want. We both know you did everything that could be done," she retorted vehemently.

"You're overlooking the fact that the fat was in the fire in the first place because of me," Travis felt obliged to point out.

"That doesn't matter. You had your reasons for doing what you did."

"Revenge is a good reason?"

"Well, certainly it's a good reason. You had a right to get even for what happened five years ago. One can hardly hold that against you."

"Your logic is incredible. But who am I to argue with it?"

Her smile was brighter than the parking lot lights. "Does this mean you're going to come back inside The Treasure House and celebrate your engagement to me in front of all those people?"

He touched the toe of one of her glittering high-heeled shoes. "Yes, ma'am, that's exactly what it means."

"Then what are we waiting for?" She held out her arms. Travis felt the joyous laughter well up from somewhere deep in his gut. For a soul-shattering instant he knew the meaning of pure happiness. He reached out and scooped his lady off the hood of the car, paying no attention to the small paint scars left by her heels.

"You know something, Juliana? You make one hell of a hood ornament."

She laughed up at him as he set her on her feet. With great care he retied the huge satin bow at the small of her back. When he was finished he traced the elegantly bare line of her spine with his finger. She was warm and silky and so magnificently feminine that he ached for her. But there were a lot of people waiting inside The Treasure House, he reminded himself.

He reparked the car. Juliana reached for his hand as they started back across the parking lot but Travis forestalled her. He'd never felt more swashbuckling in his life. So he picked her up and carried her into the restaurant.

A cheer went up as Travis strode into the crowded room with Juliana in his arms. The band immediately struck up a waltz. Travis set Juliana on her feet and took her into his arms. He whirled her out onto the empty dance floor before she had quite realized what was happening.

"I didn't know you could waltz," Juliana murmured as the applause rose around them.

"Neither did I. But I think that tonight I could do just about anything." *Except save Flame Valley from myself.*

Out of the corner of his eye Travis caught glimpses of Elly and David and the Grants watching with anxious concern. By now they must have realized that their precious resort was history, he thought, but no one made a move to stop Juliana from dancing with him.

Then a sense of exultant satisfaction swept through

him. Of course no one was going to try to come between him and Juliana. No one in his or her right mind got in Juliana's way when she wanted something, and she was making it very clear tonight that she wanted him.

Juliana had made her choice.

Several hours later Juliana was still humming a waltz to herself as Travis took her key and opened the front door of her condominium. He looked at her, amusement and something far more intense gleaming in his crystal eyes.

"Enjoy your engagement party?" he asked as he followed her into the hall.

"Had a lovely time. It was a perfect engagement party. The engagement party to end all engagement parties." She did one or two twirls on the carpet, enjoying the way her rhinestone shoes glittered beneath the green skirt of her gown. "What about you?"

Travis folded his arms and leaned one shoulder against the wall. He watched her dance around the living room. "It was a hell of a party, all in all."

"I thought so." She came to a halt in the center of the room and studied her long-nailed fingers. A diamond ring sparkled in the lamplight. "You even remembered the ring."

"I bought it right after I asked you to marry me. I've been carrying it around ever since."

"And you brought it to the party with you tonight even though you were only planning to stay long enough to say the engagement was over." Juliana smiled, feeling deliciously smug.

"I'd put it in my pocket earlier before I went to the office to call Bickerstaff one last time," Travis explained.

"Maybe it was your good-luck charm."

Travis's smile came and went. "If it was, it didn't do me much good when it came to dealing with Bickerstaff."

"Forget Bickerstaff. The business with the inn is over." Juliana walked toward him. "Now that we've settled the little matter of our engagement, I think it's time we ironed out a few small details of our relationship."

Travis's brows rose. "Such as?"

She looped her arms around his neck and looked straight into his eyes. "I love you, Travis. Do you love me?"

Travis unfolded his arms and put his hands around her waist. His eyes were startlingly serious now. "I love you."

"Is this a forever kind of love or the kind that lasts until the divorce?"

He pulled her hips tightly against his thighs and kissed her hard on the mouth. "It's the forever kind."

She relaxed, believing him. "You've never said, you know. I got a little nervous there for a while."

"That day on the beach. The day we talked about babies. That's when you started getting nervous, didn't you? I could feel you retreating from me, pulling back emotionally. I thought you were finally beginning to realize I might not be able to save the resort."

"I got scared, all right, but not because of Flame Valley. It occurred to me for the first time since I had met you that I might be making a mistake. You didn't seem ready to make a complete commitment. You were afraid to talk about anything as permanent as a baby. That's what made me so nervous."

He lifted his hands from her waist to spear his fingers through her thick hair. "I'll be honest, honey. The thought of having kids makes me uneasy."

"Perfectly understandable, given your background.

That I can handle. We can work on your fears together. But I was worried that maybe you weren't sure of your commitment to me. And that terrified me."

"There was never any doubt in my mind about my feelings for you. But tonight when I talked to Bicker-staff and realized Flame Valley was going under, I didn't want to hear you tell me the engagement was off. So I decided to tell you first. I should have known you wouldn't let me get away that easily."

Juliana brushed her mouth against his. "Yes. You should have known. How could you do it, Travis? Would you really have walked away from me tonight and never looked back?"

"I figured I didn't have a prayer of marrying you, at least not anytime soon, but I sure as hell didn't intend to walk out of your life."

"Because you knew I'd come after you?"

His smile was slow and tantalizingly wicked. "No, not because I knew you were going to throw yourself on the hood of my car. I knew I'd be seeing you again because I'm your partner in Charisma, remember? We have a deal, you and I. I am supposed to collect my fee regard-less of whether or not I saved the inn. There's nothing like business to make sure two people see a lot of each other."

She laughed up at him, delighted. "Very clever."

"A man has to be clever to stay one step ahead of you."

"Who says you're one step ahead of me?" she purred, liking the way her new ring flashed when she stroked her fingers along his shoulders.

"Right now I don't care which one of us is ahead of the other. I just want to get together. It's time we really celebrated our engagement."

His mouth closed once more over hers, and Juliana

felt herself being lifted up into his arms for a second time that night.

"I'm a little big to be carried around like this," she murmured against his mouth.

"You're just the right size for me," he said as he carried her into the kitchen.

"Funny, I was just thinking the same thing. What are we doing in here? The bedroom is the other direction."

"Open the refrigerator," he ordered.

She did so and saw the bottle of chilled champagne inside. "Ah-hah. This beats crackers in bed anytime."

"Don't forget the glasses."

Juliana plucked two glasses off the counter and cradled them, along with the champagne, as Travis carried her down the hall to the bedroom. Inside the white-on-white room he set Juliana lightly onto the bed. She pulled her legs up under her green skirt, and the rhinestone shoes glittered in the shadows. Travis watched her as he stripped off his clothing. Then he reached out and took the bottle of champagne and the glasses out of her hands and put them on the nightstand.

"Definitely the world's most stunning hood ornament," he muttered as he came down beside her on the bed.

"You don't think I was a bit gaudy? For a Buick, I mean?"

"Juliana, my sweet, you're always in the best of taste."

He kissed her shoulder and simultaneously found the bare skin of her back. Juliana trembled as his rough fingertips traveled down the length of her spine to her waist. Then he slowly undid the satin bow.

She stretched languorously, her pulse throbbing with anticipation as Travis slowly lowered the bodice of the green gown. "Your hands feel so good," she whispered.

"You're the one who feels good. Soft and silky and sleek." He leaned down to kiss the slope of her breasts as he bared them.

A moment later the dress was on the floor along with the rhinestone heels and Juliana's filmy underwear. Her breath was coming more quickly now in soft little gasps as her senses reeled with the gathering excitement.

"You always go wild in my arms," Travis said, sounding thoroughly pleased and deeply awed. "You make me crazy with the way you want me. You know that, sweetheart? No one's ever wanted me the way you do."

"I've never wanted anyone this way before," she confessed, clinging to him as he slid his hand down toward her moist heat.

"We agreed the first time that what we have is special. We were right." He parted her gently and found her sensual secrets.

Juliana clutched his arms and arched herself against him. *"Travis."*

He raised his head to look down at her. "I'll never get tired of watching you when you're with me like this." He stroked his fingers into her and withdrew them with calculated slowness.

"Oh, Travis, I can't seem to wait, I want..." Juliana felt the small convulsive contractions seize her with little warning. She cried out.

"No need to wait," Travis assured her, pulling her hips close to his thighs again. "There's more where that came from and we've got all the time in the world tonight. Go wild again for me, sweetheart."

"Not without you." She reached for him, sliding one of her legs between his, searching out the heavy, waiting length of him.

When she touched him intimately, cupping him and caressing him, Travis sucked in his breath. After that there were no words, only soft sounds of growing need and spiraling desire.

Juliana was lost in the wonderland of passion when she felt Travis open her legs with his strong hands. Her nails sank into his shoulders as he thrust boldly into her, and the delicious shock set off another ripple of release that seemed to travel throughout her whole body.

She heard him mutter her name as he surged into her again and again, felt his body tighten under her hands and then there was only the marvelous sense of free-fall that always followed the peak of their lovemaking. Juliana welcomed it, losing herself in her lover's arms even as he lost himself in hers.

The rhinestone shoes lying on the white carpet glittered in the shadows, the small stones sparkling as if they were diamonds.

"Juliana?" Travis said her name softly in the darkness a long time later. He was sitting naked on the side of the bed, pouring champagne into the two glasses they had brought from the kitchen.

"Ummm?" She was feeling deliciously relaxed and content. She studied his broad shoulders and strong back with a loving eye. He really was just the right size, she told herself happily.

"If you did happen to get pregnant, hypothetically speaking, I'd be the happiest man alive."

"It's just too bad you couldn't appreciate the expressions on everyone's face last night when you went racing out the door chasing Travis and then returned ten minutes later in his arms. It was an absolutely priceless scene. A scene of legendary proportions, as far as the management of The Treasure House is concerned." Elly sipped at her coffee latte and shook her head in wonderment.

"Sometimes a woman has to go after what she wants." Juliana savored the rich color of the Keemun tea in her cup and then automatically glanced around Charisma's pleasantly crowded serving area with an appraising eye.

Saturday mornings had typically been light until three months ago when she had put in a full range of newspapers and breakfast pastries. Customers had surged into the shop ever since on Saturdays to take their morning coffee and a croissant while reading something exotic and foreign like the *New York Times*.

"Your parents and my father were a bit stunned, I'll have to admit," Elly continued. "Especially after I told them that Travis was not going to save Flame Valley after all. You know what your father said?"

"What?"

"He told Dad to wait and see. 'It isn't over until the fat lady sings,' I believe were his exact words."

"I hope the rest of you aren't holding any false expectations," Juliana said gently. "Travis said there really was nothing more he could do except find a buyer for the resort. That way, at least, we won't all lose our money. But you and David aren't going to own and operate Flame Valley, and the inn will definitely go into new hands."

"I know. David and I had a long talk last night about our future," Elly said. "We settled a lot of things we probably should have settled much sooner."

Juliana frowned. "Well? How did it go? Are you still worried about him leaving now that the resort is dead in the water?"

Elly smiled sweetly, her eyes clear. "Oh, no. He never was thinking of leaving me. The poor man was scared I might leave him. That's why he was so uptight these past few weeks. Can you believe it?"

"Yup. I always knew the two of you were meant for each other." Juliana sat back. "So what are you going to do?"

"Well, one possibility, if Travis finds us a buyer, is to take the money and try the resort business again, this time on a much smaller scale. Maybe a little bed-and-breakfast place on the coast. Another possibility, according to David, is to see if Fast Forward Properties can negotiate us a contract with the new owner, whoever it is, to run Flame Valley. Under Travis's guidance, of course. We don't want to make the same mistakes we made last time."

"Would that bother you, Elly? To stay on at the resort after it goes to a new owner?"

"I think I could handle it and so can David. I'm not sure Dad or your parents will like it. It will probably gall them to see family members reduced to being just the managers of Flame Valley."

"On the other hand," Juliana pointed out, "Uncle Tony and my folks aren't the ones who have to make the decision, are they? It's you and David who have to decide what to do with your future."

"That's exactly what David and I told each other last night. I feel amazingly relaxed about the whole thing now that it's over. It's as if because of this mess David and I have finally stepped out from under Dad's shadow. Whatever happens now, our marriage will be the stronger for it."

"Uncle Tony always means well," Juliana said, "just like my parents always mean well."

"True. And we know they love us. That's the most important thing. But there's no denying they can be a little overbearing at times."

"Look at it this way, as irritating as the situation can be, it's better than winding up with parents who couldn't care less about what you do with your life."

"Who's got parents like that?" Elly asked in amazement.

"Travis."

Elly looked at her. "Oh. That's right. I suppose you have plans to fix the problem?"

Juliana smiled with cheerful confidence. "Let's just say I've got plans to give Travis's parents one more chance to dance at this wedding."

"And if they don't show up?"

"They'll show up."

"How can you be so sure?"

"Because thanks to a talk with Sandy I decided no more Ms Nice Guy. I'm going to blackmail Travis's folks into showing up and behaving themselves."

Elly's eyes widened. "You're going to blackmail them? I should have guessed. You don't lack the nerve, Juliana. You always go after what you want, no holds barred."

"It's one of my best features," Juliana agreed. "Just ask Travis. Say, I was planning to start the big hunt for my wedding gown this afternoon after Charisma closes for the day. Want to come with me? I guarantee this is going to be one special dress."

"Now I know for certain you're back to normal," Elly said.

"Strange how some of the things you fear most in life aren't the ones you have to worry about after all, isn't it?" David took a long swallow of his beer and looked out over the harbor.

"Life's funny that way sometimes." Travis was sitting next to David at one of the outdoor tables of the Golden Keel, a trendy pub near the marina. Both men had repaired to the bar by mutual agreement to discuss the future of Flame Valley. But so far all they'd talked about was their relationships with the women in their lives. "I take it you and Elly have come to an understanding."

"She was worried I'd leave if we lost the inn. I think some part of her had never been completely certain I hadn't married her because of Flame Valley."

"Juliana was always sure the two of you were in love right from the start."

David chuckled. "Juliana is always sure of everything."

"Yeah." Travis grinned fleetingly. "And sometimes she's right."

"I've got to hand it to you, Sawyer. I don't know of any other man who could handle Juliana Grant."

"If any other man ever tries, I'll break his neck," Travis said calmly.

"That's assuming Juliana doesn't do it first."

"True. So what now, Kirkwood? You want me to try to find a buyer and see if I can get you a contract to manage the inn?"

David lounged back in his chair. "I've got a proposition for Fast Forward Properties."

"What's that?"

"How about letting me and Elly run the place after you take possession of the property? Hell, nobody knows the resort as well as we do."

Travis studied the condensation on his beer glass. "It wouldn't be the same as owning it," he warned. "I'll have a responsibility to my investors. It would be my job to make sure the resort got back on its feet. I'd be on you all the time. Looking over your shoulder. Watching every move. I'm good at what I do, Kirkwood, but the fact is, I'm hell to work for."

"I think I could deal with it." David looked unperturbed. "Who knows? I might learn something about financial management from you."

"I'll think about it. Run it past my investors."

"Fair enough," David agreed. "So when's the wedding?"

"Juliana's got it scheduled for the end of the month."

"The end of the month? Why so soon? You're engaged and you're practically living together. Why is Juliana rushing the wedding?"

"It was my idea," Travis said. "I'm not taking any chances. When I sew up a business deal, I sew it up tight. No loopholes."

David grinned. "I know. You sewed up the deal on Flame Valley so tight even you couldn't find a way out. Juliana doesn't stand a chance."

"That's the whole idea."

# *Eleven*

"He's going to stand her up at the altar, I just know he is." Beth Grant, looking every inch the mother of the bride in mauve lace and silk, paced back and forth in the small church anteroom.

"Uncle Roy and Dad will get a shotgun if Travis tries to duck out now," Elly declared with a small smile. She was fussing with the satin train of Juliana's gown.

"Relax, both of you. Travis isn't going to stand me up." Juliana scrutinized her image in the mirror. The sweetheart neckline had been the right choice, after all. She'd had a few second thoughts yesterday when she'd tried the gown on one last time. But today it looked perfect. The wedding dress was everything a wedding dress was supposed to be, spectacular, frothy and extravagant. She'd spent a fortune on it and didn't regret one dime.

"I'm not so sure Travis wouldn't walk out at the last

minute," her mother said. "It would be the ultimate revenge on the Grant family, wouldn't it? First Flame Valley falls into his clutches and then he leaves you at the altar. Where is that man?"

"He'll get here on time if he knows what's good for him," Elly murmured, giving the train another small twitch. "He knows that if he doesn't show there'd be no telling what Juliana would do. He's still complaining about the scratches her heels left on the hood of his car."

"I'm not worried about Travis getting here," Juliana said, feeling perfectly calm as she bent closer to the mirror to check her lipstick. She wondered if she should have opted for a more vivid shade. The coral looked a tad pale. Then again, brides weren't supposed to go to the altar looking as if they'd just walked out of a makeup ad, she reminded herself. Angelina Cavanaugh had made that very clear to her a week ago. *"Tone it down, Juliana. Brides are supposed to look sweet and demure, not like an empress claiming her empire."*

"You don't look concerned about anything except your makeup," Beth sighed, watching Juliana….

"Well, to tell you the truth, I am a little concerned about one thing. I was wondering if Travis's parents had arrived. Any sign of them?"

"I'll check with the usher," Elly said, heading for the door. She disappeared out into the hall, obviously glad to have something useful to do.

Beth came toward Juliana with a misty, maternal gleam in her eyes. She hugged her daughter briefly. "You look beautiful, dear. I'm so proud of you."

"Thanks, Mom."

"I will personally throttle that man if he doesn't show up."

"He'll show up." Juliana spoke with complete confidence. Nevertheless, she was touched by her mother's unusual protective instincts. "The thing about Travis is that you can always count on him."

Beth shook her head wonderingly. "I cannot understand how you are always so certain of him. As far as I can tell he's done absolutely nothing to warrant your total confidence in him. He didn't even save Flame Valley."

"He did everything that could be done. At least with him in charge of Fast Forward Properties the transfer to new ownership will be as smooth as possible. And David says he and Elly are going to get the contract to run it."

"I suppose that's better than nothing. Maybe someday we'll find a way to get the resort back into Grant hands. Your father still thinks there's every possibility this will all work out in the end. Even your uncle Tony seems amazingly optimistic. But I still don't see how you could have had such faith in Sawyer right from the start."

"You don't really know him. I do."

"What makes you think you're such an authority on Travis Sawyer?"

"We have a lot in common," Juliana said simply, adjusting a straying curl beneath her veil. "We trust each other and we love each other. It's all really very simple."

"I wish I could be sure of that. I hope you know what you're doing, Juliana."

"I always know what I'm doing, you know that, Mom. Would you hand me my flowers, please? It's almost time."

Beth looked more anxious than ever as she handed the bouquet of exotic flame-colored orchids to her daughter. "You can hardly walk down the aisle in front of all those people if Travis isn't waiting at the other end. I won't allow it. The humiliation would be unbearable for the entire family."

"He'll be there."

Beth eyed her daughter's serene expression and smiled reluctantly. "Your complete faith in him is getting contagious."

"You'd better go take your seat, Mom. Dad and Uncle Tony will be getting nervous."

Beth looked at her. "You're absolutely certain Travis will show up today?"

"Absolutely certain."

The door burst open and Elly stuck her head around the corner. She was excited and amused. "They're here, all right. The usher says he just seated the groom's parents. All four of them. And a bunch of stepbrothers and stepsisters."

Juliana nodded, content. "Good. Another example of winning by intimidation. Mom, run along now. It's time."

Elly bit her lip. "Uh, Travis's folks are here, but Travis isn't here yet, Juliana."

"He'll be here."

Beth cast her daughter one last worried look. "You're sure?"

"Yes, Mom, I'm sure."

"You do look lovely today, dear." Beth smiled tremulously and went out of the room.

Elly gave Juliana a hard stare. "*Are* you sure?"

"Of course I'm sure. Would I be standing here in this dress if I thought I'd get stood up at the altar? Travis would never do that to me."

"Well, there was that little incident at the engagement party," Elly reminded her delicately.

"Travis showed, didn't he? He didn't stand me up. He just didn't plan to hang around very long after he got there, that's all."

"That's a very charitable view of the situation. If you hadn't run after him and thrown yourself on the hood of his car, I don't know what would have happened that night."

"A woman has to go after what she wants."

"And you really want Travis Sawyer, don't you?" Elly said with soft understanding.

A knock on the door interrupted Juliana's reply. "We're ready, Miss Grant," said a muffled voice on the other side.

Juliana nodded with satisfaction and pulled the waist-length veil down over her face. "Right on time. Get your flowers, Elly."

Juliana opened the door and walked confidently down the hall to the point where she would make her entrance with her father. She peeked down the aisle toward the altar and was not at all surprised to see Travis standing there, waiting for her. He looked incredible in formal clothes, she thought fondly. She'd have to find a way to get him dressed up more often.

"He just drove up two minutes ago," Roy Grant muttered, shaking his head as he took his daughter's arm. "Tony and I were just about to go after him. Thought for sure you'd been stood up."

Everyone was feeling protective of her today, Juliana thought happily. It must have had something to do with her role as a bride. Parental instincts coming out, no doubt.

"There was no need to worry, Dad. Travis said he'd be here."

The music swelled. Juliana smiled her most brilliant smile and started down the aisle on her father's arm.

Travis never took his eyes off her as she came toward him. Her gaze met his through the veil. When she reached the altar he accepted her hand as Roy Grant released her.

"Sorry I'm a little late," Travis murmured very softly. "Got held up at the office. Bickerstaff changed his mind."

"He *what*?" Juliana hastily lifted the gossamer veil so she could get a better look at Travis's laughing eyes.

"You heard me. Flame Valley is technically again in Grant hands as of about fifteen minutes ago. Got a hell of a load of debt hanging over it, but David and Elly are the official owners."

Juliana threw her arms around him, laughing with surprise and delight. "I knew you'd pull it off, Travis. There's nobody like you in the whole world."

A ripple of astonishment went through the crowd as Juliana hugged Travis. The minister coughed to get everyone's attention. "I believe we're ready to begin," he said with a touch of severity.

Juliana released Travis, grinning. "First you have to make an announcement," she informed the man of the cloth.

The minister's brows rose in amused curiosity. "What sort of announcement would that be?"

"Just say that Bickerstaff changed his mind."

The minister looked out over the crowded church. "Bickerstaff," he intoned solemnly, "has changed his mind."

Juliana thought she heard a small gasp from Elly and then the bride's side of the church broke out in wild applause. Anxious not to offend, the rest of the guests quickly followed suit.

When the applause finally faded the minister looked

sternly at an unrepentant Juliana. "Now may we begin the wedding service?"

"You bet," Juliana said.

"Hang on a second," Travis said and reached out to lower the veil back down over Juliana's dazzling smile. When he was finished arranging the filmy stuff he nodded, satisfied with the old-fashioned, demure effect. "A man's got a right to insist on a little tradition once in a while."

"I'm thinking of buying an interest in this restaurant," Travis muttered some time later as he stood, champagne glass in hand, surveying the throng of guests at the reception. "At the rate we're using this place, we might as well own a share of it. One of these days you're going to have to arrange a party at one of the other restaurants in town. Just for variety."

"Now, don't grumble, Travis. The Treasure House always does a wonderful job with wedding receptions."

"Uh-huh." He sipped his champagne. "At least I'm finally putting an end to your hobby of collecting proposals here."

She batted her lashes at him. "Yours was the only proposal that counted."

"Damn right."

Juliana beamed. "Do you realize this is the first moment I've had you to myself since the wedding? I thought I'd never get you away from David and Uncle Tony and Dad."

"They wanted all the details about the Bickerstaff deal."

"I'll bet they did. Why did Bickerstaff change his mind?"

"It's complicated and I don't really feel like going into it now, but to sum it up, I called in an old favor from a banker friend of mine. When he found out Bickerstaff was interested in the resort, he agreed to restructure some of Flame Valley's debt. That, in turn, tipped the scales as far as Bickerstaff was concerned. He decided to go ahead with the deal."

Juliana whistled faintly in appreciation. "Sounds tricky. What about your investors?"

"They'll be paid off the same way they would have been in a buy-out. It's complicated, but I think it's going to work. Assuming Kirkwood cooperates."

"He will."

"Yeah, I think he will." Travis glanced over Juliana's shoulder and his eyes hardened faintly. "Here comes Mom and her second husband."

"I like your mother. And your father. We all had a nice chat earlier." Juliana turned to smile at the attractive, champagne-blond woman who was approaching with a slightly portly, well-dressed man in tow.

"Hello, Mrs. Riley. Mr. Riley. Enjoying yourselves, I hope?"

Linda Riley returned the smile and so did her husband. "Very much, dear." She looked at her eldest son. "You've chosen a very lovely bride, Travis."

"She chose me," Travis said, not bothering to conceal his satisfaction. "Glad you and George and the kids could get here today," he added a little gruffly.

"Wouldn't have missed it for the world," Mrs. Riley said dryly as she slanted an amused glance at Juliana. "We never see enough of you, Travis. You really ought to come visit more often. The kids are always curious about their mysterious big brother, you know. They admire you. I believe Jeremy wants to talk to you about going into land development."

"Is that so?" Travis looked wary but interested.

Mrs. Riley's smile deepened with understanding as she turned back to Juliana. "Thank you very much for inviting all of us, Juliana. You know, sometimes families drift apart without really meaning to. People lose perspective in the heat of selfish emotion. Pride becomes far more important than it should. But that doesn't mean any of us want it that way or that we can't see the light eventually."

"I know, Mrs. Riley," Juliana said, returning her mother-in-law's smile. "As I told Travis, people change. Weddings are great opportunities for getting families together, aren't they?"

"Better than funerals," Travis remarked.

Juliana wrinkled her nose at him and then helped herself to a canapé from the buffet table while he talked to his mother and stepfather. She was quite pleased with the way things had turned out, she decided. Everyone had been well behaved at the church and seemed to be acting like adults here at the reception.

Travis's father, a tall, distinguished-looking man who had introduced himself earlier, was at the other end of the room with his second wife. Both were in deep conversation with Roy and Tony Grant.

Travis's stepbrothers and sisters, ranging in age from the late teens to early twenties, were a lively, talkative crew who appeared to regard the brother they shared with some awe and fascination.

"So how did you do it?" Travis asked as his mother and stepfather drifted off to join another group.

"Do what?"

"Don't play the innocent with me. I know you too well. How did you get both my mother and my father to attend the wedding?"

"Travis, I think you should make allowances for the fact that reasonable people are quite capable of change over a period of time. It's been years since they refused to attend your first wedding. They were probably still very bitter toward each other back then. Now they've had a chance to mellow and mature. Intelligent people grow up sooner or later."

Travis picked up a cucumber and salmon canapé and popped it into his mouth. He considered Juliana's words carefully and then dismissed them. "I'm not buying it. What you say about their maturing may be true but I don't see you just sending out invitations and hoping for the best. You wouldn't take any chances. You wanted them here, so what did you do to make certain they showed up today?"

"Blackmailed them."

Travis grinned. "With what?"

"I made it very clear that neither your mother nor your father would be invited to see their first grandchild if they didn't have enough courtesy to attend the wedding."

"I should have guessed." He put down his champagne glass. "Care to dance, Mrs. Sawyer?"

"I would love to dance, Mr. Sawyer."

Juliana went into his arms, the heavy skirts of her wedding gown whirling around her low-heeled satin slippers.

"I see you decided not to wear high heels today," Travis observed as he looked down slightly to meet her eyes.

"I figured a bride should be able to look up to her husband on her wedding day," Juliana explained demurely. "Tradition, you know."

Travis laughed and the sound of his uninhibited masculine pleasure turned the head of everyone in the room.

"Are you sure you didn't wear the low heels because you wanted to be prepared to run after me in case I didn't show up at the church?"

She looked up at him with all her love in her eyes. "I knew you'd show. I never doubted it for a moment."

Travis's gaze grew suddenly, fiercely intent. "You were right. Nothing on earth could have kept me from being at that church today."

"I love you, Travis."

He smiled. "I know. I've never been loved by anyone the way you love me. Just for the record, I love you, too."

"I know," she said, pleased. "Hey, you want to sneak out of here early and start on our honeymoon?"

"That depends. What, exactly, are you planning to do on our honeymoon? Toss me in the marina? Chase me through parking lots? Dump guacamole over my head?"

"Gracious, no. I was thinking we could spend the time going over the plans for my chain of Charisma tea shops."

"You never give up, do you?"

"Never."

"I've got a better idea," Travis said. "What do you say we go someplace private and talk about babies?"

"While it's true I never give up," Juliana responded smoothly, "I can be temporarily distracted. I would love to go someplace private and talk about babies."

"It's a deal," Travis said.

He came to a halt in the middle of the dance floor, took Juliana's hand in his and led her toward the door—and their future.

*Everything you love about romance...*
***and more!***

*Please turn the page for Signature Select™*
*Bonus Features.*

# Lady's Choice

BONUS
FEATURES
INSIDE

Here's a sneak peek...

4

# *Her Perfect Life*
## by
## Vicki Hinze

*Katie Slater's life is perfect. She's a wife, mother of two and a pilot in the United States Air Force. But then she's shot down by the enemy, left for dead by a man she trusted, and taken as a prisoner of war in Iraq. Now, six years later, she's back home—only, home isn't there anymore...and her perfect life has become a total mystery.*

*From Signature Select, in bookstores April 2006.*

## PROLOGUE

LIFE SHOULD COME with warning labels.

*Warning!* At fifteen, you're going to be tempted to give your virginity to Donald Simoneaux at Mel Ott Park behind the baseball bleachers. Don't. He's an arrogant idiot with a big mouth, and if you do it, you'll never hear from him again. You won't anyway—it'll be a one-date train wreck—but if you sleep with him, you'll feel you wasted your first, be down on sex for the next decade and be ticked off about it forever. If you don't, you'll thank the gods for sparing you from a second date with the jerk, meet a great guy at eighteen who has finesse, and the first time you two twist the sheets, you'll totally understand all the fuss about sex.

*Warning!* At seventeen, avoid the Pink Daisy. It's a cute club with cool people, but you'll get busted because Marianne Demsey will stuff her dope in your purse when the place is raided and she won't admit that it's hers. You don't smoke anything, including pot, but you'll never convince your dad of it, or the police. On the up side, you'll test clean, get community service and your mom will know the truth. She's psychic, remember? She knows everything. But she won't be able to convince your dad she's not covering for you, and he'll choke you nearly to death trying to keep you on a tight leash until you're twenty-one. You will *not* be a happy leashee.

And oh, while we're talking about twenty-one, skip the Mardi Gras frat party at the LSU campus in New Orleans. You'll save yourself an ex-husband. That's where you'll meet Wonder Dick, who considers fidelity a rule just for women.

*Warning!* At twenty-four, you'll be a pilot, just as you've always dreamed. Air force all the way, baby. And right after pilot training, you'll meet a jock who makes you weak in the knees. You'll marry him three years later, have two great kids—a girl and a boy— and you'll love your life.

Okay, so in a few years you'll get a little wistful now and then because your relationship could be better. Jock—aka Dr. Sam Slater, leading gynecologist in Willow Creek, Florida—isn't perfect, but unlike Wonder Dick, he's worth keeping. He's a faithful husband, a decent if uninspiring lover, a good dad so into having the perfect image he still hides flaws from his parents, and if he's a bit selfish and seemingly unconscious about what's important at times, well, you're not perfect either.

Actually, his faults are relatively minor compared to those of the spouses of many of your friends. If you looked at vaginas and dealt with hormonal women all day, you probably wouldn't get overly enthused on nights at home, either.

As compensation, you'll have the coolest copilot in the air force, C. D. Quade, who is a walking violation to the libidos of women everywhere. He's totally irresistible—gorgeous, sharp, funny, sensitive and straight. You two will be nuts about each other, and on occasion you'll wonder what it would be like to be with him instead of the jock, but loyalty and vows keep your wedding band on your finger and your panties up around your hips. C. D. Quade isn't the kind to trespass on another man's turf anyway, so it's just as well you keep your blood cooled to a simmer around him. Regardless, with the jock, the kids and your beloved garden at home and C.D. at work, you'll be reasonably content. That's not bad for real life.

Now for the grand slam, "kick your ass and pad your knees because you're going to be on them for the duration" *Warning!*

Love your family so fiercely that it almost hurts, and do all those things you keep saying you'll get around to someday—like finding a way to make a living with your gardening, taking that Alaskan cruise you've dreamed about since your eighteenth birthday

BONUS FEATURE

and making that pilgrimage you promised your grandmother you'd make to Scotland to see where your dad's ancestors lived. Don't wait. Do it all now. *All* of it.

Because if you don't, when you're thirty-four, on June 23, you're going to be assigned to fly a mission in Iraq and your plane is going to get shot down. You'll be with your devoted sidekick copilot, C.D., who will still be incredibly sexy and single, but... well, the bottom line is he's going to be rescued, and you're going to be dead.

At least, that's the way it's going to seem for a long, long time. And many times during this dark period of your life you'll remember the little list you made when you were eight, the one that detailed all the things you wanted when you grew up. Remember? You wrote it shortly after you completed the magical leap from the fat pencils you conquered in first grade to the brand-new Number 2 slim-and-sleek writing machine.

This list was the most important document of your life, and to mark the rite of passage in creating it, you pulled out your most prized possession: the black-ink, clear-barrel, comfort-grip, Bic medium-point pen you'd been saving to first use on something really, really special. This was that life-defining moment. That momentous occasion you would forever recall as the one moment in time when you knew exactly what you wanted to be content.

You felt it the moment the tip of the pen touched the page and you printed in bold, broad letters.

KATIE COLE
AND
HER PERFECT LIFE

I'm sorry to say that many times during these trials you'll have to fight hard not to lose hope and heart and let your spirit be broken. It won't be easy. It will be hell. You'll curse that list and your life, and you'll wish you were dead.

Oh, yeah. Life definitely should come with warning labels.

But it doesn't.

And that, Captain Katie Cole Slater, is the most important *Warning!* of all.

## CHAPTER 1

*Six Years Later*

Her prison cell was dark and dank.

Weak moonlight cut through the tiny barred window, barely casting a thin strip of a shadow on the sand-packed floor. The air lay still, silent and heavy, yet compared to the days of 120-degree temperatures, it seemed blissfully cool.

In just a few hours, dawn would come and the desert heat would again turn her cell into an oven. Trapped between the walls in this armpit of hell, the heat swelled and seemed to suck all the oxygen out of the air. Day or night, Katie felt choked. Midday she often spent strangling, and when the sandstorms came, the misery increased tenfold.

*That which is endured is conquered.*

She gently held the photo of her husband, Sam, and their children, Molly and Jake. It was far too dark to see it, but that didn't matter; she'd memorized its every detail. Though it made the ache in her heart so acute she swore it would kill her, each night she forced herself to remember every quirk and expression and sound they made, terrified if she missed even one night she'd forget and never again be able to recall them. She relived each memorable moment and the way it had made her feel—the way they had made her feel—at least a million times, and prayed it would be enough to last her the rest of her life.

*Eyes are unnecessary to view that stored in the heart.*

The photo's edges were frayed and the images worn smooth in places—one on Molly's hair and one on Jake's nose. Katie had always done that—stroked Molly's hair and dragged her fingertip down the slope of Jake's nose. Back then she'd been comforting them. Now she stroked their photo trying to comfort herself.

In the past six years there had been little comfort.

But there had been an abundance of nightmares.

Nightmares of the crash, of her injuries. The pain of setting her own broken bones. When she'd discovered she'd gone down in a lawless tribal area, she'd known that there would be more pain to be suffered. And there had been. Much, much more pain suffered.

Despite the warlords' bets that she wouldn't last a week, she had endured and conquered every single violation. She had survived. Yet each abuse had created horrible images that didn't fade from her memory on awakening. Images that ignited resentment and anger and made it burn as strongly in her as the loneliness of isolation and the constant fear of what the sadistic bastards holding her prisoner would do to her next.

General Amid had been a godsend.

Still, it had taken a couple of years to come to grips with being left behind. C.D. had to be dead, or he'd have found her by now. She still mourned him. Mourned losing Sam and their kids. Mourned having her life stripped away from her and being left with… this.

It had taken a couple more years to give up hope of ever being rescued. But on the fifth anniversary of her crash and capture, she'd reached critical-crisis point: accept it or go insane. That night, alone in her cell, she had slogged her way through a minefield of emotions and faced the truth. No one could reach her here. No one would even try—not anymore, if they ever had. Too much time had passed, and living in this cell, cleaning General Amid's home, shopping for his household at the market—that was her life now, and likely that's all it would ever be. She refused to think about his leaving. Without his protection, the guards would revert to the way they'd treated her before he'd stepped in, and that incited more nightmares, more withdrawing deeper and deeper inside

12

herself, closing even more shutters in her mind, locking away the memories of torture to stay sane.

Yet on still August nights like this one, where she lay alone in her cell on a bare cot with but one thing of her own—the photo—she silently wept inside, crushed under the weight of her darkest fears. She *would* die in this god-awful place, still wearing her tattered flight suit because it made the guards feel superior and powerful to hold her—the U.S.—captive. She would die here just as surely as C.D. had died in the desert the night of the crash.

She would never again see Sam or Molly or Jake.

She'd never again know the joy of watching them play while she worked in her beloved garden. It too likely stood as withered and overgrown as the day she'd first found it. Sam was not a master gardener. He wouldn't even remember to water the lawn if it was not on an automatic sprinkler system. She'd worked two years on that garden. But… Reality hit her. Everything in her life ceased to be when she had ceased to be.

Except for Sam and the kids.

Yet even with the most heartfelt and resolute rationalization, she couldn't convince herself that they weren't gone from her life forever.

On her cot, she curled on her side, pulling her knees to her chest, trying to shut out despair. *God, how long must I endure to conquer this? How long?*

BONUS FEATURE

*If this is the way it's to be, why am I here? I'm of no use to anyone. Why can't I die, too? I don't work without them. Nothing works without them. Please, just end this pain....*

For the hundredth time that long, sorrowful night, she swallowed a sob and buried her hopelessness. The guard was apt to come in at any time, and she didn't dare let him see her in tears. She'd made that mistake once early on and would kill herself before doing it again. He and the other guards had tortured her for six hours straight.

Shaking head to toe at the memory, she crossed her chest with her arms and squeezed. The sensation of pressure swept sweet relief through her body. She was awake, not asleep, not dreaming those haunting dreams. She had survived.

*That which is endured is conquered.*

Rubbing the U.S. flag patch on her sleeve, she wondered. What were the children doing? Was Sam home from the hospital, tucking them into bed, singing them night-night songs? Did he notice that Molly showed signs of being as psychic as Katie's mother? Did he remember that she hated the crust on her sandwiches and Jack had to have orange juice every morning to jump-start his sugar? Did he remember to kiss them good-morning as well as good-night? How often did he remember to tell them he loved them? He'd seldom slowed down long enough to give Katie the words, but love had always been there in his eyes. Always there in his eyes. Molly would sense that. But would Jake?

A tear splashed onto Katie's cheek and her heart ached. *God, how can I keep taking this, day after day? Please, please let what happened today matter. Please let that French doctor report seeing me.*

He *had* seen her. Hadn't he? He definitely had made eye contact, been startled and quickly covered it up, then pretended not to have seen her at all.

General Amid, who ran the prison camp, had sent her to the market for his fresh vegetables. There was no danger of her running away. There was nowhere to run and no one to run to, and anyone foolish enough to try would die in the desert or be slaughtered by the lawless hiding out in the region. Either way, the runner would be dead long before reaching help. In the market there had been a small group of medical workers treating the sick, passing out medicine. That's where she'd seen the French doctor. He *had* to have reported seeing her....

But nothing happened that night to verify it.

Katie consoled herself. It took time to notify people. Time to identify her and to debate options on what to do. Warning herself she was being a damn fool, she couldn't seem to stop hope from flickering to life inside her.

Nothing happened the next night, either, and doubt seeped in. Maybe she'd just seen what she'd wanted to see, and the Frenchman hadn't seen her at all. Or maybe it was just taking a little longer to get the wheels moving. It *had* to be taking just a little while longer....

But a week later, when still nothing had happened, her certainty disappeared. The Frenchman hadn't seen her, or if he had, he'd chosen to ignore it or he'd thought nothing of it.

The most important glimpse of her life—but to him it'd been too insignificant to even notice.

*You've got to stop this, Katie. Stop hoping. It's insane. Nothing is going to happen. Keep hoping, and how are you going to handle the letdown? Hope is a luxury you can't afford.*

She paced her cell in the darkness, bitterness burning her throat, her chest so tight she could barely breathe. *Die, hope.* She pushed a fisted hand over her heart. *Die!*

And whether it did, or it was buried so deep she couldn't feel it anymore, she put the Frenchman from her mind, locking him behind the shutter to forget him, too, and then returned to stroking her worn photograph in the sweltering heat, missing Sam and the kids, mourning C.D. and scrubbing General Amid's quarters, longing for her weekly bath and swearing she'd trade her eyeteeth for a hamburger, cola, or a

16

bottle of skin lotion. And conditioner for her hair. She squeezed her eyes shut and indulged in heartfelt longing. She'd give a molar for one squirt of conditioner. Just one…

While she hadn't dared to hope, she had put herself in General Amid's presence as often as possible, in case he wanted to send her back to the market. The medical workers still being around was highly unlikely, but it wasn't impossible.

Yet whether or not they remained close by quickly became a moot point. The general watched her with an odd look in his eyes, but he never sent her back to the market. Instead, just before she was to return to her cell one night, he stopped her. "Katie," he said. "I am to be transferred to a new prison soon."

Fear sliced through her heart like a knife and she had to fight to find her voice. "Will you take me with you?"

Regret burned in his eyes. "I am sorry. That is not possible."

Disappointment raised terror and tears clogged her throat. She couldn't speak, and so nodded. He would leave, and things would return to the way they had been before he had learned what was happening to her. *Oh, God. I can't stand it again. I can't.*

*Shutter, Katie. That which is endured…*

"I am sorry," he whispered. "I have done all I can do to protect you."

He had. Here, and maybe in sending her to the market. Maybe he'd meant her to be seen. On the chance he had, gratitude swelled and her chin quivered. She cleared her throat to hide it. "Thank you."

He, too, had given up hope. She was lost. Lost, screwed and defeated.

Knowing it, she walked the dark pathway back to her cell. The defeat had her despairing, but even more than despairing, she was terrified.

Long after midnight that night—exactly two weeks after she'd seen the Frenchman in the market—Katie paced her four-foot-wide cell until her feet ached, and then collapsed onto her cot, exhausted. Her stomach growled. She hadn't been fed since yesterday, and hadn't been able to steal anything from General Amid's. If he ever noticed food missing, he never mentioned it. But she didn't flaunt stealing his food in his face, either.

Holding the photo over her heart, she ignored her rumbling stomach, closed her eyes and shut down her mind.

For the first night since she'd seen the Frenchman, she didn't drift to sleep seeing his face in her mind. Every other night she had alternated between praying he'd think of her and the thought of her would nag at him until he did something to help her, and cursing him for not being more aware, seeing her and doing something to set her free. But this night she didn't think of him at all. General Amid, the man whose protection had kept her alive and safe, whose food had kept her from starving to death, was leaving. A new commander would take his place and things would return to what they had been.

She would be dead within a month.

If God was merciful, sooner…

A SCUFFLE STARTED outside her cell door.

Katie awakened abruptly. Every nerve in her body sizzled, hyperalert and warning her to hide, but she forced herself to stay still. For her own protection, and until she discovered what the hell was going on, she best served herself by not letting anyone know she was awake.

"Colonel Katherine Slater?" a man said in a crisp, sharp voice.

*Colonel?* She didn't respond. It could be a setup for torture.

A second man's hushed voice carried through the bars to her. "Call her Captain. She doesn't realize she's been promoted."

Katie stiffened. As a P.O.W. she would automatically be promoted, but the enemy knew that, as well. And Americans considered her dead. Unless the Frenchman… She stifled a gasp. *Oh, God! Was it possible?*

"Captain Slater," the first man said, then recited her code word that only she and her superior officer knew.

*American! He had to be an American!* She sat straight up. "Yes? Yes, it's me." She strained to see him, but it was a moonless night, and she could barely make out his silhouette. What did this mean? Had they engaged the tribal warlords in the lawless area and been taken prisoner, too?

"Captain Daniel Wade, ma'am," he said, his husky voice catching. "We're here to take you home…."

*Look for* HER PERFECT LIFE *in bookstores April 2006 from Signature Select.*

20

...NOT THE END...

# Stroke of Midnight
by Julie Kistler

C

*It's New Year's Eve, and though they've not yet met, in a few hours everything will change for Trey Jameson and Susannah Quincy....*

Susannah knows it's time to break off her engagement when her jerk of a fiancé stands her up on the last night of the year. But dumping Carter means risking her job. Will a fantastic midnight kiss from another man convince her the risk is worth it?

Meanwhile, Trey's made a New Year's resolution to seize the day and live out his dreams. But when fate leads him to the lips of a beautiful but conservative woman, will he give up his plans—or entice her into joining him on his next adventure?

SUSANNAH QUINCY was furious. She smacked down her copy of *Blissfully Single,* the new guide for women who wanted to maintain their independence, keep their sanity and never, ever get married. Who could read at a time like this? Her gaze landed on the back cover photo of the author, a stunning blonde who looked entirely blissful.

22

"Probably because she's *single*," Susannah said angrily. Tossing the book farther away, she glared at her sparkling engagement ring. Pretty diamond. Signifying absolutely nothing!

She rose and checked the clock. Eleven thirty-five. "Carter is *so* not coming," she muttered. "Carter is *so* a dead man." He had always been a little unreliable, a little inconsiderate. But this was the last straw.

Susannah sashayed over to the mirror. She'd chewed off all her lipstick, but other than that, she still looked really good, if she did say so herself. A red dress with her flaming red hair was something she didn't usually do, but tonight she'd been willing to take the risk. It was New Year's Eve, after all. If you couldn't shake it up on New Year's Eve, when could you? She loved her dress, she loved how her hair looked, all soft and wavy, with tiny sparkles that matched her dress scattered here and there. And yet here she was, home *alone* on New Year's Eve.

The clock now said it was 11:40. She felt certain Carter must already be at the party, because there was no way he would skip something as important as the New Year's Eve party thrown in the penthouse suite at the Hotel Marceau when absolutely every major player at Manley & Marceau International would be there, including both Manley *and* Marceau. Carter was way too much of a company man to miss this prime occasion for sucking up.

BONUS FEATURE

If he was already there, that meant he had gone without her, simply neglected to pick her up as planned and not even bothered to call. "Carter is a dead man," she repeated, with more energy this time. Suddenly she decided. "I am going by myself. I work there. I am entitled to be at the party. I am going to go in there, find Carter and throw the ring in his face!"

After applying a new coat of lipstick, she swept out of the apartment, fuming the whole way to the Hotel Marceau. Once there, she zoomed up in the elevator to the lavish, wraparound penthouse suite.

When the doors opened, Susannah saw a crowd of well-dressed people sipping champagne against the twinkling backdrop of a big Eiffel Tower centerpiece. She tried not to soften her mood. But she did love this place. Tonight it was more romantic than ever, dark and lush, with the tension of midnight fast approaching.

Intent on finding Carter before she lost her nerve, she squeezed into the party. Luckily Carter was tall enough that even in this crowd, she quickly spotted the top of his head. Getting ready to confront him, she tried to wrest the ring off her finger, but it was too tight. How could she throw the ring in his face if it wouldn't come off? So she gave up, marched over and tapped him on the shoulder. The minute he turned, she hauled back and slapped him across the face. Hard. "How do you like *that,* Carter?"

Except it wasn't Carter.

It was a gorgeous man, a man she'd never met who happened to be about the same height and coloring as Carter.

Around her, people went crazy, chanting, "Ten! Nine! Eight!"

Staring at the man she'd just smacked, Susannah began, "I—I'm sorr—"

But the count hit Two and then One, and the penthouse exploded with horns and blowers and noisemakers. Everybody shouted, "Happy New Year!" as the man she'd never met bent closer.

And then he pulled her into his arms and kissed her.

Susannah found herself tangling her arms around his neck, sliding herself up into his embrace…. And kissing him back.

*Kissing him back?*

There was so much noise and music. All around, people were laughing and shouting and hooting on their horns. This man, whoever he was, was a fabulous kisser. Was it her fault if she was overwhelmed by the atmosphere and the timing and the man?

As he slanted his mouth across hers, he shoved his hands into her hair, tipping her face so that he could take the kiss deeper. Was it the magic of the kiss that made her see stars? Or was that tiny, shimmering crystals cascading from her hair?

Susannah hung on for dear life. Who knew New Year's Eve could be like this? Who knew a kiss could be like this?

BONUS FEATURE

Finally, so dizzy she could barely see, she had to break away to breathe. She drew back, pushing a hand against his chest. "Who are you?" she whispered, eyes wide, drinking in the gorgeous man.

There was no way she should have mistaken him for Carter. He was tall, maybe an inch taller than her fiancé, with broader shoulders and an easy grace that made him look elegant even though his clothes were casual. Where most of the men at this party wore tuxedos, he had a white shirt with an open collar and a simple black jacket over jeans. Jeans? At the Hotel Marceau's posh, black-tie New Year's party?

And yet he looked perfect. His hair was light caramel brown, a bit darker than Carter's sandy shade, and he had blazing blue eyes. Amazing blue eyes.

26

How funny that she was still having trouble getting enough air. "Who are you?" she asked again.

He worked his jaw, massaging it with one hand. "Maybe you should've asked that before you slapped me." He smiled. "Who are *you?*"

"Maybe you should've asked that before you kissed me." She touched her tender bottom lip with one finger, wondering if her lips would ever be the same.

"It was the stroke of midnight," he said dryly. "I had to kiss you."

She took another step back. "It's not exactly a law."

"Aw, come on." His tone was light and teasing, which made him even more charming than he already was. Which ought to have been illegal. "It's New Year's Eve. Everybody is kissing everybody. "

"I'm not everybody," she protested, trying to keep her wits about her.

"I already know that," he mused. His eyes raked her up and down, and she wished she'd chosen a more conservative dress. This one dipped low in the front, plunged scandalously in the back and was held up only by tiny threads of crystal beads. "You're definitely not just anybody."

Susannah felt naked in the middle of the party. She glanced up at Mr. Great Kisser, feeling bewitched and bewildered under his heated gaze. He had narrow, clever lips. Excellent kissing lips. With her red lipstick still on them.

Without thinking, she extended her thumb to rub away the traces. But he caught her hand.

"What's this?" he asked, glancing down at her ring finger and then back up at her face. "Are you engaged? Who to?"

He waited for her answer.

"Am I engaged?" she echoed. She was staring at her ring as if she didn't know herself.

"Just a hint," Trey Jameson said tactfully. "It looks real to me. Not like something you got out of a gumball machine."

The redhead he'd kissed at midnight, the one with the sparkling hazel eyes and the pale, glowing skin, was instantly wary. "How would you know whether it's real or not?"

He shrugged, enjoying keeping her off balance. Even if she *was* engaged, she was just too lovely not to play with. "I'm a good judge of jewelry," he told her. Which only made her look at him with more suspicion. He noticed she still hadn't answered his question. "So, are you engaged? Or did you just wear an engagement ring to hold off any strange guys who might kiss you at midnight?"

"I'm really engaged," she insisted. But she stopped, considered, then started again. "For now."

Interesting answer. She was stunning, mysterious and a hell of a kisser. His New Year's Eve just kept getting better and better. "Oh, I get it. That's who you meant to slap," Trey said, suddenly realizing. "The fiancé."

"Well, yes, but… No." Her eyes clouded. "I didn't plan to slap him. That was more spur of the moment."

"But you're only engaged to him for now. Hmm…" He let his gaze sweep her again, lingering on the place where the shocking red of her dress slashed across the creamy white curve of her breast. God, she had gorgeous skin. "So the question is," he began, tearing himself away from the view with difficulty, "how long were you planning to stay engaged?"

"I—I don't know."

"Is he here?" Trey inquired.

28

"I don't know that, either. I—I think so," she stammered. "I was coming here to break up with him, actually, to give back the ring, but—"

"Good for you," he interrupted.

"Good?"

Trey nodded. "I think people should take risks. And you're way too beautiful to be engaged to some guy who doesn't appreciate you enough to find you at midnight on New Year's Eve." His smile widened as he bent close to her ear. "His loss, my gain," he whispered, enjoying the sparkle in her eyes and the way she seemed to catch her breath when he stood too close. "That's what I'm doing. Taking risks, crashing parties, kissing women I've never met before. It's a lot of fun."

"I'm not a risky sort of person, and…" She edged away from him. "Now that I'm here, kind of out of the heat of the moment, I don't know whether I can do it or not. Give him back the ring, I mean."

"The fact that you stormed in here and slapped me because you thought I was him is a pretty good indication to me that you want to break it off," he said logically. He nabbed a glass of champagne from a passing tray and handed it to her. "I think you should definitely dump the guy."

"Oh, no." Her eyes widened. "Oh, no."

"What is it?"

"The guy." She gulped down the whole glass of champagne. "My fiancé, Carter. He just spotted me. And he's headed this way."

Susannah held her breath. It really didn't matter if Carter had seen her with another man. She hadn't done anything wrong. Well, she had kissed him back, whoever he was, but that wasn't her fault. Was it?

She scanned the crowd. Had anyone else seen her canoodling with a stranger when she was engaged to someone else, someone who worked at the Hotel Marceau along with her and most of the rest of these people? Her boss, Joan, the director of sales, was right over there, giving her a speculative glance. How much had she seen?

*Damn.* Just when she'd had all the righteous indignation on her side, she'd gone and kissed some other guy and turned Carter into the injured party. Now she was even more confused about whether she should break up with him or not. Maybe he would save her the trouble and break up with *her.*

"Susannah," Carter said heartily, making a beeline for her through a narrow break in the crowd. "Darling, where have you been?"

"Where have I been? At home, waiting for you to pick me up!" she returned. "I finally drove myself, and I just got here at the stroke of midnight. Carter, where were you?"

"Not now, darling. Manley is right behind me. I've been shepherding him around all night." He rolled his eyes. "Duty called. You know how it is."

"Well, Duty didn't bother to call me. And neither did you. There I was, sitting at home all by myself, while New Year's Eve withered away. Would a phone call have been too much to ask?"

The handsome stranger hovered right there. "Doesn't sound like too much to me," he put in as Carter turned and glared at him.

Pointedly ignoring the other man, her fiancé took her elbow. "Suze, don't be this way. I need your support, not some petty disagreement. You know as well as I do that Manley can put me at the top. But not if my wife isn't behind me."

"Sorry to interrupt," Mr. Great Kisser said kindly, "but I think I should point out that Susannah is standing next to you, not behind you, and she isn't your wife. Not yet." He smiled as he added, "Maybe not ever."

"Suze, who is this guy?" Carter demanded. "What's going on here?"

She wondered if there was a convenient hole she could sink into. "He's no one," she tried. "I mean, we just met, while I was looking for you."

"Yes, that's exactly right," her mysterious man agreed. "I'm no one. But Susannah ran into me while she was looking for you, and she gave me something that was intended for you. So I think I'll give it back to you if that's all right."

"What?" Carter asked in confusion.

Susannah was every bit as mixed up as he was. What in the world was this guy talking about? "Something I gave you that's meant for him?" And then it all made sense. "Oh, no," she murmured. "Oh, no."

But it was too late.

Mr. Great Kisser pulled back his arm and walloped Carter, right in the jaw. As she watched in horror, her fiancé went down like a ton of bricks.

"I didn't ask you to hit him!" she cried as people swarmed around Carter.

Okay, so punching the guy was probably a bad move on his part. "He's a jerk," Trey explained, holding her back. "And he'll be fine. You're way too good for him. And you were going to break up with him, anyway."

"Oh, my god," she whispered. "My life is over. My fiancé is flattened by a party crasher and probable lunatic, my boss may have seen the whole thing and will probably fire me out of solidarity with my wronged ex-fiancé, and I don't even know your name."

"Hey, you were intending to hit the guy, too," Trey protested. "I just did it for you."

"I wasn't going to sock him," she countered. "Just a little slap. Not this big melee, this whole public brouhaha."

Trey laughed. "Oh, yeah. Slapping him and throwing an engagement ring at him is so discreet and inconspicuous."

"Well, I…" She frowned. "You're right."

"Susannah, listen, maybe this is for the best. Did you ever think sometimes fate has your number and calls your name?" he asked, running a hand down her smooth, silky arm.

"No," she said slowly. She brought up her gaze, meeting his squarely. "I don't believe in fate. I believe in creating your own destiny through hard work and careful planning. Fate is for people who just aren't strong enough to control their own lives."

She looked perfectly serious, too. And why shouldn't she? He'd once felt exactly the same way. Trey shook his head sadly. "Then I take it this is not a good time to ask you to run away to Paris with me?"

"Paris?" Her mouth fell open. "You *are* insane. I don't even know your name!"

"Trey," he said softly, watching her expression. "My name is Trey."

"What happened?" Carter asked, holding his jaw as one of the waiters hoisted him to his feet.

The waiter shrugged. "I didn't see it. I just heard a scuffle and then you fell down. Maybe you hit your head."

"Yes, that's it," Susannah said. "You fell down. I think you tripped." To Trey, she whispered, "Don't you think you'd better go before he remembers or someone else tells him you hit him? You're a party crasher, for goodness' sake. They could throw you out. They could arrest you!"

"I don't care." Trey shrugged. The least she could do was give him credit if he was going to knock down someone on her behalf.

"Can somebody get me a drink?" Carter mumbled. "Scotch, rocks."

"Yeah, sure. Why don't you come with me?" the waiter suggested. "We can get you some ice for your jaw." And he and Carter began to move away through the crowd.

"Okay, everyone, that's enough. Nothing to see," ordered a tall, slender brunette in an outfit so hideous it had to be expensive, as she elbowed her way to the center of the controversy. "Susannah? What was that all about? Is Carter okay?"

"Yes, Joan, he's fine. See? He fell and he's getting some ice for his, uh, head."

Trey could tell by the way Susannah snapped to attention that this Joan woman was someone important. Joan narrowed her eyes at Trey and then Susannah. "Aren't you going to tell me who your friend is?"

Susannah smiled stiffly. "He's not with me. He's, well, he's an old friend of Carter's. Trey, meet Joan Sanders." She paused. "My boss."

The woman arched one dark eyebrow. "A friend of Carter's? Is that why he kissed Carter's fiancée and then knocked him down?"

34

Uh-oh. Busted.

"Oh, the kiss. New Year's Eve, you know." Susannah hastened to assure her boss as Trey offered, "Nothing important—midnight, that kind of thing" at the same time.

She looked at him, he looked at her, then he added, "And there was no fight. Parker and I—"

"Carter," Susannah muttered.

"Right, right. Carter and I were just fooling around," Trey offered. "Old pals. Roughhousing. Haven't seen each other in a while."

"Boys will be boys," Susannah said brightly, her heart sinking. Joan had seen the whole thing. The jig was up. She didn't like Joan anyway, and she'd known very well if she broke up with Carter she could risk losing her job, but she hadn't planned to go out quite so dramatically. She snagged another crystal flute of champagne.

"Uh-huh." Joan didn't appear convinced, but at least she didn't shout, *You're fired!* or anything. "Susannah, do you have a minute? Maybe Trey can go check on his old friend Carter while I steal you away. Okay?"

"Oh. Sure." Susannah smiled, trying to be brave. "Trey was just leaving. Right, Trey?"

He nodded, sticking his hands in his pockets, ambling away as requested. She sighed with relief, telling herself she was glad to see him go. It would make her life so much simpler. And yet... She also felt a good deal of regret watching him disappear into the crowd. He was one good-looking man who knew how to kiss like nobody's business. Who was he? What was he doing here? And why in the world had he asked her to run away with him to Paris?

She'd gone to work for the Hotel Marceau in the first place because the Marceau part of Manley & Marceau International was headquartered in Paris. She'd harbored this silly dream about moving up the ranks and ending up in Paris. Had Mr. Great Kisser known that? If so, how?

Too late to find out now. He was gone. And she didn't even know his last name.

36    "I was talking to Mr. Marceau, and I wanted him to meet my reps," Joan announced. "*If* you can take your eyes off that man for five minutes. Oh, and by the way, your lipstick is smudged. And your dress is kind of, you know, falling off one shoulder. Whoever he was, he left behind some major devastation."

Feeling like an idiot, Susannah righted her strap, brushed little sparkles off her shoulders that had fallen from her hair, and pulled a compact out of her tiny evening purse. As she redid her lipstick, they were joined by Kerry, another of the convention sales reps. Kerry was very sweet, and Susannah actually liked her a lot, even though she felt sorry for her sometimes. Kerry was shy, and it wasn't easy being shy and trying to succeed in sales.

"Hi, Susannah." Awkwardly Kerry added, "Joan, were you looking for me?"

"I was just rounding up all my reps to meet Mr. Marceau," the boss noted.

"Well, I'm here." Kerry sighed. "I lost my date a while ago, but it doesn't matter. It's just my brother."

"You brought your brother on New Year's Eve?" Susannah asked. And she'd thought she had it bad.

Kerry smiled. "It's not like it sounds. It's just, he's leaving for Paris tomorrow, so this was his last night in town and I thought…"

She was starting to get a bad feeling about this. "Leaving for Paris tomorrow?"

"Uh-huh." Kerry perked up. "Oh, there he is. Over by the bar. Isn't he adorable?"

Before she even followed the path of Kerry's finger, Susannah knew who she would see. The mystery man. Mr. Great Kisser. And Kerry's brother. Who'd ever have guessed?

As Susannah stared, Kerry explained, "He's a commodities trader. You know, Chicago Board of Trade. Or I should say, he *was* a trader. Made a fortune, lost a fortune, made a fortune again. Decided to quit and move to Paris, buy a bookstore and live in a garret on the Left Bank." She laughed. "My brother! He's always been a little, you know, whacked." Then she stopped, noticing the expression on Susannah's face. "What's wrong?"

"Nothing." She sipped champagne as she tried to process this new information. Not a party crasher. Not a bad boy right off the street, mingling and making nice while he planned to steal people's jewelry or something. Just meek little Kerry Jameson's brother.

Joan smiled her most wicked smile. "Don't worry, Kerry. She's just realized that the man she slapped the hell out of, the man she was giving mouth-to-mouth to at midnight, is your brother." She chuckled. "I actually saw him first and was kind of hoping to move in on him myself, but then Suze nabbed him."

Kerry was staring at her as if she had three heads. "You—you nabbed my brother? You made out with my brother? But you're engaged, Susannah."

"I didn't mean to. It was just a mistake," she rushed to assure her. "See, Carter never showed to pick me up and I was really mad and I came here to throw the ring at him and break up with him, but the ring wouldn't come off, so I slapped him instead, only it was Trey. Your brother, I mean," she added. "Then he kissed me because it was midnight. That was the only reason. And Joan, I was not trying to nab him. I swear."

"No prob, Suze," Joan offered, patting her on the shoulder. "He's leaving for Paris tomorrow. What would I have done with him anyway?" Giving him another look, she made a tsk-tsk noise with her tongue. "It is a shame, though, that all the cute ones

38

seem to escape before I get a chance. But, hey, if his dream is to live in a garret, he's not my type anyway." She glanced at Susannah. "Or yours. Our sensible, responsible Susannah Quincy would never go for a guy like that. Right, Suze?" Joan laughed.

Susannah sighed. She had no idea *who* she would go for at the moment. She'd thought that driven, ambitious Carter was her type. Until he'd decided business was more important than she was and stood her up on New Year's Eve. Meanwhile, Trey's kiss had been pretty spectacular. Way to rock her world.

Maybe it was just spectacular enough to change types altogether. Or maybe that was the champagne talking.

Was it champagne that was making him look so sexy, lounging there in his jeans, leaning on the bar? He turned, saw that she was looking, raised his glass and winked at her.

And she felt the impact slide down her from the top of her head to the end of her pointy red stiletto heels.

"Susannah, are you coming?" Joan waited expectantly. "We're off to see Paul Marceau and score some brownie points with our charming conversation."

"You go on ahead." She couldn't seem to break away from Trey Jameson's intoxicating gaze. "I have something I need to take care of."

"So…" TREY SWIVELED on his stool far enough to gaze at her, and Susannah wondered what in the world she thought she was doing, passing up a chance

BONUS FEATURE

to schmooze with one of the company presidents, just so she could try to get a handle on someone whose own sister thought he was nuts. Lazily he inquired, "Did Kerry tell you all about me?"

"Not really. A little."

"Sorry I'm not some party crasher off the street? Did that blow my excitement quotient?" he inquired with a certain edge of sarcasm.

"I—I don't know what you mean."

"Sure you do." He gave her that devilish smile again, and she had to clench her jaw to stop from drooling on him. "I've got you figured, Susannah. Especially now that I got a gander at the boyfriend."

"Fiancé," she corrected.

40

"Not for long." His lips curved in a mocking smile. "You think you want the go-getter corporate mover-and-shaker guy, the guy you can buy an SUV with, have a nice house in Oak Park and maybe a lake house in Wisconsin. Kids later. Private schools. You think that's what you want for yourself. Because you think you're a good girl right down to your white cotton undies."

She could feel her face suffuse with rosy color. "I don't wear white cotton undies."

"Prove it," he whispered, his blue eyes raking her.

"Well, I could if I wanted to," she contended, which was actually true. This dress required a certain lack of foundation garment. Which was both scary and exciting. Not that she planned to show him what was or was not under her dress. Not even for a second. But wouldn't he be surprised? "I don't feel the need to prove anything to you," she added hastily.

"Too bad." His smile widened, growing cockier. "Fess up, Susannah. When you saw the way I was dressed, when you thought I crashed the party, when you thought I was up to no good and rotten to the core, you loved the idea of hanging out with the bad seed."

"You're still the bad seed." Deciding she was probably as certifiable as he was, but unable to walk away, Susannah took the stool next to him at the bar, sliding her dress up to manage it, careful not to reveal more than she wanted to. "You may be a slightly less bad seed now that I know you're not a jewel thief, but you're still a bad seed. Kerry told me how you ran away from your good, steady, cushy job to smoke black cigarettes and argue existentialism in cafés on the Left Bank."

"Okay, first, I don't smoke. Second, I want to run a bookstore, not argue existentialism, which went out of fashion, what? Forty years ago?" As she began to object, he raised a hand to hold her off. "And third, you don't know much about traders, do you?"

"Commodities traders?" She admitted, "No, I don't."

"It's not a good, steady job. It's like gambling. And it's a lot crazier and more reckless than moving to Paris." He shook his head, chewing on the stem of a maraschino cherry he'd stolen out of a bowl on the bar. "So you thought I was a jewel thief, huh?" He grinned. "I give you points for creativity. That's a new one."

"Well, you said you used to work with diamonds, or something like that. I don't know, I…" Embarrassed, she grabbed a cherry, too, twirling the stem between her fingers. "Plus you seemed awfully interested in my ring."

His gaze softened. "It wasn't the ring, Susannah. I was awfully interested in you."

She didn't know what to say. Whichever way she turned, Trey seemed to throw her a curve. "You really are nuts—you know that, right?" she inquired, leaning closer to him at the bar, somehow thinking that if she stared at him long enough, she would figure him out.

"Nope. Not nuts. Just willing to take a risk." He took a healthy swig of his drink, which looked like water with a slice of lemon in it. Didn't smoke, apparently didn't drink, and she'd thought he was a bad boy?

"But Trey, you asked me to run away to Paris with you. Tomorrow! You don't even know me," she persisted. "Don't you think that's pretty crazy?"

"Nope. I just believe you have to seize the moment and go for what you want when you see it." He spun his stool around so that he was looking out into the party. "Look at this place, Susannah. Framed posters of cancan girls, a miniature Eiffel Tower, curvy red

42

velvet chairs right out of Maxim's... Somebody was trying to make us think of Paris, don't you think?"

He'd lost her again. "Yes. So?"

"So here I am, bumping into you on New Year's Eve, offering you a chance to go to Paris, and there's Paris all around you. Don't you get it?" he asked impatiently.

"No, I don't."

"It's kismet, it's fate, it's your destiny looking you right in the face." He slid his stool her direction, taking her hands, holding them between his own, staring at her intently. "I know what your job is like, because my sister has the same job. I know what you think you want—to climb higher in Manley & Marceau and run a hotel of your own. Am I right?"

"Yes, but—"

"It may be what you want, but it's not what you need," he argued, and she began to be very angry with him. How dare he presume to tell her what she needed? How long had he known her? An hour? "Your heart was telling you, tonight, to come here and get rid of your insensitive, uncaring boyfriend, even if that meant risking your job at the same time."

She shook her head vigorously. "You don't understand—"

"Yes, I do. Better than you think. I believe, deep down, you wanted to dump the guy and get the job dumped for you." He pressed her hands tighter. "I think you knew before you got here that you wanted

BONUS FEATURE

out. And guess what? You ran smack-dab into the one guy who was offering you a free trip, nonstop, right where you wanted to go."

"I think you are making a lot of assumptions based on what *you* want," she argued, snatching her hands back, placing them on the edge of the bar and holding herself very straight and still. "Yes, I wanted to lose my boyfr—" She stopped and started again. "My fiancé."

Trey reached for her hand, but she pulled it away before he could catch it.

"I was reading this book before I came. *Blissfully Single.* Excellent book," she declared, really starting to work up a head of steam, to think straight, finally. "All about how women don't need men, except for sex and fun, how marriage is a trap and a drain. I totally saw some of my own patterns in that book. And I think I saw tonight, for sure, that Carter was not someone I wanted to spend my life with, and that I had made a mistake."

She pushed herself away from the bar, rising from the stool. "And, yes, I knew that there was a possibility that could make things uncomfortable for me here at the hotel, and that maybe I would be looking for a new job. But it never meant, for even one second, that I would consider throwing away my whole life to run away with some juvenile delinquent nut-job following some misguided, immature dream to run a beatnik bookstore."

There was a long pause. "Flattering portrait you've painted of me."

"Yeah, well, maybe you ought to consider this." She lifted her chin. "Instead of tucking me in your luggage and taking me on a one-way flight to Café Cliché, maybe, if you're so interested and all, you ought to give up Paris and stay here with me."

WELL, THAT HADN'T GONE WELL, had it?

She'd slapped him by accident, she'd kissed him on purpose, he'd slugged her fiancé, she'd lied to her boss, he'd asked her to go to Paris with him on a whim and then, to top it off, she'd called him immature and basically asked him to stay in Chicago and be her boy toy, although she wasn't entirely sure she was serious when she asked it. She could've been trying to insult him. Not that it mattered. Trey had stalked away from the bar and told her he had better things to do with the dwindling moments of his New Year's Eve than talk to a stick-in-the-mud princess.

Stick-in-the-mud princess. Ha! Was that the best he could come up with?

Meanwhile, all of this had taken place while she still had a fiancé somewhere at this same party. A fiancé she really, really needed to break up with sooner or later.

"Susannah?" someone behind her asked in an acid tone.

Speak of the devil. She turned. "Hello, Carter. How are you?"

BONUS FEATURE

"Not well." He looked a little fussy, that was for sure. "My jaw is throbbing," he said tersely, and she could see the big bruise on his cheek. "That guy who was hanging all over you hit me, remember? Now, if you'll just tell me where he is, I will go pound the snot out of him and get this over with."

If she were to be honest, she thought Trey could take Carter down nine times out of ten, even if Carter had backup and a baseball bat, but she didn't want to say that and make things worse than they already were. If that was even possible.

"Carter, I…" She had no excuse. "I'm sorry he hit you. I actually planned to slap you myself, because I was angry that you ditched me. On New Year's Eve. When I looked really, really good."

"Let's not start that again," he snapped.

She glowered at him. "Okay, let's make this simple. Again, I am sorry that he punched you out of some misguided attempt to impress me. The man has an emotional maturity level of, like, three. Men. Jeez Louise." But she was getting off track again. She took a calming sip of champagne before she went on. "This really has nothing to do with him, okay? I need you to know, before one more second of my New Year ticks off, that we are not—"

"Enough!" he roared. "Tell me where he is! I called the cops. They're on their way. Assault, battery, attempted murder—your boyfriend is going down,

Susannah! No one makes a fool of Carter Lyons and lives to tell about it!"

No one except Carter Lyons, apparently. "You called the cops?" she repeated. "For a little scuffle at a New Year's party? Like they don't have enough to do with people shooting guns off at midnight and setting off illegal fireworks and potentially burning down half the city?"

"Where is he, Susannah?" he asked again, gritting his teeth so hard his whole jaw looked out of whack.

"I don't know." She scooted off the bar stool and slipped past Carter with all due haste. "But I'm going to find him and get him out of here before you get your grubby mitts on him." She turned back. "I'm thinking of making him my boy toy, you know. I don't want you messing up his pretty face."

Carter lunged, and she took off as fast as her red stilettos would carry her.

SUSANNAH WAS AT HER WIT'S END when she finally found Trey, standing alone on the balcony, staring off at the skyline. He said wistfully, "You can just see the Ferris wheel at Navy Pier if you twist your head and squint."

It was freezing cold out here. Chicago in January was not a place to be standing on balconies. Below them, revelers were shrieking and screaming and drivers were laying hard on their horns. Happy New Year, she thought to herself. Happy freakin' New Year. Your life is a mess, you may end up losing your fiancé and your job and catching your death of cold in one fell swoop, and all because you chose to save the life of this insane man rather than think of your own well-being.

But she didn't have time for self-righteousness. Quickly she gave Trey her spiel. "Carter is on the rampage, and we need to get you out of here."

"Yeah, right." Trey stayed where he was.

"He's looking for you. He's really mad that you hit him." She hugged herself, trying vainly to stay warm in her skimpy dress as she ventured another step out onto the balcony. "Please, Trey. I know you can take him in a fight, but you're on a balcony, and he could get lucky and knock you over or something. Plus he told me he called the police. So let's go in, let's find your coat and let me get you out of here."

Trey edged around, propping his arms on the railing behind him. "Let *you* get me out of here? Does that mean we leave together? As in, you've changed your mind and decided to come with me?"

"To Paris? Or out of the building before you get arrested?" she asked in a dark tone. "Neither. Although I might come with you as far as the street if you're lucky." She felt like stamping her foot at how stubborn and ridiculous he was being. "Come on, Trey. Let me help you. You need to leave. Now."

"Just curious, but why do you care?"

"Trey, listen to me," she said carefully, slowly, trying to be persuasive. "He called the police. If you get arrested, you won't be on your flight to Paris tomorrow, will you?"

"And this matters to you?"

"Well, if we get you safely on your plane, at least you're not around here, driving me crazy and messing up my life, are you?" She started to shiver, and she rubbed her bare arms with her hands. "And if you come in off the balcony, I can go in, too, drink about ten Irish coffees and hopefully defrost from my current Popsicle state, which would be a real bonus."

That declaration didn't move him in the least. "How interesting. I can see the ring from here. So you haven't broken the engagement yet, have you?"

"I tried," she said softly. "He cut me off. He was more interested in telling me all the ways he wanted to pummel you."

Trey's heated gaze held her steady, almost enough to warm her up in the frigid air. He really did have the most beautiful blue eyes. "He wants to pummel me for kissing you?"

"Not hardly." She let out a short, unpleasant laugh. "He wants to pummel you for punching him in the nose."

"It was the jaw."

"Right." She hopped and jiggled a little, trying not to let her teeth chatter. She failed.

"Susannah, you're not dressed for this. Go in, will you?" he ordered.

But she shook her head. "Not without you."

"Why haven't you given Carter back his ring yet?" he demanded. "Why are you still dragging your feet about this breakup?"

Susannah had about had it with men and their idiotic need to tell her what to do. "I can't get the stupid ring off my finger, okay? Believe me, I have every intention of very calmly handing it over as soon as I get it off. Or if you want to go for it right now, maybe we can throw it over the balcony." She held up her hand. "Maybe the cold will shrink my finger enough, you think?"

"Worth a try."

"Not that it's any of your business," she snapped, "but I have come to some major conclusions about that man tonight, and one of them is that he doesn't care or notice what I am or who I am or what I want. It's all about Carter. He never even told me I looked nice tonight, do you believe it?" She spread her bare arms, ignoring the cold. "I know I'm a little wrecked by now, but when I first got here, I looked amazing."

He smiled. "Yes, you did." His gaze flickered over her, lingering on her breasts, and she knew her nipples were peaking in the cold. She tried to remember to breathe, but the chilled air couldn't seem to make it to her lungs. Trey's voice was rough and husky when he said, "You still do look *amazing*. And the fact that Carter didn't notice? It makes me glad I punched him in the nose."

She smiled back, crossing her arms, shivering again, and not from the cold. "It was the jaw."

"And you're still not dressed to be out here." He crossed to her in about a second flat, pulling her into his arms, gathering her close and trying to wrap his jacket around her, sighing with frustration and annoyance as he held her and rested his head against her hair. "Susannah, you keep calling me nuts, but you know, I'm not the one running out on the balcony wearing nothing but a dress that's so sheer you can see through it."

"Will you come in now?" she asked through seriously chattering teeth. "Will you leave the party so I can know for sure you're okay and Carter didn't have you arrested?"

"No." He shrugged out of his jacket, draped it over her shoulders, then slipped his hands inside it, one hand skimming the bare skin at the small of her back where the red dress swooped so low, and the other sliding up in front, cupping her breast where her nipple pushed against the slippery silk, taut and rigid in the freezing air.

She trembled, pressing into his hand, offering herself more fully to his fingers. The hand at her back dipped below the edge of her dress, tracing the line all the way down, dancing under the fabric, exploring the curves of her bottom

"I guess you *don't* wear white cotton undies," he murmured, sliding his thumb under the delicate string of her thong panties, pulling the ribbon enough to make her flush with even more heat and desire.

Lord, this was incredible.

It was so cold, so unbearably cold, and yet she was melting from the inside out. She had never wanted a man as much as she wanted Trey, now.

"Come in with me," she breathed, grazing his lips with hers. "Please?"

Bending closer, Trey covered her mouth completely, refusing at first to actually meet her lips or complete the kiss, just hovering there, driving her mad. But then he plunged in, branding her with his whole mouth, his tongue swirling around hers, tasting her, warming her, his kiss slick and deep and delicious.

Far more intoxicating than any Irish coffee. "Come inside," she tried again, backing up, trying to tug him with her, unwilling to lose the connection between them for even a second.

"Where can we go to be alone?" he whispered, and she knew exactly what he was asking.

"There are bedrooms in the back," she offered, feverishly running through the floor plan in her mind. "I give tours of this place. I know every nook and cranny. Like the butler's pantry. No one knows about that. No one would bother us. Or we could go downstairs and get a key, to a room of our own." Trying to keep a clear head and not be too undone by champagne and the nearness of Trey, she sent him a speculative, hopeful glance. "Or would getting a room take too long?"

Was she as crazy as Trey? Sensible Susannah Quincy ought to be the last person trying to find a quick lovers' hideaway at the company New Year's party. And yet it seemed so impossible to resist the idea of being alone with Trey.

"We can find something," Trey murmured, pressing his lips into the slope of her neck, breathing into her ear, sparking terrible hunger and desire all over again. She trembled against him, but he pushed her back through the door, into the party, her hand still clasped in his, his jacket still over her shoulders.

"Be careful," she reminded him, pitching her voice low and secretive. "The cops could be here by now, looking for you. Oh, god. Did you see Carter?" She tipped her head into his to hide both their faces. "He's over by the grand piano. Do you think he saw us?"

Trey held her securely against him. "No. And I don't think he called the cops, either. But I do see hotel security blocking the elevator. I guess we're not leaving that way, are we?"

Susannah suppressed the need to giggle. Now was not the time for giggling. And yet it *was* kind of funny. Staid, responsible Susannah Quincy, ducking her head and trying not to look suspicious so she and her illicit lover could avoid the cops. What was the world coming to?

"If we skirt around the outside," she whispered, "I think we can get into the back rooms that no one uses. We could, um…" She licked her lips. "We could hide out there for a while, till Carter gets tired of looking for us."

"Hide out?" They both knew exactly what she meant, and it had nothing to do with hiding. It had to do with what they'd been practicing on the balcony, only with more steam and a lot less clothing. He kissed her quickly, and then navigated a stealthy path through the thickest parts of the crowd.

Finally, after what seemed like forever, they reached the fringe of the party. One more turn and they were all alone in the dark, quiet, empty part of the penthouse. Susannah released a pent-up breath, but her body still tingled with anticipation.

54

Pulling her past the butler's pantry and the coatroom, he propelled her instead into a beautiful little powder room. Safely inside, behind a locked door, Susannah let his jacket slip off her arms, walking straight into his arms. He quickly pushed her up against the sink, trapping her boldly with his body, and her eyes widened. Whoa. He was a man in a hurry. His fervor both frightened and excited her, and she reached for the front of his shirt.

But he grabbed her left hand, holding it up in the air between them. "Did you really think," he growled, "that I would make love to you while you're still wearing another man's ring?"

"Trey, what are you doing?" she demanded as he stuck her left hand under the gold faucet and turned on the water. It struck her again how stupid men could be. And so ridiculously territorial.

"I'm getting this ring off." He interrupted his mission long enough to kiss her fiercely, framing her face with his wet hands, but then set back to work, soaping her finger, sliding the ring back and forth.

She could only look on in complete shock. She'd thought he was as turned on as she was, as desperate to find a place to be alone. But no! It wasn't her clothes he wanted to get off. It was her engagement ring!

"Got it!" he exclaimed in triumph, holding the diamond ring up under her eyes.

"Are you happy now?" Susannah balanced against the marble edge of the vanity, staring down at her naked finger. Her hand felt weird without the weight of Carter's ring, and yet a part of her also felt relieved to be rid of it. Relieved, bereft, happy and sad, success and failure. All at the same time.

Trey hesitated. "What should I do with the ring?"

"I don't care. Throw it in the wastebasket. Leave it on the sink." She shoved away from the vanity, moving toward the door. "I think it's worth a few bucks, so you could always stick it in your pocket now and sell it on eBay later. Maybe I was right in the first place, and you were only coming on to me to get to my jewelry."

"Susannah, it's yours," he said awkwardly, pressing it into her hand. "Maybe you should give it back to Carter." His voice dropped into a huskier range, and he settled his arms around her from behind, rubbing his jaw against the top of her head. "The way you look, the way you smell, the way you feel," he whispered roughly, "I'm starting to feel sorry for the guy who's losing you."

She steeled herself, angry with him, unwilling to give in so easily. But his voice tickled her hair and ruffled her nerves, and the rock-hard feel of his embrace was so very welcome. "Maybe this wasn't such a good idea," she managed to say, reaching for the doorknob. "The two of us, sneaking off to…" She let her voice trail off, not quite sure she wanted to make it concrete by putting it into words.

Trey was not so reticent. "Sneaking off to make love?" he finished for her. He spun her around in his arms, so that she had to face him. His eyes searched hers. "You made it clear you won't come to Paris with me."

"Trey, I can't—"

He laid a finger against her lips, stopping her words. "I know, I know. You have your reasons, and although you don't believe me, I do respect that. I won't push you again."

"Thank you," she said softly, not sure she respected her choices as much as he did, not sure she wanted the question closed so completely. What did that leave them? Was this his way of saying he would walk out of the party and out of her life as soon as the coast was clear?

"You're welcome." He smiled, dipping his head to touch her lips with his, so briefly and sweetly it took her breath away. "Susannah, we both know I'm leaving in the morning, so there can't be a tomorrow for us."

He crooked a finger under her chin, tipping her head up, staring right into her eyes with the full force of his seductive, electric-blue eyes. "What do you say, Susannah? I know you won't give me tomorrow, but will you give me tonight?"

In the full flush of passion, Susannah had actually considered running away to an unoccupied bathroom on the far side of the penthouse and making mad, crazy love with Trey Jameson. Now, after he had literally dumped cold water on the idea—or at least on her ring finger, long enough to remove her engagement ring—she wasn't so sure.

"I have to get back to the party," she hedged, trying to back up far enough to reach the door handle, needing to be away from Trey and out of this intimate space.

"But I thought you wanted…"

To be alone. To make love. To give in to this incredible dizziness and desire. She'd thought so, too. Until sanity had returned. She gripped Carter's ring inside her fist. She might not have a romantic future.

But she had a small chance at keeping her career prospects on track.

"Somewhere out there," she declared, "my ex-fiancé has hopefully gotten tired of looking for you and gone back to trailing around after Mr. Manley, one of the two presidents of the company. While Joan, my boss, has glommed on to the other one, Mr. Marceau. If I had a brain, that's what I would be doing, as well. Looking out for my career and my future. I came after you instead. But you're safe now." She jiggled the knob behind her back, trying to work the lock so she could escape gracefully. "And I can go back to what I should be doing. Without you."

But his hand closed over hers. "Are you sure that's really what you want? You're free of Carter. Why not take your chance to be completely free, to gamble on something better than being a corporate drone?"

"Oh, no. Don't start this again," she said angrily, ducking under his arm and pacing in the small bathroom. "I already told you, I want to go places and be someone. What's wrong with that? You said you respected my choice. Just because that isn't your dream is no reason—"

"I don't think that is what you want," he argued.

"Trey, I'm sorry, but you don't get to say what I want, okay?"

"But you're the one who suggested…"

Suggested sneaking off for a romantic interlude that turned into hand washing. Yeah. Delish. "I changed my mind," she shot back.

Shaking her head, she slipped around him, now totally intent on leaving, as he reached out a hand to try to catch her shoulder. But all he caught was the thin beaded strap of her gown.

As she flashed past, he pulled in the opposite direction. They both heard the "ping" of her strap breaking and the "zing" of tiny crystal beads flying every which way. She stumbled backward, he held on to the remains of her strap and a hunk of fabric decided to go his way in this tug-of-war. A nasty *rrrip* sounded as the bodice of her thin silk dress slashed wide open.

Susannah gazed down in horror. Her breast was completely exposed. A fact that had not escaped Trey, whose eyes were absolutely glued to the spot.

In a moment, a mere second, everything had changed, as the mood in their small hideaway seemed to darken and shift. The air crackled with the reverberations of that ripping sound.

"I—I'm sorry," Trey managed, although his words came out kind of choked and strangled.

"Oh, my god!" Dropping Carter's ring, letting it roll away somewhere on the floor, she clamped her hand over her bare breast. Her other strap still held, but she was uncovered all the way from her neck to her hip, all in one fell swoop of ripped red fabric.

"No, I'm not sorry. You are the most beautiful thing I've ever seen in my life," he said raggedly. "Susannah, there is no way in hell you're walking away from me. Not now. Not when we both feel this way."

She didn't ask what he meant or how he felt. She already knew. How did they both feel? *On fire, enraptured, entangled, out of their minds.*

His fingers brushed the torn edge of her gown, sending shivers down her body. It was the scorching look in his eyes, the smoky tone in his voice, the way his hand shook as he lifted it to touch her… All of it seemed to mix together and overpower her, dissolving her good intentions. Before she knew what had happened, her resolve had vanished, and renewed hunger pooled deep inside her, pulling her back to Trey.

Her back against the door, Susannah surged into him, wrapping her arms around him as his lips and teeth found her neck and ear and jaw. They were both desperate and greedy in their desire to touch and feel and taste. His hand moved over her breast and ribs, closing on her nipple, making her ache with longing, and she shoved her hands inside his shirt, popping buttons, pushing the stiff white fabric out of her way, loving the feel of him, so smooth and yet so hard.

As his tongue flicked over the taut tip of her breast, Susannah moaned, giving in to the incredible sensations, wanting him, wanting to be with him, no matter what it took. She slipped her hand to his belt and then to the clasp of his jeans, rubbing her hand

60

down his rigid length. Things between them were getting out of control fast, but somehow it didn't matter. She knew what she wanted. Him.

Melting, she began to slide down the door, but Trey's embrace tightened. He shifted her around, away from the door, boosting her onto the marble vanity, the trailing skirt of her gown scrunched up under her, with his sweet, warm, wet mouth still slanted over hers. He broke away for just a second, staring into her eyes.

He may have been wordless, but he was still asking a question, giving her an out if she wanted to take it. Did she know what she was doing? Did she care?

"I—I think I love you, Trey," she whispered. "Could you please make love to me? Now."

Trey smiled. He reached for her. She reached for him, too, almost falling off the sink in her haste to be with him. He reached under her skirt, stripping her thong off all the way down her legs and over her shoes in one fluid motion, tossing it aside as she scrambled to get his zipper down. Frantic, frenzied, clumsy—it didn't matter. He brushed her hands away and took care of his own zipper, still kissing her, devouring her as he positioned himself between her thighs.

Susannah gripped his shoulders, tangling her legs around his waist, urging him in. She simply couldn't find a way to hold him tightly enough.

He plunged, she took everything he had and, twisted together, precariously balanced on the edge of the sink, they began to find their rhythm. Susannah's pleasure and need climbed and climbed with every thrust. It was almost too good, too hard, too devastating, and she didn't know how long she could stand it, to have so much sensation, so many feelings, all tumbling on top of each other.

Finally finding release, she shattered into an incredible, mind-blowing climax. And shouts and cheers and another countdown began somewhere outside their small paradise.

Trey still stroked inside her, as if pushed on by the applause. What in the world was happening? Ten, nine, eight… Oh, god, she was hovering on the brink again. Five, four, three… Was she hallucinating? "One," she cried out. "One!" Tremors rippled through her. "Oh, yesss, yesss…"

His arms were so tight around her she could barely breathe, but Trey tipped his forehead into hers. Gasping for air, he began to laugh, too. "Happy New Year," he said with a great deal of amusement. "What a way to bring in the New Year, huh?"

"Were there really cheers? Did I really hear the countdown again?" she asked, totally confused, but too satisfied and dazed to really care.

"Good timing, Susannah. It must've been the West Coast celebration." He shook his head, touching the few remaining bits of glitter in her hair. "And I really did see stars. I'm not sure I believe it myself. I make love to the most beautiful and exciting woman I've ever met, I get a countdown to ecstasy *and* I see stars. How lucky can you get?"

She sagged into him, not sure whether to laugh or cry, whether to be embarrassed at how wild and noisy she'd been or just very, very happy.

"We'd better get you down from there," Trey commented softly, giving her a hand.

As he scrounged his shirt up off the floor and zipped himself back up into his jeans, Susannah tried her land legs. How nice to know she actually could still stand up. She hadn't been sure.

"What next?" she asked him.

His smile was lazy with contentment, but he found her hand and raised it to his lips. "Where can we possibly go from here?"

She didn't have a chance to answer or even think of a possible response. Voices and loud footsteps interrupted them, as if the entire Hotel Marceau New Year's party had decided to take up residence outside their door.

"Susannah?" a voice she recognized as Carter's bellowed, followed by insistent pounding on the door. "Are you in there? Darling, we're here to save you. I'll kick down the door if I have to."

Rejecting panic and moving onto hysteria, Susannah looked down at her ripped dress, all twisted around her body, at the pair of panties on the floor, at Trey in his shirt with most of the buttons torn off.

They were in deep, deep trouble.

"Susannah? Open the door! We don't want to have to break in, but we will if we have to."

Preparing for the onslaught, Susannah tried to hold the pieces of her dress together, but it was a losing battle. Without comment, Trey slipped his jacket around her shoulders, buttoning down the front of it.

It wasn't perfect, but it would have to do.

And then he kissed her cheek, whispered, "It will be okay," and opened the door.

Carter almost fell in, backtracked and stumbled into Joan, Kerry, Mr. Manley *and* Mr. Marceau, along with about twenty other people who had gathered out there. Carter's eyes swept up and down her unortho-dox outfit. He couldn't seem to stop blinking.

"We were so worried about you," Joan said with saccharine sweetness. She squeezed in front of Mr. Marceau, who looked more mystified than mortified, bless his heart. Joan went on, "We thought you'd been stolen away from the party by a criminal." Slyly she asked, "Or is that what happened, Susannah?"

"N-no." She pressed her lips together as she tried to think of a way to explain this. No. There simply wasn't any explanation. "I—I wasn't stolen. And he isn't a criminal. Just a misunderstanding. Just…"

"Too much champagne. New Year's Eve," Trey in-terceded. "I take complete responsibility. All my fault. I should know better than to take advantage of a tipsy woman."

64

Since he was standing there with his shirt hanging open, Susannah figured he didn't have any more credibility than she did, but, hey, at least he was in there swinging. "He's right," she piped up. "A, uh, romantic interlude. Most unfortunate." It was at that point that she spotted her panties crumpled near her foot, and not far away, her ex-engagement ring. Wasn't that ironic?

Trey edged in front of her, blocking the doorway. "We don't really need a crowd, do we? Would everyone mind moving along now?"

"I'm not going anywhere," Carter blustered.

As most of the other onlookers disbanded, casting back glances filled with a mixture of sympathy and horror, Susannah quickly bent and gathered the ring and her undies, stuffing the thong in the pocket of Trey's jacket and holding out the ring to Carter. "I think you'd better take this," she said awkwardly. "I've been trying to do this all night. But anyway, I don't want to marry you."

"Did you really think I still wanted to marry you?" he said savagely, grabbing the ring from her extended palm and shoving it into his own pocket. "After the way you've behaved tonight?" He seemed to have more to say, but he choked it back, stalking away, trailed by Mr. Manley, who was patting him on the shoulder and offering condolences.

"Well, I guess he got what he wanted," Trey noted cynically. "Manley is his big pal now."

Susannah didn't know where to go or what to do. "This is so terrible, beyond my worst expectation of what terrible could be," she mumbled, lifting a weak hand to her head.

"Susannah, don't you see? It's perfect." Trey was actually laughing.

What in the world was wrong with him?

"Come on!" he said happily. "You have to see now how much we belong together." He took her by the arms. "No fiancé, no job, a man who is crazy about you and with whom you just had amazing sex. What's not to like? So *now* will you run away to Paris with me?"

66

This time when she slapped him across the face, she meant it. She meant it *for him.* Nobody else.

"You're as bad as Carter," she yelled, smacking him on the shoulder for good measure. Trey ducked, trying to shield himself, but she knew she'd made her point.

"Come on, Susannah. I'm nothing like that jerk," he scoffed.

"No? He didn't love me, but he thought if he dangled a fancy engagement ring in front of my face, he could buy someone who would validate and support his dream of being a big honcho inside Manley & Marceau," she said smartly, just starting to get wound up. "It didn't matter what *my* dreams were or whether I minded if he didn't call or didn't care or left me at the bottom of his priority list."

"Exactly," Trey agreed, "and I didn't do any of that!"

"I fell for you, hard. I really thought I loved you. I admit, your plan was a little more devious." She clutched his jacket over her front, wishing it didn't smell like him, didn't make her want him all over again. Damn jacket. "You thought you could bewitch me with fabulous sex," she argued, "and earn yourself someone—wife, playmate, whatever—to validate and support your dream of being a romantic expatriate in Paris."

There was a long pause. "Did you really think the sex was fabulous?" he inquired hopefully.

"Yes," she shot back. "It was fabulous, okay? Gold star for you!" Pulling together the shreds of her pride, she added, "But it doesn't matter. I will not be bought, not by a diamond and not by fabulous sex."

"Susannah, I don't get this," he said in a bewildered tone. "I do love you. I know it's crazy and sudden and unexpected, but I do love you. And I want you with me, not to support my dream, but because I want you with me. I know I can't promise it would work. Who can ever promise? All I can do is try. Susannah…"

He grabbed her by the shoulders, pressing his lips into hers with what struck her as one last, desperate attempt to convince her. She held her breath and tried to be strong. Don't let him get to you.

"Sometimes," he whispered, "you have to take the risk. You have to gamble on someone. Sometimes you have to have faith that your destiny is right there, waiting, and it will all fall into place the right way if you just reach out and embrace it."

He really was good at this. But Susannah thought about the Hotel Marceau and how much she liked her job and how much she would mourn losing it. She thought about the expressions on the faces of the people she worked with, all lined up to see her humiliation when the door to the powder room swung open. "Embrace my destiny." She spat out the words. "Oh, and will the Easter bunny and Santa help me with that embrace?"

But Trey was still in there, trying. "I know it seems like a big leap, but… I'm asking you to gamble on me." His smile was rakish. "And I can promise lots of fabulous sex."

That was all she needed. "No, thanks," she said coldly, already moving past him, ready to close the door.

"Susannah… Take the risk."

But she walked away.

SHE ACTUALLY HAD A GLIMMER of hope she might make it to the elevator without getting caught, but luck was not on her side. Big surprise. It was Joan, her boss, who stepped into her path.

"I'm sorry, but I don't have time for this," Susannah told her. "I have to find my coat and get out of here."

"This is important." Joan twisted her lips into a semblance of a smile. "I'm going to be brutally honest here, Suze. I thought once we caught you, in flagrante, so to speak, that would be the end of you at the Hotel Marceau."

Couldn't anyone make anything easy on her tonight? Not anyone? "You don't need to fire me, Joan. I'll just quit and take my besmirched little self out of the hotel right now, okay?"

"No. Not okay." Joan crossed her arms over her narrow chest, giving Susannah the once-over. "I was chatting with Paul Marceau after the, uh, incident, and he… Well, he's French, what can I say? He thought you were all, you know, mistreated and put upon, *toujours l'amour,* all that, and he wants to poach you for the Paris hotel, blah blah blah."

Susannah saw stars again, and this time she knew there was no more glitter left in her hair. "He wants to *what?*"

You could tell Joan was not enjoying this. Not for one minute. Sourly she announced, "He wants you to be director of sales for the Hotel Marceau in Paris. It's a small hotel, but it was the first one, it's the flagship and it *is* exquisite…."

But Susannah could not comprehend a word of this. "What are you saying?"

"Bottom line, you can make us both happy by getting out of my department and taking this job. It is a major, major opportunity," Joan said flatly. "You in?"

"Oh, my god." It couldn't be real, could it? "Yes, yes, I'm in!" She was so swept up in the incredible, bizarre reality of it, she actually hugged Joan. *Joan.*

But this was so strange. She'd always wanted to work at the Hotel Marceau in Paris. And here was her opportunity, tossed like New Year's confetti. Almost like… Destiny.

Susannah had only one thought on her mind. She had to find Trey. Destiny! He would understand this, even if she had said mean things. He would understand, wouldn't he?

70

He was making his way out of the penthouse, just as she was, and he looked very pensive. "Listen," he said warily before she had a chance to speak. "I've been thinking about what you said, and you're right. You have dreams, too. But I still think we belong together. So if you want to stay here, then I can find a way to live in Chicago. I can give up Paris, and…"

She waved his words away. "You're not going to believe this. Okay, this is not what you want. I am still not Ms. Free Spirit Beatnik and I am not living in a garret. But…I have a job offer in Paris," she said gleefully. She screamed and threw her arms around him. He felt a lot better than scrawny Joan, though. In fact, he felt so good she almost forgot to tell him the rest of it. "It just fell into my lap, Trey! I can't believe it myself. And I won't till I actually talk to Mr. Marceau. But this is so cool, isn't it? Me, in Paris. Director of sales for the Hotel Marceau. I guess I'm going to have to learn French. You'll teach me, right? I can't bel—"

Trey cut off the rest of it, covering her mouth with a hard, unyielding kiss that would've knocked her socks off if she'd been wearing any.

She took a step back. "Is that a yes?" she asked, wide-eyed. "You still want me?"

"It's destiny, Susannah." He pulled her back into his arms and kissed her again, leaving her breathless. "I'm afraid if I say I told you so you'll smack me again, but…I did tell you so." He dropped another kiss on her nose. "Let's get out of here, okay? It's still a long time till morning and my flight… *Our* flight. You know, it will be New Year's somewhere every time the big hand goes straight up." He grinned. "And I know how you like to do the countdown."

"Happy New Year, Trey," she whispered.

* Originally published online at www.eHarlequin.com.

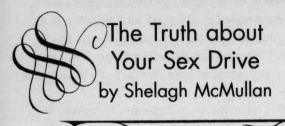

# The Truth about Your Sex Drive
## by Shelagh McMullan

*Can the vitality of spring breathe new life into your sex life? Are you and, more important, your sex drive influenced by Mother Nature's whims? Read on and discover our extraordinary findings!*

Chilly winter weather causes dry skin. A rainy spring ruins leather shoes. Summer sun leads to premature aging. And a windy fall day means it's going to be a bad-hair day. But can the changing of the seasons send your arousal levels up and down like mercury in a thermometer?

Dr. Sandy Scantling, a clinical psychologist and certified sex therapist, says we aren't slaves to the season. "Unlike many animals, humans don't have a mating season per se." While the human animal should be able to happily mate all year long, women can't expect to have the same sex drive each day.

Each season brings new challenges that can take a toll on your libido, from hosting the in-laws to getting the kids to soccer practice. Scantling, author of *Extraordinary Sex Now: A Couple's Guide to Intimacy* and creator of the *Ordinary Couples, Extraordinary Sex* video series, explains that women's sexual needs are affected by more than the temperature.

"Sexual desire, arousal and response is due to emotional readiness as much as biophysiological receptivity." To keep things from cooling off in your climate-controlled bedroom, you're going to have to work on your intimate side 365 days of the year.

### Spring Fever

Spring fever is a reality, according to sex therapist Dr. Carole Altman. Altman, the author of *You Can Be Your Own Sex Therapist* and *101 Ways to Make Love Happen* says, "Spring is exhilarating and stimulating, so the result is more sexuality."

Make the most of this stimulating season by reviving the mood in the bedroom. Altman suggests taking some time to set the mood. "Keep the windows open, feel the breeze and put aromatic spray on your sheets."

If you and your lover have to get outside, Altman asks, "Why not plan a picnic in an isolated country getaway?" We trust you'll know exactly how to make the most of this isolation.

## Summer Fun

It seems as the temperature rises so do some women's sex drives. There are scientific and practical explanations for this.

"In the dark, the pineal gland secretes the hormone melatonin, which inhibits the production of testosterone and estrogen necessary for sexual desire," says Scantling. Sunlight means less melatonin is produced. "It would follow that sexual interest would be increased during brighter days or seasons."

Getting a booster shot of self-esteem from a summer tan or a flattering swimsuit also helps put a woman in the mood. Altman notes, "During the warm months when lighter, more revealing clothing is worn, a female feels more sexy and more appealing, and this can affect her sex drive."

Even the hot sun is a turn-on. Altman adds, "Heat is one of the components of passion, and passion is aroused by it." It may be the sun, it may be the holiday spirit or it could be the free time, but a beach vacation can be a wonderful way to reconnect with your partner.

"Many of my patients describe wonderful lovemaking after a day on the beach and chalk it up to the vacation, not the sunlight," concludes Scantling.

## Fall and Winter Wonderland

There's no need for your love life to cool down when the weather does. Try to keep the spirit of summer fun alive with your man, despite the busy fall schedule. Scantling says there is no excuse for failing to fit in intimate moments. "Couples need to do "touch planning" in the same way we do meal planning. None of us are too busy to give our partner a six-second kiss," says Scantling.

Some people look forward to a winter wonderland, but many women dread the snow, cold noses and static-stricken hair. Scantling says that while some people have the "winter blahs," other people have seasonal affective disorder (SAD). She explains, "Many of my patients with SAD report not wanting touch, holding or other physical connection during the winter months."

If you suffer from SAD or are experiencing a period where you don't want intimacy, Scantling says you have to share your feelings with your partner. "If there's an understanding that your partner may have a diagnosable (and treatable) condition, this will ease some of the tension in the relationship."

Keep in mind that not all aspects of winter are bad. A winter storm might be just the excuse you and your lover need to stay in bed all day.

Altman says research has shown that married couples have more sex when they are storm-stayed at home. "It seems that it is not the weather per se but the inability to do anything else during storms." However, if winter has left you with nothing but chapped lips and a low libido, Altman suggests that you enlist your partner's aid.

Prepare by placing a bowl of kosher salt, baby oil and aromatic oil by the bed. Go get your partner. Altman says, "I suggest that the man...wash his partner with it, scrubbing her skin with the oil and salt with a loofah, then sponging it off, telling her how beautiful she is, how soft her skin is, etc."

You can bet everything will go a lot more smoothly in your bedroom after *that* rubdown.

76

## Year in Review

If you capitalize on spring fever, turn up the heat in summer, take time to touch in the fall and have rubdowns instead of meltdowns during the winter, it will be a very good year.

Altman adds, "It is planning. If you build the romantic moment, he will come, just like the ball field."

# With these women, being single never means being alone

Lauren, a divorced empty nester, has tricked her editor into thinking she is a twentysomething girl living the single life. As research for her successful column, she hits the bars, bistros, concerts and lingerie shops with her close friends. When her job requires her to make a live television appearance, can she keep her true identity a secret?

# The Single Life
## by Liz Wood

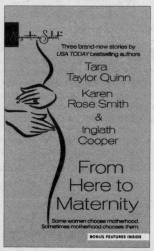

If you enjoyed what you just read,
then we've got an offer you can't resist!

# Take 2 bestselling
# love stories FREE!
# Plus get a FREE surprise gift!

# COMING NEXT MONTH

**Signature Select Collection**
**FROM HERE TO MATERNITY** by Tara Taylor Quinn,
Karen Rose Smith, Inglath Cooper
Some women choose motherhood. Sometimes motherhood
chooses *them*. Enjoy this heartwarming anthology—just in time
for Mother's Day!

**Signature Select Saga**
**HOT CHOCOLATE ON A COLD DAY** by Roz Denny Fox
Despite their high-maintenance families and high-risk jobs, Megan
Benton and Sterling Dodge find plenty of ways to stay warm during
the blustery month of March.

**Signature Select Miniseries**
**A LITTLE BIT NAUGHTY** by Janelle Denison
Two sisters find blazing chemistry with the two least likely men of
all in TEMPTED and NAUGHTY—two sizzling page-turning novels
that are editorially connected.

**Signature Select Spotlight**
**HER PERFECT LIFE** by Vicki Hinze
Katie Slater's life is perfect. She's a wife, mother of two and a pilot
in the United States Air Force. But then she's shot down by the enemy,
left for dead by a man she trusted and taken as a prisoner of war in
Iraq. Now, six years later, she's back home...only home isn't there
anymore...and her perfect life has become a total mystery.

**Signature Select Showcase**
**SWANSEA DYNASTY** by Fayrene Preston
Built on the beautiful, windswept shore of Maine, the great house
of SwanSea was built by Edward Deverell as a monument to himself,
his accomplishments and his family dynasty. Now, more than one
hundred years later, the secrets of past and present converge as his
descendants deal with promises, danger and passion.

### Juliana was ecstatic

"That was glorious. Everything I imagined. You are a fabulous lover, Travis."

Telltale red stained his high cheekbones, and she laughed softly. "Now it's time to talk."

"Talk about what?"

"Our future, of course." Travis went very still against the pillows as Juliana continued blithely, "I need to start making plans for our marriage."

"Our what?" He leaped from the bed in all his naked glory.

There was a heartbeat of silence during which Juliana abruptly lost her sensuous afterglow. "You seem rather skittish about the idea, Travis. I hadn't suspected that the best sex either of us has ever known would make you turn tail and run."

"I'm not running anywhere. I'm also not going to be pressured into marriage. Look—" suddenly he seemed distracted by the gorgeous redhead before him "—can't we just...go back to bed and shelve this nonsense?"

Juliana took a last, lingering look at Travis's magnificence. "Sorry, I find I have other plans...."

Dear Reader,

It's hard to believe that the Signature Select program is one year old—with seventy-two books already published by top Harlequin and Silhouette authors.

What an exciting and varied lineup we have in the year ahead! In the first quarter of the year, the Signature Spotlight program offers three very different reading experiences. Popular author Marie Ferrarella, well-known for her warm family-centered romances, has gone in quite a different direction to write a story that has been "haunting her" for years. Please check out *Sundays Are for Murder* in January. Hop aboard a Caribbean cruise with Joanne Rock in *The Pleasure Trip* for February, and don't miss a trademark romantic suspense from Debra Webb, *Vows of Silence* in March.

Our collections in the first quarter of the year explore a variety of contemporary themes. Our Valentine's collection—*Write It Up!*—homes in on the trend to online dating in three stories by Elizabeth Bevarly, Tracy Kelleher and Mary Leo. February is awards season, and Barbara Bretton, Isabel Sharpe and Emilie Rose join the fun and glamour in *And the Envelope, Please....* And in March, Leslie Kelly, Heather MacAllister and Cindi Myers have penned novellas about women desperate enough to go to *Bootcamp* to learn how *not* to scare men away!

Three original sagas also come your way in the first quarter of this year. Silhouette author Gina Wilkins spins off her popular FAMILY FOUND miniseries in *Wealth Beyond Riches*. Janice Kay Johnson has written a powerful story of a tortured shared past in *Dead Wrong*, which is connected to her PATTON'S DAUGHTERS Superromance miniseries, and Kathleen O'Brien gives a haunting story of mysterious murder in *Quiet as the Grave*.

And don't forget there is original bonus material in every single Signature Select book to give you the inside scoop on the creative process of your favorite authors! We hope you enjoy all our new offerings!

Enjoy!

*Marsha Zinberg*

Marsha Zinberg
Executive Editor
The Signature Select Program